BABY GIRL LAUREN

John O'Neill

iUniverse, Inc.
Bloomington

Baby Girl Lauren

This novel is fiction, its institutions and characters imaginary. There are no intended similarities to real institutions or real people. Although the story's medical technology is in current use, the events are, of course, also imaginary.

iUniverse books may be ordered through booksellers or by contacting:

iUniverse
1663 Liberty Drive
Bloomington, IN 47403
www.iuniverse.com
1-800-Authors (1-800-288-4677)

ISBN: 978-1-4759-2188-5 (sc)
ISBN: 978-1-4759-2189-2 (ebk)

Printed in the United States of America

iUniverse rev. date: 05/08/2012

BOOKS BY JOHN O'NEILL

Blue Death
Protocol Ichor (2012)

WAY PAST VISITING HOURS

For a moment they stood motionless, staring at each other.

The doctor moved first, turning and fixing Wukich with his oil-black eyes. "I'm Dr. Garcia," he said. His gaze went to the infant. "I'll only be a moment with the baby. You can wait—"

By the time their eyes met again Wukich was backpedaling to the door. After three steps, he turned to run, but he slammed into the edge of the door with his forehead and reeled sideways. Cradling the baby in his right arm away from the man, he groped for the open doorway. Yet even as he stumbled forward he knew he wouldn't make it, and he wrapped his other arm around the baby like a fullback going for a goal-line stand.

As he fell to the floor from the weight of the man pushing and clawing at him, all he could hear was his high-school football coach screaming, "Cover the goddamn ball!" And he did.

There was no way the baby was coming out of his arms . . . . He curled up on the floor against the wall like a frightened armadillo, but he didn't care. A metal tray crashed against the exposed portion of his head. He clenched his jaw and curled up tighter. Then there were voices outside the door . . . .

PROLOGUE

February 1990

Dr. Brendan Gallagher pushed through the first set of double doors and stopped, letting the sudden starkness, the bright light emanating from the main operating room of the Washington Fertility Institute, settle over him. The inner doors were ajar, and he could see that Ashton was already there, gowned, gloved, and seated on a stool his hands clasped expectantly in front of him. He was watching Jennifer Barton, the anesthetist, as she hovered over the patient's arm with a long coil of plastic tubing and a syringe. Alice, the scrub nurse, was there too, but Lindsey Baines, Ashton's chief nurse, was nowhere to be seen, and Gallagher felt a twinge of disappointment. In the short week he had worked as a rotating resident at the institute, she had always come in to make sure her boss was content, his room impeccable. With Ashton already scrubbed, Gallagher turned toward the large metal sink in the outer room.

A practiced push of his left knee against the metal claw sent a surge of water over his upheld hands and forearms, first cold, then warm, then hot. He opened a sterile sponge and began the ritual. One always started at the fingernails, the dirtiest place on the hands. With the plastic bristle brush on the reverse side of the sponge, he stroked underneath his nails, thirty swipes for each one. Thirty more with the sponge to each fingertip before moving to the fingers themselves.

Cleaner, all four sides of every finger took twenty strokes each. Then to the hands proper.

"Are you all right?" It was Lindsey, who had arrived in the operating room through the back door.

Gallagher let the water slow down and strained to listen.

"Sure," he heard Ashton say, sounding surprised. "I'm just thinking. She's a little complicated." Pause. Then, "And Fernandez is in town. We were up late."

"Oh," said Lindsey, dragging but the word. "Now I get it. Is he coming in today?"

"Later, maybe."

"How was he?"

"Okay. We went to The Blue Marlin. He had all the tables around us in stitches."

"Did he come up alone?"

"Yeah. Why? Do you want to go out with him? You know he adores you."

"Hmmm. Anyway, he's married, or so I hear."

Twenty strokes on all sides of the wrists before starting the long sweeps of the forearms. Gallagher softened the swish of the brush.

"Well then?" he heard Ashton say.

Then Lindsey: "I was just wondering . . . you know, how old is she, Richard?"

Ashton snorted. "*I* don't know. I didn't ask him. What difference does it make?"

"Guess."

"Well, he compared her to the best bottle of Beaujolais Nouveau he's ever tasted."

"What does *that* mean?"

"She's young. And fresh."

"Oh, give me a break. Is she out of high school at least?"

"I think she's around twenty-five."

"Well, he's making progress. What was Monique, nineteen?"

"I don't know,"

"What happened to *her*?"

"She turned to vinegar."

"What?"

"Carlos said she turned to vinegar. He said even good bottles from great estates sometimes turn to vinegar."

"Vinegar? What a chauvinist!"

"He said he used to think she was a great cabernet sauvignon, but in fact she was really vinegar. He actually spat when he said it."

"I see, Maybe his taste buds are dead."

"Could be."

"Is the new one pregnant?"

"I don't know. You ask him."

"I don't want to ask him. I just want to know if I should continue being nice to him."

"And if she *is* pregnant?"

"Then he's an asshole."

Gallagher let his arms drip before backing into the room.

"Good morning; Brendan," said Dr. Ashton, standing up so that he could look down the full six inches he had over the younger man. As usual the greeting sounded calculated to underscore Gallagher's manifest inferiority to the distinguished surgeon. At forty-four Ashton was strikingly handsome, his light brown hair full but for a slight frontal recession, his skin taut and glowing. Tall and lean, he somehow managed to look well dressed even in his surgical scrubs. Gallagher, on the other hand, though he was not unattractive, would never be called particularly handsome. His sandy hair and mustache were nondescript, his nose bordered on pug, his fair Irish skin, incapable of a tan, was speckled from the summers of construction work. Stocky from his head to his compact thighs and calves, his scrubs always seemed to be too tight or too long. Yet neither did this bother him. He was solid, he liked to think. In every way.

"I thought you were going over to the hospital for that lecture I told you about," Ashton said pleasantly enough.

"I stopped by on my way over here. I didn't realize it was Dr. Schaumburg speaking. I heard her on the same topic a while ago, so I thought I'd come over and scrub with you."

"I see." Ashton glanced at his watch. "Well, Susan will be here in a minute, and we'll get started. I believe we have some of the other rooms going today, as well. If you'd like, you can go back and forth."

"Thanks. I'd like to stay here for a while if you don't mind. I worked with Dr. Simpson all day yesterday."

"No, not at all."

Lindsey approached him, smiling. "Good morning, Brendan," she said, loud and cheerful. As she passed him, she whispered, "I hope you're feeling better than *he* is."

Ashton went to the head of the operating table and stared down at Sarah Morick's drowsy face. Gallagher had seen that same triumphant posture in other surgeons, that same enjoyment of power over the patient, helpless under the lights, eyes pleading, "Do what you must, but please, please, go carefully." With some Gallagher had seen the pleading begin during their first visit to the consultation room. Others had remained resolutely wary until the gurney wheels stopped sliding on the slick linoleum and the light was overwhelmingly in their eyes. And he suspected that it was with these patients that Richard Ashton took particular pleasure in playing God. At them he would stare a few seconds longer, so they would never forgot.

This woman was probably just a patient. Now, flat on her back on the operating table, she summoned a hopeful smile. Although her short dark hair was covered by a surgical cap, her slim figure covered down to her thighs by the blue paper gown, Gallagher could tell she was a very attractive young woman. He let his gaze linger as it ran across her face and torso. There were only minor imperfections: a few shallow creases in the forehead and lateral orbits; an almost-too-angular nasal bone; a well-defined Cupid's bow, but the lips a little thin, lusterless. Below her mandible were even fewer flaws. Her neck muscles were firm and clearly demarcated, the overlying skin a rich, creamy shade of shell white with almost no marks from the sun. Breasts were full and rounded with nipples erect from the chill of the room, tenting the flimsy paper gown.

"I'm sorry I didn't get to see the patient preoperatively," said Gallagher, "but I didn't think I'd be here this morning."

"I understand," said Ashton. "I think I'm going to do this one myself anyway."

Gallagher nodded. "Do you mind if I look at her record? I'd like to be a little familiar with the case before we start."

"What would you like to know?"

Gallagher hesitated, knowing that the woman was probably still semiconscious. Softly he said, "The beginning, I guess. Who has the problem?"

"She was in a car accident, years ago. Her uterus was lacerated, and at least one fallopian tube."

"But her ovaries are okay?"

"Right. Her eggs should be fine."

"Have they been trying to conceive?"

Ashton shook his head, "It's too risky with her uterus full of scars. They've known all along they were looking at an in vitro fertilization or artificial insemination, They've just been waiting until they were ready. Or until her father was," Ashton added more to himself.

"I'm sorry, I didn't hear you."

"I was talking to myself. Her father's paying for it."

"Oh. What if the fertilization is successful? Are you going to take the chance—"

"There's a surrogate mother—Mrs. Williams. A surrogate *gestational* mother I should say, since the egg will come from Mrs. Morick. We only need Mrs. Williams for her uterus."

"So both Mrs. Morick and her husband will be the biologic parents."

"Right."

Gallagher was quiet. Then he said, "This must be a pretty unusual situation. I'm not sure I remember reading about any similar cases."

"It's not the first, but it's definitely unusual. And with scars from her accident, it's going to be a difficult retrieval."

"At least the surrogate-mother situation should be simpler. If Mrs. Williams isn't the biologic mother, it'll be easier for her to give up the baby."

"That's true, but you're jumping the gun. Even if I can retrieve some eggs and get one fertilized, I still have to implant the embryo in Mrs. Williams's uterus. The timing with her menstrual cycle has to be exact. All in all, the odds aren't very good. Every step is complicated. *And* time-consuming."

Ashton glanced at Lindsey and mumbled something Gallagher couldn't hear. She smiled and left the operating room, then returned with aspirin and a glass of water.

"I told you," she mouthed to Gallagher as she untied Ashton's mask and held the glass to his lips.

Susan, the ultrasound technician, arrived, and soon the room, was busy with the coordinated movements of professionals accustomed to working with one another. Alice arranged the retrieval instruments on the sterile table next to the patient. At the head of the table, Dr. Barton fine-tuned the cardiac monitor and injected two milligrams of Versed into a vein in Mrs. Morick's arm. Her eyes closed, and the anesthetist relaxed in a chair behind her head, surrounded by monitors. Susan was already busy with the ultrasound transducer, passing over Mrs. Morick's long abdominal scar with familiarity. As she worked, she watched the screen where the sound waves were formed into the image of the patient's pelvis and ovaries.

"I'd still go for the left one," she said to Dr. Ashton. "I can see, at least two good follicles." Seated between the patient's legs, Ashton waited for nods from all involved. Gallagher positioned himself behind the surgeon. He'd be damned if Ashton was going to shut him out of this one. At this point in his residency, it was the difficult cases he wanted to do.

"Ready, Susan?" asked Ashton. She nodded, and he pushed the trocar, a sharply pointed instrument containing a needle and tubing for the egg aspiration, through Sarah Morick's vaginal wall below her cervix.

"You're fine." Susan watched the trocar tip as it appeared on her screen. She adjusted the angle of the transducer, and the trocar came into focus with complete clarity.

Slowly now, millimeter by millimeter, watching the ultrasound screen and simultaneously feeling the subtle variations in the tissue resistance to the trocar, Dr. Ashton advanced toward Sarah Morick's left ovary. The trocar suddenly met firm resistance, and his hand stopped. He and Susan looked at the screen, then at each other. Ashton shrugged and made a minuscule downward adjustment of the needle angle. "Probably scar tissue," he said to nobody in particular. The trocar tip slipped free, jumping slightly on the screen.

"How does it feel now?" said Gallagher. "It looks as if you're only about five millimeters from the inferior pole."

"Fine. It must have been a scar from her surgery. Actually, I'm surprised there's not more scar tissue. The first time I saw her in the office, she brought in her old records from the accident." Ashton paused as the trocar tip came within a millimeter of the ovary. "From what I could tell, she came pretty close to dying. She was only eight."

"Which follicle are you going for first?" Susan asked.

"I haven't decided yet. What do *you* think, Brendan?"

"The two follicles that we see most clearly are about the same distance from where you are now," Gallagher replied immediately. "I might go laterally first to avoid the ovarian artery. Then you can go over the anterior surface if you need to get to the other one."

Ashton nodded. "That's not a bad idea." He directed the trocar toward the lateral follicle and readied to puncture it.

Gallagher studied the ovarian follicle on the ultrasound screen. Most of the patients were given hormones to stimulate the development of the eggs, and Sarah Morick appeared to have responded appropriately. The follicle

Ashton was about to enter was large, ripe, and most likely full of eggs.

"Ready, Alice?" Ashton grasped the hub of the needle.

"All set."

With a deft millimeter advance, the needle entered the follicle. Ashton accepted from Alice a syringe attached to a short length of plastic tubing. Alice steadied the trocar while he gently sucked out the contents of the follicle, and within a minute there were several milliliters of blood-tinged fluid in the syringe. Alice placed the syringe on the table and handed Ashton another that was filled with a culture medium solution. With the second syringe he flushed the follicle and repeated the aspiration to get any remaining eggs. When he was finished, Alice called over the intercom into the adjacent laboratory. A man in a scrub suit and a white coat came into the operating room.

"I'm going to do a couple more, Fred," Dr. Ashton said. "Wait for me, will you?" I'd like to look at these myself."

"Okay. I'll get the aspirate in the culture medium while you're finishing."

Dr. Ashton turned toward the patient's pelvis and began to move the trocar. Once the second follicle had been aspirated, he headed for a third Susan had found on the top of the ovary.

"Don't you think you might have enough eggs in the fluid you already have?" said Gallagher.

"Probably." Ashton didn't look up. He paused as he readied to puncture the third follicle. "But I don't want to take any chances."

"Is it really worth the risk of a concealed hemorrhage from another puncture when you don't yet know if it's necessary?"

"Well, first of all," Ashton said as he inserted the needle, "I've never had anybody bleed using these needles and this approach. Not to say that it couldn't happen, but I think the chance of a clinically significant hemorrhage from this procedure is minimal. Actually, for this procedure I think the anesthetic risks are higher than the surgical ones. And that's what I'm trying to avoid. I don't want to be in here doing another egg retrieval next month."

Gallagher hesitated, then persisted: "But if there *are* extra eggs, you can freeze them. You wouldn't *have* to do another egg retrieval."

"The Moricks don't *want* the eggs frozen," said Ashton, a sudden edge in his voice.

"Even though—"

"I gave them all the statistics. But if there was a problem with a baby that came from a frozen egg, they don't want to be questioning themselves the rest of their lives."

"I see. But . . . ," Gallagher stopped. Then, lightly, he said, "Do you have any more cases this morning?"

"Yes. There's one more egg retrieval to do." Ashton's tone was pleasant again. "While I work on this with Fred, why don't you go see the patient and get a little familiar with her? She'll be a transvaginal approach also. You're welcome to do the retrieval."

"Thanks," Gallagher. "I'd like that."

At nine o'clock, the time Dr. Ashton had said the egg retrieval would be completed, Nathan Morick left the waiting room and walked down the hall to a corridor leading to another wing of the Fertility Institute. Once, during his and Sarah's first visit, he had chuckled over the gold-lettered words on the door leading into the wing—MALE REPRODUCTIVE STUDIES. Now they didn't seem funny in the least. In fact, the whole morning was disturbing to a degree he had not anticipated. The cloying personal attention of the staff grated on him with each successive smile; details of the furniture and fixtures disconcerted him with their sleek, impersonal look.

The woman with the ridiculous blond hair held rigidly in place by various aerosols was, as usual, behind the desk just inside the door. "Good morning, Mr. Morick," she said, showing her gums. "Mrs. Morick should be in the recovery room in just a few minutes. Are you ready to help her out?" Her eyes flicked humorously.

"Down the hall and to the right," he said.

"Right." She flashed her gums and handed him a bag labeled with his name. "Come on back!" she called after him.

He had been in this part of the institute on one other occasion and received a similar bag. Just to make sure *he* was okay. But it was the guided tour by the receptionist when he and Sarah had committed themselves to the program that he remembered best. First she had showed them the sperm bank. Then just before the bathroom, the lab, wherein Darwinian forces had reached their finest tension. Before eggs and sperm could be mixed for fertilization, the receptionist had explained, the sperm had to be what they called "capacitated." In something called "the centrifuge," only the best sperm—the ones that swam "fastest and farthest"—were collected to be incubated with the eggs. At that point, with the image before him of thousands of tadpolelike sperm engaged in the race of their lives, Nathan's mind had gone numb.

Finally he had been shown "the bathroom," to which Sarah had decorously excused herself entry. It had resembled more the periodicals room of a men's club than a place of bodily release. The walls were richly paneled and decorated with fine framed prints, the floor carpeted with oriental rugs. Just inside the door stood a magazine rack with *Newsweek, Time, and U.S. News and World Report* spread across the top. Below—"for the college students," the receptionist had said—were copies of *Playboy* and *Penthouse*. It will be like jerking off in DeLozier's library, he had thought, smiling to himself. When he had told this to Sarah on the way home, she hadn't been amused.

Now, as entered the bathroom, he wasn't smiling. He took the plastic cup out of the bag, found the toilet, and sat down. Breathing heavily, he leaned back with his eyes closed and took out his penis. It was soft—dead—and he forced himself to conjure up some semblance of tender emotion he might relay to Sarah. Suddenly he felt like destroying the whole room, the whole fucking institute with its hushed efficiency, its receptionists with their cheerleader smiles. Through no doing of his own, he had been cheated, debased. Pulling and pushing on a penis that seemed to want nothing to do with the whole business, he felt humiliation of the last few months well up. He and Sarah were like frogs on a dissecting table, with no secrets left unprobed. Now they wanted *her* eggs, *his* sperm, to make this child whom fate had robbed them of.

But it would, he made himself say out loud, be "our child." His and Sarah's. "I love my wife!" he almost shouted. "I *do* want us to be happy! I want to have *our* baby!" Some inner wall collapsed, his back involuntarily arched, and Nathan Morick shot the seeds of their miracle into the plastic cup.

PART ONE

ONE

May 1990

There had been only one other assignment as bad as this one. At the time, Russ Wukich presumed it had fallen to him because he was the most junior member of Cecil McCormick's detective agency. Even now the memory of old Mrs. Staunton, crazier than a loon, made him shake his head in amazement. She had been sure there was a plot to steal her poodle, and for three full weeks he had watched her house and followed her and the pooch on their stupid walks. She even used to hide its little turds—"covering her trail," she said with a cackle one day. Finally her daughter found out and, after swearing at old man McCormick until he was red as a damn fire truck, called the watch off. Apparently old Mrs. Staunton didn't have any money, and her daughter ended up footing the bill. What the hell, he thought. It always made for a good story.

This one sure as hell wouldn't. What could be more boring than watching a pregnant lady go to the store two times a day and the doctor's once a week? He knew the case was important to McCormick, but for Christ's sake, then tell me what the hell's going on, or let one of the younger guys handle it. "I'm sorry, Russell," McCormick had said, "That's the way the man wants it. But between you and me," he had added, lowering his voice, "I think he's worried about the lady's husband."

1

Wukich looked at his watch, then back to the main door o the apartment complex. She should be coming out any minute now. On the appointment days she was always early, always waiting for the cab. Out of habit he turned in the front seat of his car and strained to see into the parking lot. The old red pickup truck the big guy drove had not come back. It shouldn't—the son-of-a-bitch ought to work a full day if he wasn't going to the appointment with her. But with him you could never be sure.

The door opened, and Billie Williams came out. She was wearing one of her better flowered sun-dresses, as she always did on Friday. Wukich took out his small binoculars and studied her face. She was gaining weight—just like Carla had. Get knocked up, and use that bullshit "eating-for-two" excuse. Carla still hadn't lost the thirty pounds she'd kept after the birth of his second son, Jimmy. But to be honest, the other women he'd seen during their current "trial" separation hadn't been much better. In fact, Carla had most of them beat hands down. Wukich glanced down at his own belly, feeling his belt tight and uncomfortable. He would call her this morning, he decided. Maybe they could have a cup of coffee.

A cab pulled up, and Billie climbed in. Wukich could see that Burky Jones, his replacement, was driving, and the slight sudden tenseness in his hands and arms faded. Billie was safe. Until she was chopped off at the clinic, she was Burky's responsibility.

*   *   *

At eight o'clock in the morning, there was none of the usual waiting. Billie Williams was still getting her blood drawn when Dr. Ashton called the Moricks into the exam room a few minutes ahead of schedule.

"Good morning," he said, beaming. "I'm sorry to change the appointment time on you so suddenly, but I have a meeting later this afternoon. I also thought it would be better to see you at least one time in the morning. It's generally not so rushed."

Sarah glanced at Nathan. "We haven't felt rushed." she said.

"Maybe it's just me. I always feel as if there's never enough time. Anyway, we do have more time this morning, so if you have any questions, feel free to fire away." Ashton glanced at his watch. "How are the two of you? Are things going as you expected?"

"We're fine," said Sarah, placing a hand on her husband's thigh. "And Billie's been great. We wish we could see her more, but . . ."

"I know it's hard for you, but that can get to be a pretty sticky situation."

"We understand."

"I'm glad things are going well," Ashton said.

"Actually, you've been very fortunate in all respects."

"What do you mean?" said Sarah.

"Well, your situation was odd to begin with. You always knew you had a fertility problem and were just deciding how to approach it. It's not as if you'd been trying for years. Many couples I see are very frustrated and angry by the time they get to me. One more failure, and they've had it. The fertilization and implantation also went very well. Often we have to try several times before we get to where we are now."

"I guess we have been fortunate," Sarah said slowly, looking at Ashton as if she weren't, sure how to respond.

"All of that's obviously wonderful," he went on. "I just want you to know—"

There was a knock at the door, and Billie Williams stuck her head in.

"Come in, Billie," said Ashton.

Billie smiled at the Moricks and took her place on the exam table.

"All done in the lab?" said the doctor.

Billie nodded.

"Good. How have you been?" Ashton covered Billie's legs with a sheet.

"I'm okay."

"Just okay?"

Billie grinned. "I'm *fine.*"

Ashton pulled up her dress and at the same time covered her groin with the sheet. He rested a hand on her abdomen, giving her a moment to accommodate to his slightly moist palm and fingers. "Can you pull your knees up for me, Billie? . . . Great. Now just try to relax. Don't mind me. I'm just going to feel your tummy. Try to think about something pleasant."

Gently, he palpated Billie's lower abdomen, watching his hands, glancing occasionally into her eyes for pain. The Moricks followed his every move. Once, for four or five seconds, Ashton closed his eyes and was perfectly still.

Nathan put his hand on Sarah's.

The door opened, and a rich, booming voice filled the room.

"Richard!"

He was a big man, as tall as Ashton, but with an extra fifty pounds in his thick shoulders, chest, and belly. He glanced around with a look of good-humored mischief and said, "I don't mean to disturb you. I just wanted to let you know I was here. When you get a break, maybe you can spare me a minute."

"Fine," said Ashton with a tone of dismissal.

But the man didn't move. "A family affair, this one?" he boomed, and a wide grin creased his face. "No, don't tell me," he said as Sarah started to speak. He took a step into the room. "Let me guess."

"I thought you were coming this evening, Carlos," said Ashton.

"I decided to come early. Actually, I got in late last night. I didn't want to disturb you then." He was looking at Billie. "And so serious!" he said. "You should be *joyous*, young lady. This gift of God—I suppose by way of my good friend here—is a celebration. This is life! Yes, in this room, this is *life*! Please, you *must* smile." The man's big face was radiant, as though *he* were the expectant mother.

Billie giggled and Ashton smiled. "Please forgive Dr. Fernandez," he said. "He really does try. We're almost done, Carlos. I'll see you in my office or the lounge."

"I do apologize." Fernandez cocked his head and peered playfully at Ashton. "I didn't want to be here all night and morning, Richard, and then have you tell me I'm a lousy friend."

"Carlos."

"Okay, okay. But since I won't have the opportunity to guess, please don't leave me hanging. My guess would have been that you're not a family. Too much variation in the facial bones."

"Mrs. Williams is a surrogate gestational mother," Sarah said with a quick look to Billie.

Fernandez's face grew serious for a moment. "Gestational," he said softly, looking then at Ashton. "These are the fortunate ones you told me about."

Ashton nodded, reddening.

"Strictly confidential," Fernandez put in quickly. "Please understand that we are the closest of friends and colleagues. He won't admit it, but Richard's proud of what he's done for you. A successful pregnancy with a surrogate gestational mother is something for all of you to cherish. Well, I've stayed far too long. Please excuse me." Fernandez smiled one more time and was gone.

"Sorry," Ashton said. "But that's just the way he is."

"It's okay," said Sarah with a little laugh. "He's a character. Is he also a fertility specialist?"

"One of the best. Maybe *the* best."

"Where's he from?"

"Mexico."

Ashton turned back to Billie. "So everything's okay?"

Billie nodded.

"Do you feel any different? Has anything changed?"

No. I'm gainin' some weight, but I thought I was supposed to."

"You are. But not too much. Don't go on a see-food diet."

"I don't like seafood."

Ashton laughed. "Don't eat everything you *see*."

"Is everything okay, Dr. Ashton?" asked Nathan.

"I believe so, Nathan. But I think we'll go ahead and do another ultrasound today."

"You mean you hadn't planned on doing one today?"

Ashton reached for a phone on the wall. "It's pretty standard at this time in the pregnancy. I was going to wait until next week, but we may as well do it now." He picked up the receiver, then excused himself and went out into the hall.

There was an awkward silence. Sarah removed her hand from Nathan's. "Do you need anything, Billie?" she asked.

"No, Mrs. Morick I'm fine. Thank you anyway. I'm taking good care of myself. Please don't worry about that."

Sarah smiled. "I don't, Billie."

The door opened, and Susan, the technician, backed in with an ultrasound cart. The Moricks hadn't seen the baby by ultrasound in three weeks, and they inched up in their chairs.

Susan was fast and thorough. She bared Billie's belly and guided the transducer over her skin. She was silent as she worked, concentrating on the strange gray shapes and tones with a frowning intensity they had not previously seen.

"Well," said Sarah.

"I'm not supposed to say anything until Dr. Ashton or the radiologist sees them, Mrs. Morick," she said. "Dr. Ashton will be back in a minute." She waited until the machine regurgitated copies of the selected intrauterine views before leaving the exam room.

A nurse poked her head in and said, "You can get dressed now, Mrs. Williams. I think your cab's already here. Mr. and Mrs. Morick, Dr. Ashton would like you to wait for a couple of minutes if you don't mind. He wants to talk to you in his office."

"Let us know if you need anything, Billie," Sarah said on the way out.

Twenty minutes passed before Sarah asked Dr. Ashton's secretary if she thought he remembered they were still waiting.

"He's looking for the radiologist," she said.

Another ten minutes and Ashton strode through the office door with the ultrasounds in hand. "Please come in," he said, holding the door open for them. Then, closing it firmly, he led them to armchairs across from his desk. His face was without any of its earlier joviality.

"What's the matter, Dr. Ashton?" asked Sarah immediately.

The answer came slowly. "It's possible that nothing is the matter. But it's also possible that there *is* a problem with the baby, I'm sorry to be so nebulous, but it's early in the pregnancy. It's hard to tell."

Nathan clutched Sarah's hand.

"Why do you think there may be a problem?" she asked calmly.

Ashton stood up and looked out the window behind his desk. He turned to face them. "When I examined Billie today, I wasn't sure I felt her uterus. I thought I could feel the tip of it, but if it was the tip, it didn't feel right. Several things can do that. That's why I wanted to do the ultrasound. That's also why you had to wait. I was trying to locate our radiologist to look at the different views. That's not my field of expertise. I'm sorry, but he won't be available this morning. I'll show them to him this afternoon."

"What do you think *might* be the matter?" said Sarah.

Ashton waited a few long seconds. "The fetal head may be smaller than it should be."

"Which means what?" said Nathan.

"That can mean a mew things, one of which is that it's normal for the views we have. However it may also mean there's a problem with the development of the head."

"What *kind* of problem?"

Ashton shrugged. "It's hard to say exactly, Sarah. Several developmental problems can cause similar changes. But the one we're always most concerned is anencephaly."

"What does that mean?"

"It means there is a severe abnormality of the fetal skull and, consequently, of the brain."

"If the baby's brain doesn't form," Sarah said, faltering, "then . . ."

Ashton nodded. "Then the fetus would not be viable."

Sarah bit her lip and squeezed Nathan's hand. "Did Dr. Fernandez look at the ultrasounds?" she asked tentatively.

Ashton frowned. "I don't think that's necessary today."

"I'm sorry, Dr. Ashton, but I don't understand," said Nathan. "You . . . you tell us we may have a baby that may not live, but then you also say you don't really know. Well, if *you* don't know, then who the hell does? Why are you even telling us this now if you're not sure? And when *will* you be sure?"

"I'm telling you because I feel you deserve to know now. I don't want to keep anything from you. I find its better that way. Besides, if the radiologist sees what I think I see, there are some things we need to do. I want both of you to understand why we would ask you to do them."

The Moricks were silent, and he continued: "I believe I answered one of your questions, Nathan. Let me try to address the others. The answer to your first one is, nobody knows. Its just a touch too early in the pregnancy. However, this is a period of rapid fetal growth, and every day that passes makes these determinations easier. Especially with some of our newer ultrasound technology. So, if the radiologist is unsure at all, what can we do in the meantime? First, I recommend we bring Billie back today to give us some more blood. I would also say let's plan on doing an amniocentesis as soon as possible. There are some special tests we can do on Billie's blood and the amniotic fluid to help us with this problem. And of course we'll need to repeat the ultrasounds regularly. In fact, I would recommend continuing with our weekly follow-ups." Looking down at a calendar on his desk, he said, "I'm already booked for next Friday. How about Saturday morning?" He studied the calendar again. "Actually, next Saturday would be a good day. We're hosting an international workshop this week, and Dr. Fernandez is going to unveil the latest in ultrasound machines—straight from Mexico City. It should still be here by then. Ours are good, but they're like computers. As soon as you buy one, it's out-of-date. Maybe even Dr. Fernandez can give you a state-of-the-art reading."

Sarah brightened and agreed on Saturday. She got up to leave, but Nathan stayed seated, glaring at Ashton.

"I know, Nathan," the doctor said softly. "I didn't exactly answer your last question."

"Will you he able to tell us something more definite next Saturday?"

"I hope so, but I can't promise that. Believe me, I don't want to drag this out any more than you do. But you have to realize that medicine isn't black-and—white. We do our best with what we have."

Nathan stood up.

"I'm sorry," Ashton said. "Let's hope everything works out."

"And if it *doesn't*?"

"Let's not get ahead of ourselves, Nathan."

"As you said, it's better if we know."

Returning the young man's stare, Ashton said, "Yes, then we have a decision to make."

* * *

He found Fernandez in the staff lounge, animatedly expounding on a new operative technique he had recently described in a leading journal. Dr. Simpson, the newest me of the institute's staff and the recipient of Fernandez's barrage, quickly exited with the appearance of Ashton. They were alone then, and Ashton walked to the coffeepot without speaking.

"Are you angry with me, Richard?"

"Was that really necessary?"

"I didn't know you were with them, Richard. I just wanted to tell you I was here."

Ashton turned "You don't have to lie to me, Carlos," he said. "I'm not one of your . . ."

"My what, Richard?"

"I told you. I told you I'd—"

"I know what you told me, Richard, and I told you I *didn't* know!"

"I'll see you tonight, Carlos," Ashton said, heading for the door, "Arlene is expecting you for dinner."

Two

A nurse led them to the waiting area outside Dr. Ashton's of flee. As on all Saturdays the halls of the institute were eerily still. "Mrs. Williams is already here," she said brightly.

"May we see her?" said Sarah.

"Umm, I'm not sure. Maybe you should ask Dr. Ashton."

"What would you like to ask me?" Ashton said pleasantly as he turned the corner. A sheaf of ultrasound images dangled from his right hand.

"About Billie, We were expecting to see her today. We wanted to make sure she's all right."

"Billie's fine. Why don't the two of you come into my office?"

Seated in one of Ashton's leather chairs, Sarah persisted. "What about Billie?"

"I don't think that's a good idea, Sarah. Everything's a little too emotional right now."

Sarah glared at him. "Billie's a friend, Dr. Ashton."

"I realize that, Sarah. But I still don't think it's a good idea. Neither would the surrogate agency. I can guarantee you that."

"Why did you do the ultrasound before we got here?" she said sharply.

"Because I thought it would be better that way. Less stress on everybody." Ashton spoke gently yet firmly, as if there should be no more talk of Billie Williams.

Sarah's eyes suddenly glazed with a film of tears. "You seem to have an answer."

"I believe we will by the end of the day." With each word Ashton's face was more serious. "Let me go ahead and tell you what we do know."

"*'We,'*" said Nathan.

"'We' as in the Fertility Institute. Many people are involved in your case. But yes, *I* am responsible, as much as I can be, for anything that *we* tell you."

Nathan was silent. Sarah began to cry.

"We've had the blood tests and the amniocentesis results checked twice. Both labs obtained essentially the same results. There's a protein called alphafetoprotein that we use as a marker of certain neurological defects in fetal development—particularly anencephaly. Both labs found elevated alphafetoprotein levels in the blood and amniotic fluid. Not tremendously, as we sometimes see, but elevated to where they're probably significant.

"And I believe the ultrasound today *is* more definitive. However, I do want to show it to a radiologist before I say much about it. So I may not have the full answer until later this afternoon." Ashton paused, then dropped his voice. "I do want you to be prepared. I think it is an abnormal ultrasound. I think the head is small and consistent with an anencephalic fetus."

Nathan stood up and gripped Sarah's shoulders from behind. Sarah spoke: "I believe we understand everything you've said so far," she said slowly, turning to Nathan for agreement. "But if we have, you still seem a little unsure yourself. You even said 'probably' when you were talking about the lab results."

Ashton nodded, "I'm not sure 'unsure' is the correct word, but I understand what you mean." He sighed and looked at them sadly. "First of all, let me tell you how sorry I am. I now how much this meant to both of you. But please don't give up. That's what I was trying to say the other day. You're young, you're resilient. Everything is not lost." He turned his chair toward the window for a moment, then spun halfway back to face them. "I cannot give you the kind of answers you're looking for. At least not now. You want a concrete answer—yes or no. I understand that. But I cannot give you that. I can only tell you probabilities based on our experience."

"What *im*probabilities are there? said Nathan.

"It's possible we're wrong. I cannot *guarantee* you that there is no margin of error in these tests. However, the probability that all of them are wrong at the same time is rather low."

"How low?"

"Quite low."

"But possible."

"'But possible.'"

"How long would we have to wait before it is *not* possible?"

Ashton shrugged. "That's hard to say. Again, you're looking for an answer I can't give you today. I think the best answer is weeks. How many, exactly, I don't know."

"I went to the National Library of Medicine this week," said Sarah, "and from everything I read, I came away with the idea that it should take only one or two more weeks to say for sure."

Ashton smiled. "That, Sarah, is quite simply explained. It's relatively easy to *write* about problems like this. However, it is not easy at all to sit behind this desk and try to help people make real decisions. We are now in the trenches, not the library."

"So now what?" Nathan asked.

"I'd like you and Sarah to talk it over and get a feel for what you want to do. If you decide you want to wait and see what happens in the coming weeks, we can do that. If you don't, then we've already discussed the alternative in our prefertilization counseling. Remember? We discussed potential situations like this."

Nathan snorted. "What do *you* think we ought to do, Dr. Ashton?"

"I can't help you with that decision, Nathan. I'm sorry. All I can do is give you the best information I possibly can. And be here to support you in whatever you decide."

Sarah got up. "Dr. Ashton," she said from the door, "we would appreciate hearing any of the other doctors' opinions. If Dr. Fernandez is still here, maybe you can ask him."

Ashton nodded. "I plan to."

They had agreed to have lunch at Sarah's parents', and halfway to the DeLoziers' they stopped in a wooded park. They tried at first to comfort each other with words but in the end found more solace in the firm and silent grasp of each other's arms. Finally Nathan turned on the engine.

"Are you all right?" said Sarah. "We don't have to go. I'll call them if you want. They'll understand."

Nathan shook his head. "I'm okay."

Soon they were in the long driveway. The broad expanse of grass separating the house from its neighbors was newly mown, the blades glistening in the midday sun. Warren DeLozier was standing on the back deck waiting for them. The grief on his face was almost palpable, and Nathan couldn't help feeling sorry for the man. For a brief moment he even had the urge to hold him, to absolve him. But then he saw the old, hard determination return to his father-in-law's face, erasing the sadness, and with it Nathan's tenderness.

Sarah and her father rushed at each other. "Oh Sarah. Sarah, Sarah," he said over and over as he held her to him. Nathan stood back until they were done. When DeLozier came to him, he closed his eyes and accepted the short embrace.

Dorothy DeLozier hurried down the stairs, and the scenario was repeated. She held Nathan closer, longer, and looked into his face. "I'm so sorry," she said. "I'm so sorry."

They moved into the house and sat silently around the kitchen table while Dorothy poured iced tea. Then, sentence by sentence, Sarah reconstructed the morning's events.

"Well, I think bringing Billie in like that was pretty cheap," Dorothy agreed. "I think he just didn't want to face you when he did the ultrasound."

Sarah nodded. "That made me furious. It was the first time I've really disagreed with him."

"Tell me again, what did he say about the results of the amniocentesis?" said DeLozier.

Nathan repeated what Ashton had said and watched his father in-law digest it. "It sounds as if the result wasn't very elevated, DeLozier said finally. Sounds as if he was hedging with that too."

Nathan shrugged. "I don't know. In a way I think he's right. Were looking for a hundred percent answer he doesn't have."

The older man rose and walked to the kitchen window. Then he turned to face them. "Why don't you let us drive you back there later this afternoon? We'll wait outside. You have enough to worry about."

Sarah looked at Nathan. "Sure," he said.

Dorothy ushered them into the dining room, where they seated themselves around the gleaming cherry table. It was a casual lunch—Nathan had come to recognize the everyday flatware from the "good silver," the heavy white cotton napkins from the fine holiday linen. The only food on the table was a large colorful salad of angel-hair pasta. And as he had at every other meal at this table, Nathan could not help but envision his own family in the same circumstance, his mother and the table she would set. Or not set.

It would be a noisy kitchen affair, his brothers stacking beer in a cooler, his mother laying out plates of cold cuts pulled from thick rolls of bloodstained wrapping paper. There would be large, pungent onion rolls and fresh pumpernickel for his father. She would have made fresh potato salad, laden with mustard and egg, and the odors of several kinds of pie would fill the small room. And it would all be laid out along the counter for each of them—his father, round and silent, whatever uncles or aunts had stopped by, his three brothers and two sisters—to heap onto their plates as much as they wanted. Through it all his mother would be crying, silently, but there would be no talk of his and Sarah's tragedy—that was a matter between husband and wife.

Nathan felt Sarah's foot nudging his, and he caught the last of Dorothy's question. It had something to do with his work.

"It went fine, Sarah answered for him. "Actually, there is some good news." She looked at Nathan expectantly.

"Mr. Davidson told me I'm under consideration for one of the junior-partner positions. I should know soon."

"That's wonderful, Nathan," Dorothy said, raising her water glass to him in a toast. She glanced at her husband over her glass.

"Yes, Nathan," said DeLozier, "that's wonderful. You shouldn't be so shy about these things." His glass stayed firmly on the table.

Nathan shrugged. "It's not a big deal. It's kind of expected."

"Oh, come on, Nathan," Dorothy said playfully. "Enjoy it. It *is* a big deal. You forget how many people never accomplish anything like that."

"I suppose."

"How many junior partners are there?" asked DeLozier.

Nathan took a sip of water and looked through the dining room, across the living room, and into DeLozier's library. On the far wall—DeLozier's wall—he could see most of the framed citations. Radiating from the central Navy Cross, just about the highest award a marine-corp officer in Korea could have gotten, were the Navy Commendation Medal and the others. Then, feeling Sarah's foot on his again, he looked across at her calming, reassuring face.

"It depends on how many people leave each year, but anywhere from twelve to fifteen." Nathan returned to the angel hair. At the head of the table, he knew the calculations were beginning: thirty or so people started with the firm each year; a third usually left after the first year, another . . .

"Well, that's great, Nathan," said DeLozier. "It looks as if the years are finally starting to pay off." He lifted his glass.

Nathan nodded, then excused himself. Out on the deck he breathed deeply and turned his face into the gentle breeze. Several hundred yards way a man was cutting his lawn on a riding mower, and the juicy smell of freshly injured grass wafted over him. Shortly he took one last deep breath and started back into the house. But the kitchen was so disturbingly clean that for a moment he stopped still on the ceramic tile, feeling himself caught in some strange net of order and disorder. Then he heard Sarah, smelled the subtle lemony sheen of wood everywhere, and moved toward the subdued voices in the dining room.

They were finished with Dr. Ashton shortly after five. There was not much to say. Nathan held Sarah to him as they walked through the quiet corridors of the institute. A nurse let them out the front door, and they stepped into the still-bright sunlight. Nathan shielded his eyes and saw the big Lincoln in the parking lot begin to cruise toward them.

The leather of the back seat was warm and worn slick. Nathan drew Sarah close, and the DeLoziers stared out the windshield, allowing them their privacy. Then Dorothy DeLozier started to cry, and Sarah put forth a hand to her. Nathan watched a flush spread across his father-in-law's cheeks, across the firm outline of the muscles working his jaw.

"Oh, baby," Nathan said softly to Sarah, "what are we going to do? What in the name of God are we going to do?"

DeLozier wheeled around in his seat. "What do you mean, what are you going to *do?*" His voice was so hard Nathan sat back. "Did he give you a definite answer? Did he quit the bullshit and *tell* you something?" His eyes glistened. "What do you mean, what are you going to do? This is your life, goddammit! Take control of it! He's no *God!* He makes mistakes like anybody else. Don't throw away everything until you're *sure*, for Christ's sake!"

THREE

If the increase in Billie William's comings and goings in the last few days hadn't been annoying enough, she was now running late for a Thursday morning. By ten o'clock she was always out for her first walk to the grocery store. Wukich glanced at the exit of the parking lot to make sure the battered red pickup truck wasn't exiting. Its presence on a weekday morning in and of itself was a pain in the ass. Every weekday he had covered Billie, her big Indian-looking husband named Buck had left in it by dawn. Maybe this morning he had overslept—he seemed like the type.

Or maybe they'd gone out the back door—though he had never seen Billie use it. The first week he had positioned himself so he could see both doors. But that meant spending most of the time out of his car, which wasn't his idea of fun.

Christ, how could anybody stay sharp after nearly a month of watching a pregnant woman? He had already learned more than he wanted to know when his own wife was pregnant. He decided to check the back door.

The apartment was in an old section of Hyattsville, a Maryland suburb of Washington, D.C. Comprising mostly older apartment buildings and small convenience stores, the neighborhood was run down, to put it mildly. Wukich hated the trash blown up against the walls of the buildings by the wind. He hated the corner stores, all of which seemed to be operated by someone who didn't speak English. Not to mention the *people*, standing around on the corners and the stoops, staring at his white skin as if he had just dropped trou' and peed in the street.

"Jesus fucking Christ," he had said repeatedly in the last month. "Go back to where you came from, or get a job. Yeah, get a fucking job!"

The creep on the steps of the apartment building catty-corner to Billie's was a perfect example. Nearly every day he had seen him in the same position. Occasionally the asshole stood to talk with some of the locals. Sometimes he walked to the corner and back. But he sure as hell seemed healthy enough to work. One day Wukich had watched him sprint up a set of cement stairs to rescue a baby that was about to fall out of a stroller, headfirst. The man's color suggested somewhere south of the border, but, hell, they were all spicks as far as he was concerned. Today the guy was, as usual, unshaven, his painter's overalls filthy. A baseball hat shadowed most of his face, but Wukich could tell he was returning his stare.

"Get a fucking job," Wukich whistled under his breath as he passed him.

The back door of the apartment building was locked, and Wukich headed toward the parking lot. Buck used the truck during the week, but on weekends Billie sometimes ventured out in it. The truck was still there, the back still filled with construction debris.

Continuing his circle, Wukich turned the corner and saw Billie at the entrance to the apartments. She was speaking vehemently, maybe yelling, to somebody close to the door. Cutting diagonally across a patch of dirt, he saw Buck, standing on the curb in bare feet, his hands in the pockets of his jeans. They were arguing, with Billie doing most of the yelling. Even from this distance Wukich could see the blank stare on Buck's face. An older woman exited the building and hurried nervously away.

Wukich kept to the sidewalk and slowed his pace as he came abreast of them. Now close enough to hear her words, he felt like running, felt like slamming the asshole into the wall.

"You said it was okay!" She started to cry and turn away. Then after one step she stopped and faced him. "Goddamn you, Buck! You said you understood." She was quiet for a moment and seemed to gather some control. "You know, Buck, I've learned a lot from this. One day I am going to have my own baby. But I'm really starting to wonder if it's going to end up being with you." With that she turned and rushed down the sidewalk.

Buck's face turned pensive, and he took several steps after her. Then he looked down at his feet, turned, and disappeared back inside.

Wukich was sure Billie was headed for one of the stores or restaurants around the corner, and he debated waiting in his car for her to return. What had been a threat of rain was now inevitable. Peals of thunder reverberated from the darkened horizon. The temperature had dropped maybe ten degrees in the last twenty minutes. He swore and hurried back to his car for his coat and umbrella as the rain began to spatter the sidewalk.

He caught sight of her around the corner near the Chinese restaurant where she sometimes stopped for egg rolls. She was walking quickly, faster than he had ever seen her, and he congratulated himself on his decision to follow her. After two more blocks she slowed and finally stopped to turn up the collar of her windbreaker. The rain was now falling with audible force. Without an umbrella Billie looked around for shelter before deciding on a diner across the street. He had seen her eat there several times in the past weeks. Wukich stepped into a doorway out of the rain and watched her go into the little restaurant.

The wind precipitately changed direction, blowing the rain almost sideways, right into the doorway. Wukich pressed back against the glass door behind him and studied the street. The traffic was at a near standstill, headlights blinking on and wipers waving furiously. A van stopped in front of the restaurant and momentarily blocked his view of the door. Moving on, it turned the corner only seconds after a man wearing a poncho hurried up the restaurant steps. Wukich thought about running back for his car, but he really didn't want to leave Billie in there unattended. Neither did he want to go into the restaurant and risk her recognizing him. He agonized a little longer, getting wetter by the minute, before the thought of hot coffee and a dry place to smoke propelled him across the street.

Focused on the restaurant's steps, he was five yards away when his peripheral vision picked up a man running alongside him. The man had a hood over his bent head, and as he bore down on him, Wukich thought the man probably couldn't see him. He didn't have time to think anything else. The man hit him broadside, lifting him off his feet. Ignoring Wukich's profanities, the man quickly passed him and turned the corner.

Wukich got up and looked at his dripping, grimy pants. "Fuck the both of you," he said, turning in the direction of his car. His golf clothes were in the trunk, and he would drive back to the restaurant, he decided.

He gathered his bearings. Then, taking a shortcut, he headed down the side street next to the restaurant. Crossing a narrow driveway that led into a back parking lot and delivery area, he registered several trash cans and a few vehicles. He stopped and turned to look again. The van that had slowed in front of the diner was backed up against what appeared to be the place's rear entrance. It's just a delivery truck, he told himself as he started back to the front of the diner. After a few steps he broke into a trot.

Thick clouds of cigarette smoke swirled toward a central ceiling fan in the narrow room. Wukich looked left, looked right. He wanted to scream. He studied the faces one more time before he turned to a waitress.

"A woman in a yellow jacket came in here about ten minutes ago. Do you remember seeing her?"

"You mean Billie," she said, looking him over.

"Yeah, Billie."

"I guess she left."

"She just got here."

"I think something happened to her husband. At least that's what the guy said that came in here."

"The guy who came in here just a minute ago wearing a poncho?"

"Yeah."

"Did they leave together?"

She shrugged and started to clean off a table. "Don't know. Ain't none of my business."

Wukich ran for the back door, the waitress calling after him. He barreled through a storage area and then outside onto a cement landing. The van was gone. He hopped off the landing, and for the first time in years, tears filled his eyes.

Billie Williams had no idea how many hours she had been there, slipping in and out of bad dreams about some tedious childhood car trip. From time to time she felt a bump of the road. Each brought a sharp stab of fearful pain in her belly. She concentrated on the rumble of an engine beneath and in front of her, anything to obliterate the heavy breathing of the other person she knew was there.

The terror hit her suddenly with the realization that she was tied down at her wrists and ankles. Her head was free, but useless with the tight band of cloth across her eyes. Her next thought was of Buck, that he and his friends were going way too far. Yet the pain was too real. Buck might be ambivalent about the pregnancy, but he loved her—that she knew. Still, she thought, this might have something to do with his behavior of late. The other day he had even come right out with his nonsense.

"Some of the guys were talking at work," he had begun. "About money and things. You know, like how much money it would take you do something you thought you'd never do. Well," he had said, "I'm just kind of curious. I know you wouldn't ever do it, but just how much would somebody have to pay you to give up that baby? The guys say everybody has their price. I said I don't know about you. They said I was full of shit. They said you may act like you're different, but you're not."

"What the hell are you talking about, Buck?" she had said. "I *am* giving up this baby. You know that. And why are you asking me questions like that? You know perfectly well the money doesn't have anything to do with it. Besides, I really don't care what your stupid-ass friends think."

"I know, Billie. But I ain't talkin' about our kind of money. I mean big money. Money like you never seen."

"Shut up, Buck," she had said.

"And I don't mean when you have it," he had persisted, "I mean—you know what I mean. I know what that would do to you, but . . ."

"Just what the hell are you talking about?" she had yelled.

"I'm talking about now," he had said. "Giving it up *now*."

She had never before heard Buck's voice quaver. He had then ducked the glass ashtray she flung at his head. He took the toe of her boot, aimed at his balls, in his hip.

Buck had caught her halfway down the street and apologized. "It was only a game," he had said. "It was just something we were doing at work. You know how fucked-up those guys are."

But she knew he had been lying, even though she had never figured out why. Now it didn't matter one way or another. The warm, fetid breath laden with the odor of greasy food was coming closer, was only inches from her face. A cold hand touched her belly, and her abdomen involuntarily retracted. When the hand reached up under her shirt and squeezed her breast, she bucked against the ties.

The person breathed again, right into her partially open mouth, and she felt like gagging. Knowing she had to conserve her energy, she lay still. The hand slowly moved down her abdomen. When it reached the snap of her jeans, she gathered her strength to buck, but a male's low voice from somewhere in front of her stopped the hand. Another voice—just above her head and more guttural—answered in a foreign language. The hand moved up, gave her breast one more squeeze, then retreated.

But the rancid odor of the man's breath, as though it had coated her, stayed behind and heightened the nauseating motion of the vehicle. The darkness began to spin. On the verge of vomiting, she started to lift her head for help when a dragging sound like a curtain being pulled open restrained her. A moment later somebody loosened the cloth along her temple. Suddenly it was off, and she squinted hard in the dim light. The half-second glimpse she did get, however, was enough to see that they were in a truck or van and that it was night. That meant at least eight or nine ours of traveling, she calculated, and the distance they must have traveled made her acutely afraid. The light faded from her eyes, and she began to focus. All she saw was a man, wearing a cap and mask, leaning over her and reaching for her face. He gently lifted her upper eyelids, and an incredible brightness flashed deep in her eyes. Seconds later the cloth was back and tight.

For a moment the despair was paralyzing. Then a rush of panic seized her, and she rocked her head violently from side to side. The man's big hands immediately pinned her head, and knowing there was no choice, she went limp. And in some way that she recognized as absurd, she felt safer with this man above her. His touch was soft, his smell clean. Then the knife-sharp pain was in her upper arm again, within seconds making her light-headed, and she arched in protest. But the cool, unyielding web slid over her, enveloping her like a film of blackness. Floating now, the urge to strain gone, she felt comfort in the man's gentle touch on her forehead. Again and again he stroked her hair as she drifted to the edge of total darkness. She tried desperately to cling to the brief image of his masked face, but it was dark, so dark, and she could barely remember the blur of his head. She fell, carrying with her only the sadness of his dark eyes.

When Billie came to, she knew at once that the sounds and sensations all around her were far from her dreams, and that she had been moved. There was still pressure on her wrists and ankles, but it was softer and looser than before, more like the band of pressure on her eyelids. The surface she was lying on was firmer, the angle of her body different. As was the position of her legs—the very odd position of her legs. They were up in the air, her ankles pressed against chilled steel.

Suddenly she felt her groin cold and wet in a familiar way. Then the faint odor of iodine reached her, and she realized with a sickening sensation that spread through her like an electric shock that her legs were in stirrups, and that a sponge was being slopped against her labia. A new rivulet of cold water ran down between her buttocks. The nausea she remembered from the van returned, along with spurts of bitter fluid up into her throat. She started to gag and tried to move her head, but it was held in place with a strap around her chin. Her stomach began to heave in earnest, filling her mouth with vomit.

She heard shoes moving quickly on a hard floor and felt a presence beside her. Hands grabbed at her chin and face. The ties loosened, slipped away, and sudden bright light shut her eyes. She forced them open to see the man who was turning her chin and cleaning out her mouth with a finger. He wore a blue cap and mask similar to what she had seen in the van, but she didn't think he was the same man. he was bigger in the chest and belly, and his finger seemed thicker than the ones that had stroked her forehead. When most of the vomit had been wiped away, she quieted. The man gazed down at her, studying her face without ever looking at her eyes. Then he motioned to a masked man standing between her legs to get something on the other side of the room.

Billie started to wretch again, her body buckling in uncontrollable waves. The man that had been between her legs returned and whispered to the man next to her. He swore softly and looked around the room. Billie felt new bits of food lodging in the back of her throat. She bucked against the restraining ties and shook her head wildly from one edge of the table to the other. The man beside her swore again and began to untie her wrists. The moment her arms were free, she sat up as far as her position allowed to cough and spit out what she could. "Bathroom," she gasped. "Let me go to the bathroom."

More whispering, then one of the men went to a door while the other began to untie her ankles. A shorter third man entered, his gaze on her bare groin. He came close, and Billie fought the urge to kick at his face as she recognized his smell. The other two gripped her arms and helped her down from the table. When she was standing, wobbly and faint, they put her into a gown and passed her to the short man. He grunted and led her out of the room.

The bathroom was down a hall and around a corner. Once inside, Billie fell to her knees and leaned over the toilet bowl. The man started to follow her in, but she struck at him with her legs. "I have to go to the bathroom," she said angrily, and pushed him out the door.

Besides the sink and toilet, there was little else in the tiny space. She forced herself upright and searched for something to use as a weapon. Other than a metal paper-towel container and a scrub brush, she didn't see any possibilities. She picked up the brush—it was light, useless. Then she saw a small bucket behind the toilet. She rifled through several sponges and rags and grabbed a bottle of industrial cleaning fluid. She poured some of it into a cup on the sink, tightened her gown, and faced the door. Holding the cup to her mouth, she stepped out.

The man was right there. She bent over and began to retch, aware of him leaning over beside her. She straightened and flung the fluid into his face. For a moment he was still. Then he cried out like an animal in pain and grabbed wildly at his eyes. By the time he started to stumble toward the other men, Billie was five yards past him and running for a door with an exit sign above it. Pushing through it, she found herself in another hall, this one barely lit and completely quiet. There was an exit sign down to the left, and she ran, her bare feet slapping loudly on the linoleum. She found herself in an entry hall, its front door locked. She looked around and lunged for a window behind a row of chairs. Flipping the lock, she yanked the window up and, as an alarm pierced the air, looked down to ground and bushes ten feet below. She squirmed through the window headfirst and half jumped, half fell. Gratefully she felt the bushes rip into her legs and feet.

It was dark out, the street ahead lit, but empty. Instinctively she ran for the road and some buildings on the other side of it, feeling as though she were out side of herself and watching somebody else's arms and legs propel her forward. She made it to the street. Crossing it, she saw a bright neon light and what appeared to be the sign of a gas station far down the row of streetlights. They would have a telephone, she thought. But first she had to hide. First she had to get away.

She reached the shadow of the first building and began to think about whom she would call. The cops? Maybe, but the last thing she wanted was a police interrogation in a small, strange town. She kept running. Buck was out of the question. For a split second between her retches on the table—when the man beside her had sworn in what she thought was Spanish—the unbelievable thought that her husband was involved in this had returned. Somewhere before she had heard that voice, and all she could think of was Buck's friends. But still the matching face would not come. Like her body, her thoughts seemed dulled and slow, like in the first blurry seconds after the shots in her arm.

She turned a corner, and suddenly she knew whom to call. That he would come for her wherever she was, without question or judgment, he had already told her. She turned another corner and saw a stand of trees and a town-house development, There would be plenty of places to hide until she could get to a telephone.

FOUR

Nathan Morick paced the kitchen, stopping every second or third cycle to stare out the back window. Once he went to the front door and looked out into the street.

"Will you *please* stop it, Nathan?" said Sarah. "It's okay. Really—it is. I'm fine. Dad says Billie is fine. And I *do* understand."

"I'm not concerned about you. I believe you."

"Then why in the world are you letting *him* get to you? He's not an ogre. He understands these things."

"Bullshit. That's just it, Sarah. He *doesn't* understand. He expects me to tell them to just fuck off. Except for those two years in Korea—and he probably thought he was a damn general then—he's never worked for anybody but himself. And that's what he expects of the whole fucking world."

"Oh, you're too sensitive. I work for a bank, for heaven's sake. He knows everybody can't work for themselves."

Nathan shook his head and paced. "Bullshit, Sarah. And you know I'm right. For the next twenty years, he'll be telling people he had to take you and Billie to the doctor's because I wouldn't take off from work. He stopped and stared at Sarah. "And don't even start comparing—"

"*Couldn't* take off from work, Nathan."

"That's not the way he sees it. Especially when it has anything to do with you. And it's not just now with the baby. Even though he doesn't know the first fucking thing about the accounting business, not going out on my own is the reason we don't have a bigger house. It's the reason—"

"Come here, Nathan," said Sarah, as if he were a little boy. She pulled him onto her lap and drew his face down. "*I* understand, and that's all that counts. Don't worry about him." She kissed him and rubbed his back. "Come on. Try to relax."

For a moment the tension in Nathan's face seeped away. Then he was up again, leaning against a counter, glaring at the entry hall. "You know, Sarah, it's more than work and taking off—"

"Nathan, for godsake, we just—"

"It's not that," he interrupted. "I'm talking about Billie. This whole business with her really—"

The doorbell rang, and Sarah went to the door. Nathan had not seen his father-in-law since the day Sarah had taken Billie to see Dr. Gleason. He and Dorothy had come over at first chance that evening to hear every word. Although Dr. Gleason's dissenting opinion had been far from disheartening, at the time they had all been too confused to take much hope. But now it was a week later.

Warren DeLozier definitely looked pleased. He grunted at Nathan and pulled out a map. Sarah took her place next to him at the kitchen table, and the two of them bent over the map, discussing the fastest route to Wilmington. Nathan looked at his watch. He had to leave for work in a few minutes.

"Warren," he said, "why does Billie have to see a doctor in Wilmington? Wouldn't it be better to see somebody here in town? Especially if that's where we might have the baby."

DeLozier nodded, his face stiffening with the equivocation. "Yes, I'm sure it would be. But as I told Sarah last night, Billie doesn't feel safe here."

"Not even for the day?"

DeLozier looked at him. "No, not even for the day. She doesn't trust her husband. She doesn't *want* to come back here."

"I'm not quite sure I understand that."

"What don't you understand?"

"Why she's so scared of her husband. The surrogate agency is supposed to screen for things like that."

"People lie," said DeLozier. He studied the map for a moment, then added evenly, "I don't know what happened between them, Nathan. All I know is that we have to deal with what we have, and right now that's a frightened young woman. If Billie doesn't trust

Buck, then we have to—"

"*Buck?*"

"Yes, Buck. That's her husband."

"How do you know his name?"

DeLozier looked somewhere past his cup to the table. Then he sighed and faced Nathan directly. "Because I've talked to Billie about him, Nathan. And because I've met him. And I sure as hell don't blame her for not trusting him."

"You've met him!"

"Yes, I've met him. When Billie told the agency she was concerned about him, they called me."

"But why did they call *you*? What do you—"

"Because *I'm* the one paying for Billie, Nathan. Have you decided if you're going with us?"

"I have to go to the office," said Nathan, rising from the table, "I can't miss another day."

"That's fine. I'll take good care of the both of them."

"I'll call you from the doctor's office as soon as we're done," said Sarah. "Promise."

Nathan nodded and moved for the door. The son-of-a-bitch can't help it, he told himself over and over. If it wasn't for that fucking accident—*his* fucking accident—he'd be preening over three grandchildren by now. And he knows it every minute of every day. Nathan went back into the kitchen and kissed Sarah good-bye. Six more months. He could manage six more months.

It took an hour to get out of Mexico City from the airport, another half hour before the highway traffic to the west lightened. Soon the silver Mercedes sedan was on cruise control, the apartment buildings, factories, and patches of littered, barren ground flying by. Fifty miles from the road leading to his family's hacienda, Dr. Carlos Luis Fernandez stopped at a roadside café to call his office. There was no new message from Roberto—the tramp was still missing. Four days later, and she had not returned to her apartment, the Moricks, or to Richard. Her husband—even with a blank check in front of him—had no idea where she was. Four days he had waited. Four days he had wasted. And now they were late. The seeds should have been in the ground, sprouting like the fields of fresh green corn. For a while he stared out at the road. Finally he turned for the bar. All was not lost. There was still time, still hope. Roberto was as good as they came.

At the bar he ordered a bottle of beer. He would have much preferred to have been heading in the opposite direction, to his Mexico City town home, and he felt nothing but dread. Even his sister—kind, understanding Felice—would be disappointed. And rightfully so. He had made premature allusions. He had hinted of hope, and of new life, when he should have surprised them with the gift. He drank deeply. But he had wanted to see their thankful faces. He had wanted to see Don Rafael's attempt at gratitude, though he had known it would be silent. He had wanted to feel his gaze, warm and . . . loving. Of course his mother and Felice had complied. And to his surprise Don Rafael—the devil take his soul—had smiled. But not in thanks. "You . . . you are my dreamer, Carlos," he had said. "You . . . you have always been my dreamer."

Fernandez finished his beer. This is no dream, Papa, he said to himself in the car. You will see. You will see my dream, and you will see *me*, whether you want to or not.

He exited the highway onto a winding narrow road and turned of the cruise control. Now it was only fields, broad expanses of young corn rising through the red dirt in soldierly rows. In the distance, on the foothills, the green geometric shapes of coffee fields were spaced against squares of brown.

A boy was waiting by the tall black iron gates at the foot of the driveway. Fernandez rolled down his window and motioned him close to the car. The boy accepted a coin with a sheepish grin, and Fernandez moved on. He drove the remaining quarter mile up to the main house slowly, taking in the clean air, the faint smell of recent rain, the fields of corn and soy alternating with acres of earth turned over in long parallel rows. The fields were immaculate, as were the fences and outlying sheds, and he reminded himself to compliment Octavio Monsano. Near the house he stopped to study the main barn. Several men, shouting and laughing at each other, were climbing onto tractors and huge combines. Octavio's son, Eduardo, was talking to the foreman. Seeing Fernandez, he waved.

Fernandez moved up to the circular driveway in front of the house and turned the car over to one of Roberto's nephews, who took it around to the back. For a moment he stood still, looking out over the nearest fields, feeling the crisp air on his face. Coming down from the mountains, it was a refreshing ten degrees cooler than the city's, and he sucked it in deeply. He turned to study the house. It looked as good as it had in years. A fresh coat of white paint on the old adobe brick walls was bright in the midday sun; the burnt-orange shutters and porticoes were almost fiery. Don Rafael should be pleased.

But his second son knew he wouldn't be. He would be silent, mourning the loss of one hundred years of *Fernandez* hands in Fernandez dirt. And now—in the face of death—it was a loss that seemed to tear at him more with each week.

He found his mother and Felice at the kitchen table. His mother rose and hurried to him, and he held her silvery head, the thick hair pulled back tightly with a silver clip, against his chest. After similarly embracing his sister, the three of them walked arm in arm out to the side porch.

"I don't think you learned as much as you hoped you would," said Felice. She put an arm around her brother. "Don't look so sad. He's been all right this week."

Senora Fernandez turned her head and stared at the line of scrub pines on the foothills.

Her son went to her. "What Felice says is true, Mama. There are doctors in the States with good ideas, even great ideas, but for now that is all they are. I had hoped for more." He paused. "I still do. I talked to a doctor in Mexico City just this morning. There are no promises, but . . . there is still hope."

She smiled weakly and nodded, then went into the house to dry her eyes.

Fernandez sat in her chair and sighed.

"Mama will be okay," said Felice.

Fernandez was silent.

"We'll be okay." She watched him for a minute. "Papa is not blind, Carlos. When he comes down, he sees . . . everything. He sees what Octavio has done. He sees Eduardo."

"He sees *nothing*! He sees beans and corn and . . . *Benito*! He is blind as . . ." Fernandez stood and shoved the wooden chair into the wall behind him. Felice moved for him, but he rushed past her and down the steps. When he reached the dirt path leading toward the pond, he stopped and shouted: "*You* will be okay. *I* will suffer until the day I die. Don't you understand? I want him to see *me*! I want him to let us go—to let me go!—in peace. He needs time for that! he needs *me*!" Fernandez turned and hurried down the path. "And I need him," he added under his breath. "I need him very much."

Her father had warned her, but the sight of Billie climbing out of the beige sedan waiting in the 7-Eleven parking lot was a shock. The right side of her face was swollen and turning a yellowish green; a long scratch started at her left ear and crossed her jaw near her chin. She walked gingerly toward the car, dark sunglasses shielding her eyes.

"Oh my God, Dad, why didn't you tell me!"

Billie climbed into the backseat. "I'm okay," she said. "It looks worse than it is. Same as last week?"

DeLozier answered for Sarah. "Basically, yes. Let Sarah talk about why you're in Wilmington. You just need a reason for your cuts and bruises."

Staring out the window as they left for the obstetrician's office, Sarah felt her stomach tighten. Dr. Zimmerman was the end of the line. Highly recommended by several of her father's friends in Wilmington, he was reportedly bright, experienced, and, above all, frank.

At the clinic one of the nurses tried to obtain a history from Billie, but the story became so convoluted that she quickly gave up. She left the interview room, and shortly Dr. Zimmerman met them with a grin.

"Beth says you're confusing the heck out of her and I better talk to you."

"It's not that complicated," Sarah replied. "Really."

"Okay," he said, his eyes going to Billie's bruised face. He motioned them into an examination room.

Feeling his gaze more on her now, Sarah said, "Would you like me—"

"In a minute." The nurse came in and handed the doctor a folder.

"I made up a new patient record," she said, "but I'm not sure we need a full one. I think she's just here for a check."

"You won't be delivering here?" he asked Billie.

"No, sir," Billie answered in her resurrected rural Floridian accent. "I gots to go home. I'm just visitin' my cousin."

Zimmerman nodded while he scanned the folder. When he was finished, he looked to Sarah.

"Yes, I'm her cousin. If it's all right with you, Billie wanted me to stay with her while you talked to her. She's a little scared."

"That's up to Mrs. Williams," he said, looking at Billie's thin gold band.

Billie shook her head.

"Do you live around here, Mrs . . . . Morick?" he asked.

"No. I live at the beach. Billie came to see us there, and that's how all this started. I'll let her tell you about that." Zimmerman didn't respond. "The people staying next to us are from Wilmington," she continued. "They recommended you highly. Billie hasn't had much prenatal care."

"I see. Who are your friends?"

"Ted and Carol Martin. I think they live on the Brandywine River."

"Doesn't ring a bell. But that doesn't mean anything," he added with a chuckle. "So how can I help you, young lady?" he said to Billie.

"Go ahead, Billie," said Sarah. "Just tell him what you told me."

"My sister had a baby last year. It was deadborn. Stillborn, maybe they said. She thinks they told her it runs in the family. I don't know if you can check for that or not. I was wanting to know, though. I don't want no dead baby."

"I'm pretty sure there was a problem with the development of the brain," added Sarah. "I spoke with the doctor who did the delivery. I believe he said anencephaly. And Billie's mother thinks one of her sisters had a similar problem."

Zimmerman nodded slowly. Then he said, "How many weeks pregnant are you, Mrs. Williams?"

Screwing her face up as if it were a difficult question, Billie took a few seconds to answer. "I think we figured a little over three months," she said, glancing uncertainly at Sarah.

"How long are you going to be in the area?"

"I got to take a bus back Wednesday."

"Well, what would you do if you needed an amniocentesis? That's a test where we look at the fluid around the baby. I believe I can answer your question without it, but let's play 'what if' for a minute."

"If it's necessary, I can bring her back," said Sarah. "But if you can tell her anything today, good or bad, I think it would really help. I think not knowing bothers her the most."

Zimmerman shrugged. "I should be able to answer all of her questions today. But you never know."

"If you need to see her again, I'll make the arrangements," said Sarah. "But you think you can tell her today?"

"If she's as far along as she thinks she is, I should be able to tell by an ultrasound." He squinted. "But it's a little late to be starting all this, isn't it?"

Bill stared at him blankly.

"What do you mean?" said Sarah.

"Well, I presume you're here because you're going to make some kind of decision about the pregnancy if there is a problem. It seems a little late in the game to be asking the question for the first time."

Sarah started to speak, but Billie interrupted her. "I'm sorry, Doctor. I don't know much about these things. I didn't say nothin' before 'cause I figgered there wasn't nothin' we could do 'bout findin' out. And my mother didn' tell me 'bout my sister 'till a few weeks ago. We only got one doctor in our town," she added angrily. "It's hard to get to him."

"I understand." Zimmerman moved away from the table. "Well, let's go ahead and see what I can tell you." To Sarah he said, "Ma'am, if you don't mind, I'm going to ask you to wait outside."

As the door was closing behind her, Sarah heard Zimmerman say, "What happened to you, young lady? You look as if you got into a little scuffle. Is everything all right at home?"

"Oh, sure," said Billie. "I was up on this ol' ladder paintin' and . . ."

Twenty minutes later Dr. Zimmerman came out, his face neutral. Tremulous, Sarah followed him to his office. A step from the door, she saw Billie, already seated in a chair, smiling. Zimmerman began to talk, but his words were wasted.

"So," she finally heard him concluding, "as far as I'm concerned, everything looks fine, and I would just check in with a doctor when you get home, Mrs. Williams."

"The ultrasound looked normal to you?" said Sarah.

"Yes, Mrs. Morick, as I just explained, the ultrasound looked normal. I do not appreciate any problems with the fetal head. Its size and shape are appropriate for my estimated fetal age."

"What about her uterus?"

"What about her uterus, Mrs. Morick?" He studied her for a moment.

"Does it feel the way it should, I guess?"

The doctor's eyelids narrowed. "As I said, her exam is normal. All of it. And the way I see it," he said pleasantly to Billie, "your dates are right on the nose. You probably conceived right around the middle of February."

PART TWO

FIVE

October 1990

With the early morning sun coming bright off the water, Wukich had to shield his eyes to see the motorboat churning up the bay into the wind. It passed the house and sputtered on. In another few minutes its indistinct form was just another receding shape on the horizon. Wukich stayed on the dock until the boat was out of sight. Then, hunching over, he lit a cigarette and turned for the house.

It was about time to go out for the newspaper, he thought. He tried to remember if it was Friday or Saturday, if the day before he had gone to Jake's store or Harry's, but he could not recall. Between all the moving and the slow pace of their lives in the isolated houses and communities, the days had long ago become a blur.

"I was about to come out and get you." Billie was lying on the couch on the porch, her hands resting on her belly.

"I know. It's time to get the paper." Wukich looked at the calendar on his watch. "And the lady at the store said your magazines might be in today. Man, we're going to have a high time."

Billie giggled, then was quiet.

"What's the matter, Billie? You feeling okay?"

"I don't think we should go to the store yet."

"Why? What's the matter? Are you feeling somethin'?"

"I'm having some pain. It's kind of different from anything I've had before."

"You think its contractions?"

Billie shrugged. "I guess it could be. I don't really know."

Wukich remembered his wife's visits to the hospital. "Well, is the pain there all the time? Or does it come and go?"

"It's come two or three times."

He felt his pulse quicken. "Well . . . what do you think? Should we start packing or not?"

"I don't know. What do you think? *You're* the one who's been through this before."

She looked at him in the little-girl way she sometimes did when she wanted help—when she really did not know and was in some way embarrassed. And suddenly he felt a sharp sense of loss: after this was over, he would most likely never see Billie again.

"Jesus, Billie, I don't know," he finally said. "I was getting the car ready and stuff like that."

"Well, what was your wife's pain like? Don't you remember that at least?"

Wukich heard the panic in her voice. He wanted to touch her, to comfort her. This wasn't fair. There ought to be another woman here, somebody to hold her hand, for Christ's sake.

"How'd it start for her?" Billie persisted.

"I don't know, Billie," he said gently. "I don't think I was home when it started."

"Didn't you ask her?"

Wukich saw the pain in her face. "I think I better start packing," he said. "Better safe than sorry."

When he returned to the living room, Billie was sitting up and putting her shoes on.

"Well?" he asked.

"I think we ought to go. If it stops, we can always come back."

Wukich nodded and looked at his watch, working the time in his head. It would take three hours to get to Washington, D.C., another fifteen minutes to the hospital to which he had been instructed to take her to. Since this was her first baby, they should have plenty of time. And if they didn't, then there was a hospital almost every fifty miles all the way home.

Wukich quickly straightened up the house and locked it. Then he helped Billie out to the car, feeling none of the relief he had expected. Taking a deep breath, he turned his head to back out the driveway and found Billie, tears sliding down her cheeks, smiling at him. They hugged.

Wukich finally pulled away and smiled. "Do you want to check on your magazines?"

Billie laughed and wiped away her tears. "No. I don't think I'll be needing them."

"Now, let me get this straight," the woman behind the desk was saying as Wukich returned from parking the car. "You're almost *nine* months pregnant, you don't have a doctor, you don't have any records, and you don't have any insurance."

"I have a doctor, and I have records," Billie said. "I told you ma'am, I'm just visiting here."

Wukich took a seat in the waiting area close to Billie and the receptionist.

"You mean it *never* crossed your mind that being nine months pregnant you just *might* have a baby while you're visiting? That maybe you *ought* to have brought your records with you?"

"I'm not due for another ten days."

The woman stared at Billie with disbelief. "And the insurance? How do you propose to pay your hospital bill?"

"With money."

"Whose money?"

"Somebody will be here to pay the bill before I leave . . . . I promise."

The receptionist looked at Billie's sweater and jeans and nodded. "Right," she muttered.

Wukich stepped to the desk. "Her hospital bill will be paid, ma'am."

"Are you the father?" She looked at his hand.

"No, ma'am. But I can guarantee you the bill will be paid. Somebody from the family will be here shortly."

Pain suddenly crossed Billie's face, and the woman sighed. "How often are you having contractions?"

"Every three or four minutes."

She looked hard at Billie's face and picked up her pen. "Address and telephone number, please."

Billie gave her the address of her parents' house in Florida and made up a phone number. The contractions were now doubling her over. "Ma'am, I've never had a baby before," she said between breaths, "but I don't think it's going to be much longer."

The receptionist stared at her again before standing to get a nurse.

Obviously having been briefed about Billie's state of affairs, the nurse who returned was without humor. "Has your water broke?" she said in greeting.

Billie looked at her.

"Did a lot of fluid come out of your vagina?" The nurse's voice was full of exasperation.

"No."

"None?"

"Maybe a little."

"Can you walk?"

"I guess so. I walked in here."

The nurse frowned and looked at the receptionist, who smiled. "Follow me, please."

Billie stood, then bent over for a moment in pain. When she straightened, Wukich winked at her, gave her a thumbs-up, and turned to look for a telephone. With a trace of a smile, he spotted one in the lobby and called into his office for the second time that morning. "Billie Williams is now in St. Joseph's emergency room," he reported with satisfaction, "and she most definitely is going to have a baby."

Six

Sullivan's *Text of Obstetrics* slipped off Brendan Gallagher's chest, and he caught it on its way to the floor. Opening his eyes, he blinked and looked at his roommate in an armchair across from him. "How long have I been asleep?"

"Half hour or so," said Wayne Masterson from behind a large book propped up on his knees. "Why don't you go to bed? You've read that book cover to cover three times in the last year."

"I know. Sometimes I even dream about it. Tell me that's not sick."

"It is sick. You're not supposed to memorize it. You just need to know where things are so you can look 'em up."

"Not when a kid's croaking right in front of you."

"Yeah, I guess," said Masterson, turning back to his atlas of surgical anatomy. "But that's what you have staff for."

"I'll be staff in seven months."

Masterson looked at him. "Good Cod, I keep forgetting that. But you're still sick. Half the groinocologists in town don't even remember what color that book is."

"What can I say? I'm a professional anal obsessive. If I don't know it all, I feel like shittin' in my pants when it gets rough."

"Your mother must have given you enemas."

"Every Sunday. Right before mass. I was the cleanest little altar boy that ever looked up the organist's skirt."

"Now *that* is sick. Go to sleep."

"No way. Notre Dame's going to kick the shit out of Penn State."

Masterson snorted, and Gallagher rose from the couch to turn up the volume on the television. The announcer had just finished his introduction, and the camera took a wide swing through the standing crowd, finally focusing on a cheerleader's legs.

Masterson closed his book and went into the kitchen, his six foot five inch frame almost filling the small space. "Beer here, beer here," he called. "Getchyour beer here. *Col*dest beer in town. Beer here." He opened a bottle and brought it to Gallagher.

Gallagher shook his head. "Not today. I'm on call for the junior, residents. They don't know their ass from a hole in the ground."

"That's not what we say," said Masterson, plopping back down in his chair.

"'We'?"

"Surgeons."

"Oh yeah. What do the *real* surgeons say?"

"We have a very simple motto: if you can't drink and take call, then you shouldn't be taking call."

Gallagher laughed. "Actually, for a bunch of brain-dead megalomaniacs, that's not too bad. Maybe I'll reconsider in a bit."

"If I were you, I'd do it now," said Masterson, rising to his feet as the Penn State tailback crossed the twenty with the kickoff. He broke another tackle and picked up a blocker. "'Cuz my boy Uhle is going *all* the way. Hot damn!" he shouted, turning in a circle and raising his arms. "You're in for a long damn day. You better go talk to Mr. Brewski."

"Goddamn," said Gallagher, picking up the remote control and turning the channel. "Enough of that."

"Turn it back, you asshole!" Masterson lunged toward Gallagher, spilling beer onto the rug and coffee table.

Gallagher took the remote control and slid it under the couch. "Not until the replay's over. I refuse to believe that happened."

Masterson picked up one end of the couch, tumbling Gallagher onto the floor. After retrieving the remote control with his foot, he let the couch drop with a thud that shook the walls. By the time he changed the channel back, Notre Dame was getting ready to receive the kickoff.

"That's much better," said Gallagher.

"God, you're an asshole."

The phone rang and Masterson answered it. "Well, let me see if Dr. Gallagher is still here. He may have gone to church early today." Masterson covered up the phone and smiled. "Do you want to talk to a Dr. Curry? He seems a tad excited."

"Gimme that," said Gallagher, reaching for the phone. "Hey, Michael. What's up?"

"I'm sorry to bother you, Brendan," said Michael Curry, the junior obstetrics resident on call at St. Joseph's Community Hospital, "but things are getting crazy here. I've got one lady ready to go, one fat lady whose pressure is sky high, and the ER just called with one who's completely dilated."

"Who's the attending for the one in the ER?"

"She doesn't have one. Sharon said she's just visiting here. She doesn't have any records either. Coretti's the staff today. I'll call him if you want, but I thought I ought to let you know first."

Gallagher hesitated.

"Please, Brendan," said Curry. "I don't want to call Coretti."

"I'm coming, Michael, I'm coming. What do you want me to help you with, the ER delivery or the fat lady?"

"If you could see the lady in the ER, that would really help. I can take care of the other stuff."

"Okay. Listen, send one of the medical students down there to do a history and physical. I'll be there in twenty minutes. Can she wait that long?"

"Yeah, this is her first. Sharon said she probably wouldn't go for an hour or so."

"Fine. I'll check in with you when I get there."

Gallagher hung up and looked at the television. "Son-of-a-bitch," he said. "This is the one game I wanted to watch this year."

"You're too good to them, Brendan. My chief resident would have told me to suck it up and quit wasting time on the phone."

Gallagher shrugged and began to gather some clothes and books. "He needs help."

Minutes later he headed for his old white Mustang parked a block down the street from their apartment. Parking places were sparse even in this fringe of the city, but most days Gallagher didn't mind. With the majority of his time spent either in the hospital or sleeping, he relished the fresh air and sunlight.

Comprising mostly old Victorian and three-story frame houses, the neighborhood was a pleasant transition between the city and the seemingly endless miles of new suburban houses sprouting spindly young trees and swing sets like the bizarre appendages of insects. Here the big oaks bent their arms over the sidewalks in graceful, sweeping curves, and the driveways were devoid of minivans and tricycles.

An elderly couple raking leaves waved at Gallagher as he passed. He waved back, yelled a greeting, and picked up his pace as he looked across the street to a row of narrow brick town houses. Unless it was raining in Boston, his father would have already raked and edged the little square in front of the row house. Then he would have headed down the street to Callahan's, which had recently acquired a giant television screen. Yelling with his buddies for Notre Dame to annihilate the heathens, he'd be on his second beer by now. Maybe these days, since he had lost his job, it'd be his third or fourth. Maybe he wouldn't have raked at all.

Gallagher threw his bag in the back of the car and headed down toward the Potomac River. He stopped for a moment at MacArthur Boulevard, then turned for the city and cut up to Foxhall Road. At Foxhall he turned toward Wisconsin Avenue, passing one embassy and embassy-like house after another. A mile from Wisconsin he slowed, his gaze turning to the parking lot of the Washington Fertility Institute. There was no sign of Lindsey Baines's red Honda Civic, or Ashton's baby blue Jaguar XJS.

It felt like years ago—walking through those gleaming doors and into the meticulous high-tech world of modern fertility medicine. Although some of the institute's monetary policies had bothered him, his time there had been like a refreshing dream: fresh-ground coffee in the morning; lab results back the next day; operating rooms that sparkled and ran on time. When he had left on the first of April to begin a rotation in acute-care gynecology at the city hospital, it was as if he had stepped backward in time, into another world. Most of the patients there had no money for medicine; half were prostitutes who came back every month with a different disease. By the time the first of July had rolled around, he had been more than eager to fight the traffic over to the clean halls of St. Joseph's.

Staying on Wisconsin, Gallagher made his way through Chevy Chase and into Bethesda. When he was a mile from the hospital, the top of the building came into sight, then the new west wing, white against the seagull gray of the original institution. Despite the weekend the staff parking lot was almost full, and he felt the predictable surge of nervous energy. In this big quasi-metropolitan hospital, he knew all too well that any kind of medical problem could walk or roll through the doors at any minute. Yet here, no matter how crazy things got, there was always that sense of underlying order, of some higher control at work.

He hurried by the gates of the parking garage and headed for the main entrance, the way he always chose to enter the hospital. Straightening his tie, he passed into the lobby, breathed the slight antiseptic scent of the warm air, glanced at the huge painting of the crucifixion on the wall ahead, and slowed, feeling as though he ought to genuflect. After several quick turns he pushed through the back doors of the emergency room.

"I thought you'd never get here," came the voice of Sharon, the head nurse. She stepped out of a trauma room and lowered her voice. "Would you *please* get that medical student and woman out of here? We delivered one last night. That's enough."

"Okay, okay. Where is she?"

"In six. With *Dr.* Long."

Gallagher stuck his head through the drapes of cubicle number six and motioned to Chuck Long, the fourth-year medical student. They spoke for a minute in the nursing station, then returned to the cubicle.

"Hello, Mrs. Williams," said Gallagher, and introduced himself. By the time the introduction was over, he had a glove on one hand and the other resting on her abdomen. "I'm sorry if everything seems a little rushed, but from what I hear, you're about ready to have your baby." While his fingers measured the breadth of her stretched cervix, he kept his other hand on her abdomen and watched her face. "How long have you been having contractions like the one you're having now?"

"Since about eight or nine this morning," said Billie through short, quick breaths.

So why the hell did you wait so long to come in? Gallagher thought to himself. He said, "Do you feel as if you can push it out?"

Billie nodded and grasped the side rails of the bed.

"Whoa, not yet. We have a few more minutes. Chuck, will you call the labor deck and tell them we'll be up in a few minutes?" Facing Billie again, he reviewed what Long had told him about her medical history and the pregnancy. He listened to her heart and lungs. "Everything looks fine," he said. "Dr. Long is going take you up to the delivery room, and I'll be up in just a minute."

Sharon reappeared with a gurney. As the medical student began to wheel her out, Gallagher called to her from the nursing station where he was writing admission orders. "Do you have the name picked out, Mrs. Williams?"

Gallagher thought she hadn't heard him, but then he noticed that she was blushing. "That's okay," he added quickly. "Lots of people wait to see what they have first."

"Everything happened kind of fast," he heard her say as they wheeled her into the elevator.

A minute later he finished writing and stood up to leave. "Something's a little screwy," he said to Sharon. "She's no rocket scientist, but I don't think she's as dumb as she makes out to be."

"Yeah, I can't figure her out. It isn't as if she's a month early."

"I think Chuck said she's married. Is her husband around?"

"Haven't seen him."

"Oh, well. Thanks for watching her."

In the elevator Gallagher leaned against the back wall and stared at the door. The absence of a staff obstetrician didn't bother him in the least, but the woman's abrupt arrival and lack of records had roused some medical sixth sense drawn from a thousand patients and procedures. With a week left in his rotation, and St. Joseph's in his plans for the future, the last thing he wanted was any kind of problem. Particularly with that ass Coretti. He'd better call him, he decided.

The Paseo de la Reforma, four stories below, was so crammed with cars, buses, and taxis, that even the mopeds and motorcycles were mired in the fumy standstill. To make matters worse, at the intersection of Avenida Juarez, a crowd was gathering around a taxi driver and a man in a business suit whose car he had just rear-ended. Fernandez watched the taxi driver step closer to the man, then a few seconds later push him. Moving his gaze up the wide boulevard, for several more minutes he stayed at the window, staring at the horizon of seemingly endless buildings. Then slowly, as if his body were moving on its own accord, he returned to his desk.

Roberto had found her. Roberto had returned to the States two weeks before to watch the parents. There had been no other choice. Everything else had failed. And still, there had been no others so perfect. So perfect that even now it could work. He watched the telephone. He imagined Roberto's voice, telling him that Richard's gift was on its way. Six months later than he had planned for, but . . . it was so perfect. He willed the telephone to ring. It was silent, a mound of coffee-colored plastic staring back at him.

One of his office lines rang, and he listened impassively until it stopped. Seconds later, his private line lit up, and he watched the little lights on the answering machine flick on. When he heard Roberto's voice, he interrupted the tape.

Roberto was brief. She was still in the emergency room. The only one with her was the man who had watched her at the apartment. He shouldn't be a problem.

Fernandez was just as brief. He'd be waiting for the next call at his home in the city. He reminded Roberto that she had seen his face in Ashton's office; she had heard the name of Dr. Carlos Fernandez. And who knew how much she remembered about the van or the operating room.

Fernandez hung up and called his wife, Rachel. Emilio would be coming to take her to the beach house, he told her; he would meet her there as soon as he could. Next, he wrote a detailed note to his office manager. She already expected him to be out of the office for the next two weeks, for his yearly expedition to Europe. He would be leaving a few days early, he informed her. Dr. Mendoza at the downtown hospital would be available for any problems.

SEVEN

The first order Wukich had received in response to his message—to ensure that Billie Williams safely made it to the labor and delivery suite—was only annoying. One trip to the nurses' desk had completed that task. The next was a real bite in the ass. No only was he to guard Billie throughout her hospital stay, but he was also expected to watch the baby whenever he or she was not with a "Mrs. Morick." Billie, apparently, would not be taking care of the baby. That she had decided to give it up for adoption—and had somehow royally pissed Buck off in the process—he had half expected. Why the hell else had he moved her around like a damn Russian defector. But Jesus Christ, watching a *baby*?

So who's this Mrs. Morick? he wondered, heading out into the corridor. The man he had met in Delaware after Billie's disappearance was named DeLozier. And that was who he had talked to on the pay phones every week over the last five-plus months. Wukich stopped by a wall near the receptionist's desk, out of the way of the people milling around. There was now a line at the desk and no more seats in the waiting area. With the steady parade of patients, the noise had escalated and Wukich took in the controlled din of harried voices, ringing telephones, and short staccato bursts of unintelligible summonings over the emergency radio units. An ambulance pulled up to the receiving door, its lights flashing, its siren emitting the last few decibels of a wail. In seconds it discharged a stretcher and two paramedics pounding on the bared chest of an obese middle-aged man. Wukich watched for a moment, then turned away.

He had been through the baby routine before—was familiar enough with hospitals and the steps you went through before the kid emerged and you could leave with it. After making sure one more time that Billie was in the delivery room, he asked the receptionist for directions to the admissions office.

"Which one?" the girl in admissions said in response to his introduction of himself as a "friend of the family." When he didn't respond, she read indifferently from the computer: "Mrs. Williams will be in six-A, two down from Mrs. Morick. The maternity ward is four east. Labor and delivery is in four north."

Wukich headed back to the elevators. "Mrs. Morick," he repeated to himself, arriving in the lobby as one of the elevator doors opened. He joined a quiet group filing in and at the fourth floor wormed his way out.

Following the signs to the labor and delivery suite, he found a Red Cross volunteer sitting beside a set of swinging double doors. Across from her was a large, comfortably furnished waiting area that was nearly filled up. Wukich studied its occupants. A half—dozen older couples were reading magazines or talking; several families were huddled on couches; two young men were watching television. At the moment the only people nervously pacing were a couple—an expectant uncle and aunt, he presumed—with their backs to him. He asked the Red Cross woman about the progress of Mrs. Williams and, learning that there was none to report, claimed a chair within viewing distance of the TV.

After three unanswered pages Gallagher knew that, Saturday afternoon or not, he would have to call Coretti at home. He dialed; and a minute later, the unanswered phone still ringing in his ear, he dropped the receiver back into its cradle.

He called the labor and delivery suite: Mrs. Williams was on her way into the delivery room; her blood had been drawn; her intravenous line was in place. She was ready to go. Gallagher tried Coretti one more time. Ten rings later he gave up and headed for the delivery rooms.

Chuck Long was studiously working on his fingers outside delivery room number four when Gallagher joined him. While they scrubbed, Gallagher reviewed a few points he wanted the medical student to remember when the excitement began. It would only be Long's third delivery, and with the first two Coretti had made him so nervous he could barely hold onto the instruments. Finished, their hands dripping, they were about to back into the delivery room when a door down the hall opened. Henry Kirby peered through and motioned to Gallagher.

"Go on and get gowned," Gallagher said to the student. "What can I do for you, Mr. Kirby?"

The hospital administrator looked a bit frantic. "I understand a young woman came into the emergency room a little while ago and is about to deliver."

"That's where I'm headed. Why, is there a problem?"

"Does it look like a routine delivery?"

Gallagher shrugged "Should be. She doesn't have any records with her, but she seems healthy enough. Is there a problem, Mr. Kirby? I need to get back there with her."

Kirby shook his head. "Who's the staff on call today?"

"Joe Coretti."

"Did you think about calling him? I know you're comfortable doing the delivery yourself, but since she doesn't have any records or a staff doctor here . . ."

Gallagher looked at him for a moment, then said, "I do feel comfortable doing this delivery, Mr. Kirby. But I did call Dr. Coretti."

"Good. When he comes, will you send him down to my office?"

"He's not coming. Nobody's at his house, and he didn't answer his pages."

"That's not like Joe."

"His beeper's probably broken. It's no big deal. I was only calling him to let him know about the situation. I'm sorry, but I have to get back there."

Kirby nodded. "When you're done, Brendan, would you come to my office?"

Gallagher stopped halfway down the hall. "Your office?"

"Yes, my office. As soon as you can, please."

The man wore a short white laboratory coat with the hospital logo of St. Joseph's on the front pocket and a piece of rubber tubing looped through one of the buttonholes. In his right hand he carried a tray loaded with syringes and empty glass tubes. His pants were hospital white, his shirt open at the neck without a tie—perfectly acceptable dress for a new arrival outside the labor and delivery suite. Wukich's head had started back toward the TV when something clicked into alarm mode. The man's eyes had stayed on him a millisecond too long. His head snapped toward the doors, but the face of the technician, or whatever he was, was now out of view. Then imperceptibly, except to one accustomed to following the movements of others, the man pace quickened.

Wukich was maybe twenty yards behind him when he reached the central lobby. The elevators were all closed, the lights indicating they were floors away. The man weaved between the groups of waiting people and turned a corner. Wukich lengthened his steps, rounding the corner, and stopped. Some people and a nurse were gathered far down the hall. Otherwise it was empty.

Ten yards ahead was a stairwell. Wukich hurried inside and stopped again. The man was two flights below, he guessed from the sound of heels clicking on cement stairs, then the squealing of a metal door. Taking the stairs three at a time, he exited at the second floor into a ward. At the far left end, just yards before another stairwell and exit sign, the man was striding past a nurse standing at a medicine cart. She looked up briefly as he passed.

"May I help you?" she asked Wukich, stopping him five yards from the stairwell.

"That man who just walked by dropped his keys in the lobby." Wukich took out his own keys and dangled them in front of her. "I'm trying to catch up with him."

"He's probably going to the lab. It's on the first floor."

"Thanks." Wukich reached the stairwell in three long strides and almost jumped down the first set of stairs. Stopping at the landing between the first and second floors, he looked out a window and saw the man halfway up a sidewalk leading to parking lot with large Employees Only signs. Now he was nearly running, yet in enough control to appear only to be hurrying. He took the last short set of cement stairs between him and the parking lot with two quick semi-jumps, and Wukich's stomach turned. Although he did not know the man's face, somehow he knew him. He knew his walk, the way he carried his arms, the way he leapt like a cat going up a tree. Turning, Wukich sprinted back toward the elevators.

Four voices chanting, "Push! Push!" echoed around the tiled walls of the delivery room. With each new salvo Billie Williams, her knees tucked up into her chest, her face red and swollen with the effort, did her best to comply. Between contractions she waited stoically, her mouth set firmly, her eyes lit with some inner resolve. Then the uterine monitor would spike again, precipitating another round of coaching, and she would push with an effort that made her eyes bulge.

It was no lack of effort on her part that was slowing the delivery. The baby's head was having trouble passing her coccyx, the last part of the tailbone. Billie's curved upward only millimeters more than usual, but it was enough to cause resistance. Gallagher studied her face. With no evidence that she or the baby was in distress, he was going to let her try to push it out as long as she had the energy.

Twenty minutes later she showed the first signs of tiring, and Gallagher took the medical student's place between her legs and asked for forceps. Despite his confident tone, the steel handles, cool even through his rubber gloves, were far from reassuring. At the moment, though, there weren't a whole hell of a lot of alternatives. He didn't want her too tired to push at all, and it was way too late for a cesarean section. He inserted the forceps and felt the force of six eyes beside him, behind him, watching his every movement. Shutting out everything else, he focused on the softball-sized opening in front of him and felt for the baby's head. The room was hot, getting hotter beneath his paper gown, and there were no more sounds but the rushing and thumping in his ears. Billie finished a contraction, and he maneuvered the forceps around the head. When she contracted again he applied gentle traction and the head slid a half inch. A minute later it slipped a full one.

Billie was groaning now, the urge to push the baby out almost uncontrollable. "Hold on," said Gallagher. "I'll tell you when." The uterine monitor ascended, and without waiting for the instruction, Billie grabbed her knees and with a half groan, half cry, pushed the baby's head out of her. Gallagher set the forceps aside and quickly suctioned out its nose. One final contraction and the baby was nestled in his arm, wailing with all the force its little lungs could muster. He cut the umbilical cord and held her up for Billie to see.

"It's a girl, Mrs. Williams. She's beautiful. Now you can pick out a name."

Billie lifted her head, then slumped back without responding. While the infant was being cleaned and wrapped in a blanket, she stared at the ceiling, a sense of contentment and fulfillment seeming to fill her. When the nurse was done, she held the baby only briefly. "Maybe later," she said.

Gallagher was already absorbed in delivering the placenta and planning his repair of her perineum, which had torn despite the episiotomy. Except for intermittent anatomy lessons for the medical student, he worked silently, thinking about his conversation with Henry Kirby. The incident irritated him, and he cautioned himself to stay cool before going to Kirby's office. The more he thought about it, the more he knew something was up. He had never even seen Kirby out of the administrative suite before.

Minutes after placing the last suture, Gallagher was still on the stool between Billie Williams's legs, peering into her vagina. The episiotomy site was oozing little spots of blood and, although some bleeding from her uterus was to be expected, the steady trickle through her cervix was a bit more than he liked to see.

"I know I asked you in the emergency room, Mrs. Williams," he said, "but I just want to double-check a few things. Have you taken any aspirin recently?"

"How about any drugs for arthritis?"

"I haven't taken anything in months."

Gallagher blotted away a few spots of blood from her sutures. "Have you ever had any bleeding problems?"

"Not that I know of. Why? Am I bleeding?"

"A little. But we expect some bleeding. Don't worry. It will stop." He studied the laceration one final time, then packed her vagina with gauze and reminded himself to check her sooner than he normally would. "I'll see you in the recovery room in a little bit," he said, standing up to leave. Several feet from the doors, he stopped. He walked back to the table and checked the gauze—the visible portion was white. He felt her pulse—it was regular and full. He checked the last blood-pressure reading taken just minutes before—normal. Mrs. Williams looked fine. Her color was good, and she was smiling to herself. Ten minutes, he thought. Check her in ten minutes.

*   *   *

Eight minutes later Mary Dickinson, a recovery—room nurse, wheeled Billie out of the delivery room. Blood was trickling down Billie's arm from the intravenous catheter, leaving a trail from the delivery room to the recovery room. Dickinson stopped in the hall to remove the catheter and tape a gauze pressure dressing to the puncture site. In the recovery room she put a new catheter into Billie's other arm. When she was taping it into place, she noticed the pressure dressing was soaked through with blood. She removed it with the intention of placing a tighter one, but there was a lump of blood under Billie's skin the size of a lemon. It was at that point, she later recalled, that Billie told her she felt wet. Dickinson would also remember lifting up the bed sheet to inspect the large white pad strapped between Billie's legs. She would remember seeing red—red legs, red sheets, and fresh red blood leaking around a soaked red pad. And for a long time afterward, the only other thing she would clearly remember was running for the phone to page Dr. Gallagher.

EIGHT

From the hallway Gallagher could hear two muted voices. After a perfunctory knock he found Kirby sitting behind his desk, his attention on one of two armchairs facing him.

"Brendan," Kirby said enthusiastically, rising from his chair. "You've been making us nervous. This is Mr. DeLozier. He's the grandfather. Father of the mother."

Gallagher smiled and reached for his hand. "Congratulations. You have a beautiful seven-pound granddaughter. And your daughter did just fine. She should be in the recovery room any minute."

DeLozier's ear-to-ear grin weakened. "I'm sorry," he said. "I know it's confusing, but Billie's not the mother. My daughter is. Billie was a surrogate mother. And a great one at that. You said she's okay?"

Gallagher nodded.

"Mr. DeLozier and the parents of the baby, the Moricks, are from Potomac," said Kirby. His gaze shifted, and Gallagher felt a presence behind him. Dr. Joe Coretti draped his jacket over one of the chairs.

"How do you do?" he said, shaking DeLozier's hand. "I'm Dr. Goretti, the staff obstetrician on call today."

"He's also the chairman of our obstetrics department," Kirby added.

"Thanks for the attention, Dr. Coretti. We're very grateful."

"Listen, that's what we're here for. I just wish I had been there for the delivery. Everything okay, Brendan?"

"I paged you several times, Joe," said Gallagher, noticing the disorder of Coretti's hair.

Coretti frowned and pushed a button on his pager. A burst of static and an operator's voice immediately issued forth. He shrugged and turned back toward DeLozier. "Henry's already told me about the situation, Mr. DeLozier," he said. "Although I must admit it's not an everyday occurrence at St. Joseph's, it's nothing we can't handle and handle well."

"That's why we're here, Dr. Coretti."

"I'm not sure I understand, Mr. DeLozier," said Gallagher. "If you're from the area, why didn't Mrs. Williams have any records with her? Or a doctor? I really could have used some information about her pregnancy."

DeLozier—five foot ten or so, slim, nearly gray—studied him without apparent intention to speak.

"Particularly her pelvic dimensions," Gallagher went on. "It's not quite the same when the baby's head is already there. As it is, I had to—"

"Henry, you mentioned a contract concerning the current situation," interrupted Coretti.

"Right here," Kirby lifted a legal-size document off his desk.

Coretti scanned it. Then looking up with a smile, he said, "Don't you think we better find the parents?"

"They're upstairs in the waiting room," said DeLozier. "I'll go get them."

"Why don't you relax here for a minute?" Kirby interjected. Coretti nodded his agreement. They were both envisioning the same scenario: if Mrs. Williams had relatives in the waiting room, it could get ugly. "I'll page them to the office."

Gallagher turned for the door. "I have to check on Mrs. Williams," he said on his way out.

"I'll see you upstairs, Brendan," said Coretti.

Outside, Gallagher said to himself, "I'm sure you will." A few feet from the stairwell his pager beeped, and he stopped to listen. It was Mary Dickinson's voice, and with her first words he found himself running. Billie Williams, he knew, was in big-time trouble.

Arriving back at the delivery-room waiting area, short of breath, Wukich cursed his paunch and cigarette habit. "Any news on Mrs. Williams yet?" he asked the Red Cross volunteer.

She scanned her roster. "Not yet. Are you a family member? I'm only supposed to give out information to the family."

"Well, uh, sort of. I work for the family."

"Then maybe you should speak to one of them." She pointed into the waiting area.

Wukich turned to meet the stares of an older woman and the young couple who had been pacing up and down. They had apparently overhead the conversation and seemed to be talking about him. The older woman stood up and started his way, but then stopped as a voice came over the loudspeaker: "Will Mr. and Mrs. Morick please report to the hospital administrator's office?" Tentative smiles crossed all three of their faces. Then with only a glance at Wukich, the trio gathered their belonging and headed for the elevators.

*   *   *

By the time Gallagher arrived, Mary Dickinson had recruited another nurse, who was holding pressure on Billie's arm. Mary was attempting to replace the pad between the patient's legs. "She's bleeding from her IV site and from her vagina, Dr. Gallagher," she said.

"Anywhere else?"

"I don't think so, but I haven't had time to look."

"Is the oxytocin in her IV yet?"

"It was started in the delivery room."

Gallagher looked at Billie's face. He hadn't realized it before, but she was an attractive woman. He pulled one of her lower eyelids down and checked the color. It was pale, like her complexion, but not too pale.

"How do you feel, Mrs. Williams?" he asked.

"I'm starting to get nauseous."

"Mary, do we have the results of the CBC we did earlier?"

"I haven't seen them. Karen," she yelled to the unit secretary across the room, "call down for the CBC on Williams. Tell 'em we need it stat."

"Tell them to send another tech up here too," Gallagher said, grabbing a wad of gauze and taping it down hard over Billie's second IV site. "Get her pulse and blood pressure," he said to Ellen, the nurse who had been holding her arm. Then to Mary: "Let's go ahead and get the blood. We can't wait for them. We need another CBC, a platelet count, a PT, PTT, fibrinogen level, fibrinogen split-products level, and an antithrombin three level. Get enough to type and cross-match her also."

Gallagher plucked a stethoscope from his lab coat and bent over Billie's chest. He was fairly sure he knew what the immediate problem was—disseminated intravascular coagulation. But what was the cause?

71

Straightening up, he fired question after question at her. To each her answer was no, and his memory searched for the rarer causes of DIC that finally led to this inability to form blood clots.

"Were you ill at all before you came into the hospital?"

"No."

"No fever?"

"No."

"Have you had chicken pox or anything like it recently?"

"No."

"Heart rate one twenty-eight, blood pressure one oh five over sixty-two," said Ellen.

"She's still bleeding from her vagina," added Mary as she withdrew a needle from Billie's arm and set the last of the tubes of blood on the bed.

"Mary, hang some normal saline and open it up. Ellen, will you please get me a subclavian catheter? She's going to need a central line."

"I think I'm going to get sick," said Billie, her forehead and upper lip suddenly dotted with little beads of sweat.

"Get some help, Mary. We need more hands."

A lab technician came to the bed and picked up the tubes of blood. "Run it as fast as you can," said Gallagher. "Especially the type and cross match. And tell the blood bank to get some fresh frozen plasma ready ASAP. Do you have the results of the CBC from before?"

"No. We never received a specimen for any Billie Williams."

Gallagher glared at him before looking to Mary.

"I *saw* the guy up here," said Mary. "Check again."

"We looked all over for it. We even checked with chemistry and serology."

"Then get the tech that drew it up here!" said Mary. "Ask him what he did with it."

"We can't find him."

"Forget it," said Gallagher. "We're wasting time. Just go run those as fast as you can."

Billie groaned, and her head rolled from side to side. Gallagher stared at her. Although her eyes were still open, they were without focus. "Mary," he said, "tell them at the desk to get some heparin and aminocaproic acid up from the pharmacy stat. And will you please page Dr. Coretti over the intercom? Page him to the intensive-care unit."

One look at her father's face, and Sarah Morick squealed with delight. "What is it?" she asked, her hands clasped in front of her.

"A girl. Dr. Gallagher said she's beautiful."

Sarah hugged Nathan, her father, and her mother, then turned to the man she presumed was Dr. Gallagher. "Oh, I'm so excited. Is she all right? Is everything okay?"

"The baby's fine. I believe everything went smoothly. I'm Dr. Coretti, the chief of obstetrics."

"And Billie?" said Sarah. "How is she? Is she handling it okay?"

"I believe she's fine also. She should be in the recovery room by now."

Sarah turned to her husband. "You have to call home. I promised your mother we'd call right away."

"I know your parents are planning to come out at Thanksgiving," said Dorothy, "but if they want to come now, they're welcome to stay with us."

"Thanks, but I 'suspect they'll just come next month. They're planning on making a big trip of it and seeing all the relatives on the East Coast." To Sarah he said, "Let's see her before I call. So I can tell Mom what she looks like."

"Well, when can we see her?" Sarah blurted, looking from Coretti to Kirby. "I'm so excited, I can't stand it much longer." She moved for the door, then saw the contract Coretti was holding. "There's not a problem, is there?"

"Oh, no. But it will be a few minutes before you can see the baby. She's getting weighed and her footprints taken and all that. While we wait, do you mind filling me in a little more on the situation? I'd like everything to go as smoothly as possible."

"Sure," said Nathan, putting his arm around Sarah. "What would you like to know?"

"The beginning, I guess. Were you initially working with a fertility specialist?"

"Yes. At the Washington Fertility Institute." Nathan glanced at DeLozier. "We had a disagreement with one of the doctors. But Billie has . . ."

From the cleaning crews to the director of the board, everybody at St. Joseph's carried a pager. The main purpose was to eliminate general noise, but an added benefit was to give emergency status to the rare announcement over the loudspeakers. When the intercom message called for Dr. Coretti to report at once to the ICU, he immediately started up the stairs, leaving the Morieks and DeLoziers to stand there, staring at each other in silence.

Wukich didn't know what to do. One woman he was supposed to watch was in a delivery room to which he had no access; the other was with the hospital administrator on another floor. And the baby he could not get any information about. He was about to step outside for a smoke when he was stopped by sudden voices and the flinging open of the delivery-suite doors. The bed was being pushed, as fast as it would go. An oxygen tank hung from one end, and the person next to it was holding a mask over the patient's face. The hair was the color of Billie's, all right, but Wukich couldn't see her face. It didn't matter. He recognized the doctor who was leading the way: he was the one the Red Cross woman had said would deliver Billie's baby.

"Jesus, Brendan, what happened?" said Coretti, pulling on a pair of gloves.

"She started bleeding like crazy fifteen or twenty minutes ago," said Gallagher, taping down the catheter he had just put into Billie's neck. "I'm sure she has DIC. I just can't figure out why. The only thing I can think of is an amniotic-fluid embolus, but the way everything started isn't great for that either."

"You generally see amniotic-fluid emboli in older women."

"I know, Joe."

"Did you order any blood? She's going to need a transfusion. Maybe several."

"She's getting typed and cross-matched right now, but I don't know if we can wait that long. I think she's starting to bleed into her gut. It's hard to tell with all the blood coming out of her vagina, but, she's so shocky now, she's got to be bleeding from somewhere else."

A lab technician ran into the room with two units of fresh frozen plasma. "Hang them," Gallagher said to the nearest nurse. To the lab tech, "Call down and get us two units of O negative blood."

Coretti looked from the cardiac monitor to Billie and back to the monitor. "She's really tach'ing away," he said, moving to the head of the bed. He gently rolled Billie's head while he lifted her eyelids. "Jesus, she might be bleeding into her head."

Gallagher nodded, and they stared at each other for a moment.

"Let's bolus her with heparin, Joe. I don't think we have much choice. She's going to die before the blood gets here."

Coretti looked from Billie to the cardiac monitor.

"Give her five thousand units of heparin, Angie," said Gallagher, staring at Coretti. "I also had them bring up some aminocaproic acid, Joe. What do you think?"

"I don't know, Brendan. The heparin is risky enough. You're assuming she has DIC."

"Her pressure's eighty over forty," Angie said as she injected the anticoagulant, the only hope to save the last of her clotting proteins if she did have DIC.

"Joe."

Coretti took a stethoscope out of his pocket and bent over Billie's chest.

Angie looked to Gallagher as soon as the earpieces were in.

"Give it to her," he said flatly.

Within minutes the first units of blood arrived and were added to the fluids pouring into Billie. There was nothing else to do but hope that more blood went in than came out, and that the heparin could save any last remnants of her clotting proteins. Her heart rate slowed for a minute, and the room took hope. But then blood started oozing from her nose, quickly followed by her mouth, and she started to cough. Coretti reached in the crash cart for an endotracheal tube.

"Don't, Joe," said Gallagher, reaching for his arm. "Please." Gallagher raised her eyelids and shined a penlight directly into her pupils. "She's bleeding into her brain stem and probably higher. Let her be."

NINE

The room was dark, only slivers of light from the parking-lot lights slipping through the blinds and outlining the shapes. At the window Nathan Morick watched a car pull into the lot, its lights blink off. A woman with white stockings got out and pulled her coat tight around her. He watched her hurry down the sidewalk, her breaths shooting out in steamy plumes. He looked at Sarah on the bed. In sleep her face was relaxed, almost peaceful. He returned to the bassinet.

Under the plastic hood it was even darker, Lauren's face inseparable from the blanket tucked neatly around her up to her chin. Slowly the lines of her face took form. He could see the little nose, already angular like her mother's, and the sparse strands of fine black hair over the top of her head. With the blanket too thick to see the movements of her chest, he waited for her lips to pucker and gently suck the air, searching for food even as she slept. Then he knew once more that their baby was alive, that Billie had not died for nothing. But she *had* died, goddammit. At the window again he stared at the horizon sprinkled with lights from the nearby highway.

*　　*　　*

Brendan Gallagher rolled over and again looked at the alarm clock in the on-call room. "This is hopeless," he said to himself. But what should he have done? What *could* he have done? Slipping on his shoes and coat, he left the room quietly so as not to wake the medical students.

It was five-fifteen, forty-five minutes before the cafeteria opened. In the hallway he shielded his eyes from the fluorescent light, then turned and headed toward the back stairwell, leading to the laboratory. He had intended to check Mrs. Williams's blood tests soon after she died, but another woman had come in to the emergency room in labor, keeping him and the junior resident busy with one problem after another. Finally, at one in the morning, when he had called the laboratory about Mrs. Williams's lab results, he had been told it would be another hour or so before all of them would be ready. "One of the machines," the lab tech had said, "was temporarily down."

The laboratory was immense, occupying one complete wing of the hospital and sprawling partially into two others. Normally teeming with technicians and other assorted ancillary personnel, it was always quiet during these hours before dawn. Gallagher found an unattended computer terminal and pulled up a chair.

He typed in "Williams," and a long list of names appeared on the screen. Selecting "Billie L.," he typed several commands and leaned back while the information was retrieved. The numbers—the normal values of which were so ingrained in his memory that he did not need the computer's statistically acceptable range of values to tell him something was wrong—were still scrolling onto the screen when he frowned and sat back up.

WILLIAMS, BILLIE L.
CURRY/GALLAGHER/CORRETTI

284-46-8629
23 AUG 67 DOB
22 OCT 90 DOA

TEST:
NORMAL VALUES
RESULT (UNITS)
(UNITS).

PROTHROMBIN TIME (PT):
17.0 SECS
9.5-13.0 SECS

PARTIAL THROMBOPLASTIN TIME (PTT):
25.0-39.0 SECS
166.0 SECS
CRITICAL VALUE

FIBRINOGEN: 205 MG/DL
150-450 MG/DL

FIBRINOGEN SPLIT PRODUCTS:
ABSENT
ABSENT

ANTITHROMBIN III:
55-82%

88% THROMBIN INHIBITED
THROMBIN INHIBITED

PLATELETS: 310 K/CMM
150-450 K/CMM

"Goddamn lab," he said out loud, slamming a terminal key with his index finger to continue the information display.

CBC:
WBC 12.8 K/CMM
3.0-10.5 K/CMM
RBC 3.9 M/CMM
4.7-6.1 M/CMM
HGB 8.8 G/DL
12.0-16.0 G/DL
HCT 27.1%
37-47%

Some of the lab results were as expected: they had been obtained from blood drawn just after she had started to bleed heavily, and they should not as yet show the severe hemorrhage that occurred. But whatever had *caused* her to bleed had already happened, and *that* should have been reflected in her clotting studies. Studying the screen, Gallagher continued to frown. Those results did not at all fit the predictable pattern. He scrolled the screen backward and looked again at the initial display. Then, sequentially reading each value, he shook his head in disbelief. The two main tests that measure the body's capacity to form blood clots—the PT and the PTT—did not make sense. Billie Williams had bled death. Billie Williams, he was sure, had died from a major clotting abnormality. Most likely DIC: widespread clotting followed by *no* clots since all the clotting proteins had been used up. Yet only one of those tests supported that hypothesis. Unless they were wrong, he thought. Unexpected lab values were often a result of technician or machine error.

He stared at the screen in deep concentration. Something *was* wrong. The values were just too different. One was too high, higher than he had ever seen, and one was too low, much too low.

He leaned back in the chair. He knew of only one situation capable of producing what the computer was telling him and what he had seen, and it wasn't DIC. But that was not applicable here. Or was it? Could there have been a mistake in her medications? He went to, the main computer to have the lab results printed out and made a mental note to check with the pharmacy. Hundreds of IV solutions were compounded every day for patients on the hospital wards. Perhaps there had been an error.

The cafeteria didn't open for another twenty minutes Alone in the hall he decided to check on the baby.

"The baby's with her parents," the nurse at the desk informed him. "That is, she's with her parents if I understand the situation. As a matter of fact, ever since she came from the delivery room, she's been in there." The nurse looked around to ensure that they were alone. "Basically we've been told by the supervisor to let them do whatever they want. Everyone's *real* nervous."

Gallagher nodded. "What room are they in?"

"Two. We had to move somebody, to make it into a private."

The door was partly open, and Gallagher peered inside to see if anyone was awake. Seeing a man at the window, he knocked softly and stepped inside. There were two beds in the room with a hospital bassinet between them. On the bed nearest the window was a motionless, prone figure. The man had not moved, and he was about to walk out when the figure on the bed abruptly sat up. The man turned around.

"I'm sorry if I disturbed you," Gallagher whispered when he was close. "I delivered your baby."

"It's okay," a woman said from the bed.

The man extended his hand. "I'm Nathan Morick. We were hoping we'd get the chance to meet you. To thank you, of course, but also to tell you how devastated we are about Billie. We had gotten to know her fairly well."

"I don't know what else we could have done," said Gallagher. "I'm sorry." Then a moment later, "And I apologize again for disturbing you. I wanted to see the baby, and I wasn't sure if I'd be able to get back later. I'll come back another time."

"Really, its okay," said the woman. "We wanted to meet you." Sitting up, she swung her legs off the bed and brushed back her hair with her hands.

Even in the dim light from the hall, even with her swollen eyes, red from recent tears, her face looked familiar. And the name Morick rang a faint bell too. But he could not place where they might have met before. Eyeing the bassinet again, Gallagher said, "Do you mind if I look at the baby?"

"Not at all," said Sarah. "Her name is Lauren. Lauren Elizabeth."

The new white baby blanket had slipped up over her cheek, and Gallagher gently pulled it back, letting his finger rest on her warm, smooth skin. "I'm sorry, Mrs. Williams," he said to himself. "I'm sorry we couldn't save you." Sarah Morick was talking to him, but he did not hear. In the slowly increasing light of the room, Lauren's face was taking shape. He could see the slope of her forehead, the shape of her nose, the sharp lines of her mouth. And he felt lost. Yes, even though Billie Williams had given this baby life, it was not hers.

Russ Wukich sat in a chair at the end of ward 4 east within easy viewing and running distance of room number two. His head drooped too far, and, as it had many times throughout the night, his chin jerked up in fright. For a moment the yellow walls of the ward disoriented him even further. For on the porch of the small house in Chincoteague, he had just handed Billie a bag with her magazines. And hidden beneath them, sure to bring her big, warm smile, two frozen Milky Ways and a Mars bar. But the bag had been empty. She had looked up, her eyes crestfallen, her hair flying out wildly above the oxygen mask covering her nose and mouth. Wukich briskly shook his head and stood. Stretching, he whirled as he saw a figure in his peripheral vision. Mrs. Morick was heading directly for him.

"Everything okay, ma'am?"

"Yes, everything's fine. Do you have children, Mr. Wukich?" she asked, smiling.

"Two boys. But my wife and I are, uh—"

"That's great. You must be so happy. Since you know what to expect, then, would you mind sitting in the room with Lauren for a few minutes? We want to run down to the cafeteria with Dr. Gallagher to get some coffee and a quick bite to eat."

"Well, it's been a while, and my wife did most of that," Wukich stammered.

"Oh, I'm sure you'll be fine. She's sleeping soundly now. You know how babies are. She'll probably sleep for a couple of hours."

Wukich started a reply, but she was already walking back toward the room. He followed her in, and she handed him a new bottle of formula and a cloth diaper to protect his shirt. "Just in case," she said with a wink.

Then before he had a chance to say another word, they were gone.

"Friend of the family?" asked Gallagher as they walked to the elevators.

"Sort of," said Sarah. "He's a friend of a friend of my father." She paused. "As you probably know, we haven't gotten to this point in the usual fashion. One of the reasons we wanted to meet you is to apologize for putting you on the spot with Billie. We know it wasn't right to ask whoever happened to be on call to deliver the baby."

Gallagher nodded but didn't respond. Not only had that concern paled in light of others, but he had little desire to know anything else about the Moricks or their situation. He had come into this mess with Billie Williams, had his own image of her, and he didn't want it altered. Yet, in better light now, here was Sarah Morick's oddly familiar face again—the well-defined cheekbones, the nose, the lips—all of which he knew he had studied with appreciation somewhere before.

"Try to forgive us," she was saying. "We wouldn't have done it unless we had been told all along that Billie was in good health and that the pregnancy was normal. Now, of course, we feel terrible. Do you think what happened to her could have been prevented? I mean, we weren't aware of any problems, but maybe she wasn't seeing the right doctors."

"No, I don't think so," said Gallagher. "I was able to spend a little time with her before the delivery. There wasn't anything about her history or exam that indicated a potential problem. Not that I wouldn't have liked to have seen her earlier than I did. But no, I wasn't expecting any problems. Sometimes things like this happen which we just can't explain."

They were quiet as they reached the cafeteria and made their way through the line. Gallagher was beginning to get uneasy in their presence, and he debated intentionally setting off his pager. But he needed the coffee, and sitting awkwardly with them at a table, he asked if they had used a fertility specialist in the area.

Sarah nodded. "We were with the Washington Fertility Institute."

"Billie was a surrogate gestational mother," Nathan added.

Sipping his coffee, Gallagher glanced at Sarah over the cup, imagining her on her back with a surgical cap covering her hair. "Your egg retrieval and fertilization were in February?" he said.

"February the tenth," said Nathan.

Gallagher nodded and bit into his egg sandwich. There couldn't have been two of those that month. He recalled Ashton giving him the brief bits of Mrs. Morick's clinical history. But the implantation into Billie Williams—no, he hadn't watched that part; Ashton had pawned him off on Dr. Simpson. He looked at them again over his coffee. This case had been important enough that Ashton had done the egg retrieval himself. So why had they ended up here?

"Are you familiar with the institute?" asked Nathan.

"Somewhat," he said, feeling his face warm. He really wasn't up to reminiscing about the Fertility Institute, and his previous encounter with Sarah Morick. They had obviously had a problem with Ashton. He didn't want to be their second one.

Gallagher stood up to leave. As weird as things had been with this case, there was something a lot weirder still hidden. Why were these people so silent? Why hadn't they bothered to explain the surrogate mother's emergency arrival at St. Joseph's? Well, whatever had happened before—it was none of his business. Forcing a smile, he said, "Well, good luck, the baby seems fine."

"Thanks," said Sarah Morick. Her smile seemed shy. "Thank you very much—for everything."

Wukich was too agitated to sit. Every thirty seconds he poked his head under the hood of the bassinet to ensure that the blanket was moving up and down in the expected manner. He paced to the door, the window, and back to the bassinet. Maybe ten minutes had passed when he heard the first faint rustle. "Shit," he said to himself. "Please don't." Shortly, there was another, then a series of brief high-pitched cries. His hands moist with sweat, he reached into the bassinet and lifted the baby out. Lauren's cries escalated in frequency and volume. "Shit," he uttered, glaring at the still-wrapped bottle and unconnected nipple. Looking from the bottle to Lauren, he put her back in the bassinet and fumbled with the bottle. As soon as the nipple was in her mouth, she was quiet. Sitting down in the chair with a smile, he hoped the Moricks would return to find him in such a position.

A nurse appeared in the doorway. Looking around the room, she frowned. "They'll be right back," said Wukich. "They went to grab a bite to eat."

"Did they tell you anything about a cardiologist comin' to see the baby?"

"No, but I didn't talk to them very long."

"Well, there's a cardiologist here who wants to see the baby. He says the pediatrician heard a heart murmur. There's nothin' in the chart I can see about a murmur, but then again, I can't read the handwriting."

"Do you know the cardiologist?"

"No. But there's lots of private consultants I don't know."

"They should be back any minute."

"He said he needs to see the baby *now*. He has to go to another hospital from here. Maybe you can stay in the exam room with him," she offered.

Wukich shrugged. "I don't know what else to do. I can't let this baby out of my sight. Do you think he'd mind?"

"I don't know why he would. If he does, then I guess he can wait until they come back."

Wukich nodded and followed the nurse out of the room.

"He's in there," she said when they were abreast of an exam room. She kept walking. "Just tell him the situation. He'll understand, I have to go. Somebody's calling me."

The first thing Wukich noticed was a large black doctor's bag on the exam table. Then, standing in front of a sink and mirror, a man in a long white doctor's coat adjusting his tie. The doctor saw Wukich in the mirror at the same moment Wukich saw him, and his hands stopped. For a moment they stood motionless, staring at each other.

The doctor moved first, turning and fixing Wukich with his oil black eyes. "I'm Dr. Garcia," he said. His gaze went to the infant. "I'll only be a moment with the baby. You can wait—"

By the time their eyes met again, Wukich was backpedaling to the door. After three steps he turned to run, but he slammed into the edge of the door with his forehead and reeled sideways. Cradling the baby in his right arm away from the man, he groped for the open doorway. Yet even as he stumbled forward, he knew he wouldn't make it, and he wrapped his other arm around the baby like a fullback going through a goal-line stand. As he fell to the floor from the weight of the man pushing and clawing at him, all he could hear was his high-school football coach screaming, "Cover the goddamn ball!" And he did. There was no way the baby was coming out of his arms. She started to cry as he curled up on the floor against the wall like a frightened armadillo, but he didn't care. A metal tray crashed against the exposed portion of his head. He clenched his jaw and curled up tighter. Then there were voices outside the door, and silence behind him. Envisioning the man poised above him, ready to strike, he tensed. A steel pole ricocheted off the wall above his head, followed by the sound of the bag dragging across the table. A moment later a woman in the hall yelped, and there was a thud on the floor. Wukich jumped up and ran out the door. Although he could now picture the man as he had seen him months before—bearded and in painter's garb on the stoop across from Billie's apartment—all he wanted was one more look at him.

Sarah Morick turned the corner of the maternity ward and nursery one step ahead of her husband. Then she screamed and ran for the group of people over the prostrate figure of Lauren's nurse.

"What the hell!" said Nathan, taking off after her.

Wukich had run after the man as far as the stairs. Now, seeing the Moricks, he held Lauren close to him.

"Is she all right?" Sarah cried, taking the baby. Wukich started to explain, but she ran into the room.

Gallagher came into view and picked up his pace as he saw the commotion. "Are you okay, Mrs. Potts?"

She straightened her blouse and brushed off her pants.

"What's going on?" he said, looking to Nathan Morick.

"Why don't you ask him." The nurse glared at Wukich. "*I'm* going to talk to the supervisor. And *you* might want to check on that baby," she said to Gallagher as she started for the nursing station. "Who knows what went on in there?"

"The baby's fine," said Wukich.

Gallagher looked at him, then Nathan. "What happened?"

"It sounds as if there were a misunderstanding. We weren't expecting a doctor to examine Lauren this morning—her pediatrician saw her last night. I think he surprised Mr. Wukich. He was just . . . doing his job."

"'His job'?"

"He was taking care of Lauren."

Gallagher turned to one of the nurses beside him.

"We're checking on it," she said. "All we know is a cardiologist came to see the baby. We're pretty sure he said, 'Morick.'"

"Where is he?"

"He got upset when I wouldn't give him the baby," said Wukich. "He left."

"Well, why the—" Gallagher stopped and studied Wukich's blank face. To Nathan he said coldly, "Is the baby okay?"

"Yes, thank you.

None of your business, Gallagher reminded himself, but he decided he'd better check on her, one last time.

TEN

For Gallagher the rest of the day had been interminable. He had expected to go home as soon as morning rounds were over but had sat most of the morning with one of Dr. Coretti's prominent private patients, who was in labor. When Coretti finally arrived in the early afternoon to relieve him and do the delivery, the fat lady from the previous day had promptly had a seizure. The rest of the afternoon had been spent with her, the intern, and the junior resident. Then with Coretti "tied up" with an unspecified "problem," he had been asked to lead afternoon rounds. The moment he answered the last question on the last patient, he took off for the residents' locker room.

He was unlocking his car when he was paged to an unfamiliar number. Swearing, he glanced at his watch. Technically he was no longer on call, and with the fat lady stabilized, none of his patients were acutely ill. Nevertheless, he knew he'd worry about the page all night if he didn't go back. Returning to the hospital, he called the number from the first phone he could find.

It was Kirby, who wanted him in his office, "if he wouldn't mind sparing a few minutes." Christ, thought Gallagher, it could only be about Mrs. Williams. She'd only been dead twenty-four hours, and already they were paranoid.

The door leading to Kirby's office was open, and there, toying with the goddamned wire-rimmed glasses he had recently taken to wearing, was Coretti, looking more, thought Gallagher, like a spectacled ferret than ever. Coretti's presence was bad enough, but then he saw the woman sitting across from Kirby, one plum-colored shoe pointing toward Coretti, and he knew that this must be Danielle Parker, and that things were really bad.

"Come in, Brendan," Kirby said cordially. "I'm glad you could join us." Coretti straightened up from the window. "Do you know Danielle Parker? Our lawyer?"

The woman spun around, facing him. Not having seen her close up before, Gallagher had underestimated how striking she was—and how sharp were her clear blue eyes.

"No," he said, managing a smile. "I don't believe we've ever met."

Parker's voice was cool: "This is really a precautionary meeting, Dr. Gallagher. Over the years I've developed a sixth sense so to speak. Aided by a rather large pool of information sources. It's kind of like the Indians with their ears to the ground."

Gallagher nodded, his smile gone.

"I'm concerned about the patient who died yesterday," she continued. "Even though it appears no one did anything wrong, the case is vulnerable to litigation."

"Why does it only *appear* that way?" said Gallagher. "We *didn't* do anything wrong."

"You know what I mean. Any serious complication in obstetric cases these days is essentially a lawsuit until proven otherwise. Now, I don't know whether Mrs. Williams's family will initiate litigation, but with the proper prompting they may. As a matter of fact, I have reason to believe that an attorney has already spoken with her husband."

"She only died yesterday, for Christ's sake," said Gallagher.

"I know," replied Parker, still cool, but with some empathy. "These information networks work both ways."

"Are you even aware of the way Mrs. Williams arrived at this hospital?" said Gallagher.

"Dr. Gallagher," said the lawyer, "we're on the same side. Yes, I am aware of that."

"That she had no records, no doctor?"

"Yes. Listen, all I want you to do right now is put up your guard. I would advise you not to discuss the case with anybody except Joe, Henry, or myself. We also need to ensure that we have copies of all the appropriate records, beginning with the emergency room and going on to all the obvious places from there." She saw the change in Gallagher's face. "Don't get me wrong. Neither you, nor anybody else should be overly concerned about the legal aspects of this incident. But neither should we be lax in our handling of it."

She made several more comments that Gallagher did not hear. He was one of an extreme minority of his medical-school class who had chosen obstetrics as a specialty. Most of his classmates had shied away from the field to avoid precisely this sort of horror story. He stared blankly at Parker, feeling his face getting hot. Then he turned and headed for the door "Brendan," he heard Kirby call after him, but he didn't stop.

*　　*　　*

Wayne Masterson was spread out on the couch with his atlas of surgical anatomy resting on his chest. The TV was on, an empty beer bottle was on the coffee table, and he was sound asleep. Gallagher threw his knapsack full of books and spare clothes on the kitchen table and opened a beer. Then he sat down across from Masterson and stared at his roommate's hands. After four years of looking at them, they were still awesome. Wayne was 250 pounds big, but his hands were huge. The middle fingers themselves were nearly the length of Gallagher's hands. What always fascinated him, though, was their delicacy. Their skin was smooth and hairless, the fingers narrowing to deft tips comfortable in the depths of any body cavity. Their only fault—for the patients—was their size. Nobody wanted a second rectal exam from Dr. Wayne Masterson.

Gallagher flipped the top of his beer bottle onto the book moving up and down on his roommate's chest. No response. He turned the TV up as loud as it would go. Masterson's big head jerked up as if struck.

"You douche bag," he said "Where have you been? I thought what's-her-face cut you off."

"*I* cut her off."

"Right. Then where were you? And if you tell me the hospital, I'm going to call St. Elizabeth's."

"Get a straitjacket."

"You're shittin' me."

"No."

Masterson opened his eyes. "Really?"

"Really."

"What's the matter?"

"I think I'm going to get sued."

"Jesus, lighten up. Everybody gets sued. If you haven't been sued, you haven't been doing enough surgery."

"Even as a resident?"

Masterson sat up and closed his book "Well, it would be nice if they waited until you finished the residency."

"That's what I thought."

"Actually, that's not a bad idea. Tell 'em you'll be worth a lot more in eight months."

Gallagher took a long swig of beer.

"What happened?"

"That lady Curry called about. The one that came into the ER ready to hatch without an attending or any records. She died."

Masterson cocked his head.

"The delivery went okay, but she started bleeding right afterward. I think she had DIC. Anyway, she bled out. I couldn't do a damn thing to stop her."

"So?"

"The hospital's paranoid. I think mainly because the woman was a surrogate mother, and they don't want all the publicity. They already brought their fucking lawyer in."

His roommate frowned. "What's the big deal? Did you do anything wrong?"

"Not that I know of. She was bleeding some after the delivery, but it looked to be slowing down. It wasn't but ten minutes after I left her that they paged me. I was on my way to examine her again." Gallagher shook his head. "Man, it was a mess."

"So she got DIC and died. Tomorrow morning I'm going to cut a twelve-year-old boy's arm off. He has an osteosarcoma the size of a grapefruit in his humerus. He'll be dead this time next year."

"I know." Gallagher slumped in his chair. "I don't think I'd worry about it if the hospital wasn't already so uptight."

"They've probably gotten nailed before."

"They sure act like it. Particularly the chief of the department, that asshole Coretti. He was sleeping when I tried to reach him. Now he's acting as if I didn't try."

"Don't worry about it."

"Easy for you to say. I'm also worried about the woman's lab tests. I'm not sure they *look* like DIC."

"I thought you said that's what she had."

"That's what I *think* she had. But if all you did was look at her labs, you'd wonder if maybe she didn't get some heparin. And a lot of it."

Masterson screwed his face up. "You mean accidentally?"

Gallagher nodded.

"Unless somebody fesses up, that'll be awful hard to prove."

"I know."

"So get an autopsy. That should tell you if she had DIC or not."

"We tried. Her husband told the hospital to go fuck itself. Then he said he was coming to get her and bury her himself because he knew that we—quote 'motherfuckers' unquote—would do whatever the hell we wanted anyway."

"Let him calm down, and try again tomorrow. Did he say anything about suing?"

"No. but I wouldn't be surprised. I don't think he likes doctors very much."

"Go to sleep, guy. You'll feel better in the morning. It probably won't amount to anything."

Gallagher got up. "You want to trade places?"

"Hell, no. I got enough to worry about."

"Thanks." But ten minutes later, imagining Danielle Parker's cool, beautiful face leaning into his—whether to kiss him or not, he couldn't tell—Gallagher was fast asleep.

ELEVEN

Gallagher snipped the last strand of connective tissue holding onto the patient's left ovary and dropped the organ into a steel specimen tray. With the woman's uterus already in another pan and most of the bleeding stopped, the rest of the case was routine. Thank God for that—he didn't think he could stand much more of Coretti's nit-picking attempts at edification. And if the incessant quizzing of himself and the medical students weren't enough, Coretti was continually leaning over the surgical site to inspect each suture. Forcing him out of his mind, Gallagher closed Mrs. Keaton's belly layer by layer.

As he worked, his thoughts drifted to Billie Williams. Wayne was right—an autopsy might very well allay many of his concerns. Although he knew it would not answer the heparin question—the drug was rapidly broken down in the blood and would be gone by now—autopsy should be able to determine if DIC had indeed been the main cause of death. Like it or not, one of them ought to call Mr. Williams again.

A moment later he said to Coretti, "I just remembered something I need to do that's pretty important. Would you mind staying in here with Chuck?" He finished the knot he was tying and handed the needle driver to the medical student. Then turning from the table, he began to pull off his gloves.

"Can't it wait until we're done, Brendan?" said Coretti.

"Not really. It's Mrs. Bernstein, our next case. There was a problem with her preop labs last night. I need to make sure it was a lab error. Otherwise we may have to cancel the case."

"Shouldn't you have taken care of that earlier this morning?"

"I was called to the ER about five minutes after I got here this morning. I was pretty busy."

"Okay," Coretti said gruffly, repositioning the needle holder in the medical student's hand. "I'll be in the lounge. *Call* me if there's a problem."

Gallagher hurried out of the operating room. "Fuck you, Coretti," he said under his breath.

At the tellerlike window in the blood bank, he waited for the technician to get off the phone.

"Yeah?" said the technician.

Gallagher smiled. "Two days ago I had a patient typed and cross-matched. She expired after the transfusion, so I won't be asking for any more blood. What I'd like to get is the sample we sent down to you. You still freeze the tube for the type and cross match, don't you? I'd like toxicology to take a look at it."

"Can't they do it from the autopsy?"

"No. The half-life of the main substance I want to measure is too short. I need the frozen sample."

"Well," he said, "I'm not really sure. Let me call the shift supervisor."

Twenty minutes and two signed release forms later, Gallagher found the toxicologist working alone at a laboratory bench. He described the need for a heparin assay, and the man nodded, taking the styrofoam box containing Billie Williams's blood sample.

"I'll page you," said the toxicologist. "It'll be a few hours, maybe longer."

Standing at the elevators, Gallagher scanned the printout of the dead woman's lab results once again. Maybe the abnormally high PTT value *was* a lab error. He turned and headed for the laboratory offices.

James, the head of the lab, was sitting at his desk. "Dr. Gallagher," he said, looking up. "I was going to call you this morning."

"Don't tell me—the PTT was a mistake."

"Nope. We repeated all the abnormal tests right away, and we just ran 'em again."

"Did you find out anything about the blood drawn *before* she went back to the delivery room?"

James nodded. "We have a problem there. I'm not sure whether or not that blood was in fact drawn. Or if it was, I don't know what happened to it."

"Mary Dickinson saw the guy draw it."

"I know. I talked to Mary about it late yesterday. But she doesn't think the technician she saw drawing blood was the one who was *supposed* to draw it."

James lifted a sheet of paper from his desk and showed it to Gallagher. It was an employment application form with a duplicate of a technician's hospital ID photo stapled to one corner. "And Manny Ternera," he said, flicking the photograph with his index finger, "never finished his shift. Nor did he turn in his equipment tray, his ID badge, or his coat. We haven't seen him since that morning. He was scheduled to work yesterday and today."

Gallagher took a few more steps into the office and sat down. "The blood was never logged in."

"No. And believe me, I've searched everywhere for it."

"Did you try calling the technician?"

James smirked. "His mother says he's not home. And when he does come home, she doesn't think he'll be returning to the hospital. She says he thinks he's been discriminated against. The usual bullshit."

"What can you say? Said Gallagher, shaking his head.

"I'll call him again, Dr. Gallagher. This is my lab, after all."

Gallagher nodded. "Let me know what happens, James."

In the elevator he looked at his watch. The next case wouldn't start for at least fifteen minutes—he had plenty of time. At six that morning he had made sure Mrs. Bernstein was ready for surgery. Now, exiting on the fourth floor, he headed for the obstetric recovery room. Mary Dickinson was at the desk, buttoning her coat.

"Hi, Mary. You just finishing?"

"Yeah, it was awful. We had two emergency C-sections."

"Well, I won't hold you up. I just wanted to ask you one more thing about that Williams case. James said he talked to you yesterday."

"Right. What's going on? Did somebody in the lab mess up?"

Gallagher shrugged. "I don't think so. He just can't figure out what happened to the blood that was drawn in here."

"Beats me. The picture he showed me didn't look like the guy *I* saw."

"So I gather. Do you remember who started her IV?"

She thought for a moment. "One of the nursing students did. But I think the tech helped her. We were awfully busy."

"Hmm. Well, sorry about bugging you, but I gotta check everything out too. You know, in case somebody asks me at a later date."

"Hey, don't worry about it, Brendan. What could you do?"

"Nothing, I guess."

In the nursery Gallagher found Mrs. Potts sitting at a desk, writing in a chart. "Hello, again," he said. "Did you ever figure out what happened up here yesterday morning? It looked like a fire drill."

"We should be so luck." She finished writing before she looked up. "*No*, I didn't. The family wouldn't talk to me or Mrs. Curtis. Except to say how incompetent we are. They talked with Mr. Kirby for a while, but he didn't tell us anything. All I know is I took some cardiologist to the exam room to see the baby, and the next thing I know there's a racket comin' out of there like I never heard before. Then he comes flying out like a bat out of hell and near kills me."

"Who's he?"

"The cardiologist. Then that man who's been sittin' in the hall like a damn spook comes barrelin' out after him and near knocks me over again. Now," she said, "I don't know why anything like that would require an explanation. Do you?"

"Who was the cardiologist?"

"I think he said Garcia, but I'm not really sure. And no, it's not written down anywhere. I don't think he quite finished his consult," she added with a laugh.

Gallagher shook his head. "Never heard of him."

"Neither have I, but as I told the spook and Kirby and everybody else, that doesn't mean anything. I see more doctors comin' and goin' in one day in this hospital than most people see in their *en*tire life."

"So you're saying there was more of a problem between the cardiologist and that man than he let on?"

"Listen, I'm going to tell you the same thing I told the family. And this afternoon I'm going to tell it one more time to some police detective. All I know is that this doctor told me he was asked to see the Moricks' baby. I don't go questioning doctors about things like that. Now if the family says they didn't know about any problem with the baby, I can't say nothing about that."

"'Police detective'?"

"Right. I knew that family was bad news the moment they came up here."

Gallagher looked at her. "Her pediatrician didn't write a note about a consult or a cardiac problem in the chart? Sometimes if they're not sure about a problem, they won't tell the family until a specialist sees the baby."

"I don't know. I couldn't read his chicken-scratch."

"Where's the chart?"

"Downstairs," she said, peering at him curiously.

"Are the Moricks in the same room as yesterday?"

She looked at him as if he needed his head examined. Then with a loud snort, she shook her head and returned to her writing. "Dr. Gallagher, they're *long* gone. They were out of here like greased lightnin'."

TWELVE

At seven o'clock the next morning, Wukich parked in the back lot of a Rockville Ramada Inn and radioed to Burky Jones to drive around and pick him up. A minute later Burky reclaimed his spot across from the Moricks' room, letting the engine run to warm up the car. Wukich unfolded a newspaper and leaned back in the seat. "Don't get excited," he said. "I still got fifteen minutes. How you doin'?"

"Just great. I got to watch some kids make out for an hour. What the hell's goin' on here, Wuk? How long are they gonna stay in a damn motel?"

"Don't ask me. I moved Billie around for almost six fucking months."

"Come on. You know."

"All I know is Williams is nutso. He's got somebody trying to steal the kid for him."

"So let 'em go to the police."

"DeLozier went last night. He went six months ago too, but they wouldn't do shit then either. They just don't have enough guys. Not for what DeLozier wants them to do." He read the front-page headlines.

"Anyway, Williams was at a friend's house all that morning. With plenty of witnesses. So unless they get something else to go on, the cops say they can't do anything. And with the baby okay, they're sure as shit not gonna watch him or the Moricks' house."

"Find the doctor then."

"I never said he was doctor. That's what *he* said. And I can tell you one thing, they're not gonna accuse some doctor of trying to steal a baby without something better than me saying so. Anyway, the hospital thinks I just torked the guy off."

"So what are they going to do, stay here till she's eighteen?"

"Nah. I think DeLozier thinks he can nail him. I don't know how, but he does. What the hell. We could be freezing ass some place." Wukich flipped to the sports page and read its headlines before he moved to the other sections. "But don't get too comfortable," he added. "McCormick called me this morning. If something doesn't happen with Williams pretty quick, it sounds as if the family might be heading out."

"Gimme a fucking break. And I suppose *I'm* going to be with them."

"He didn't say nothin' about that. but don't make any plans."

Burky grunted and then was silent.

"Nothin' else goin' on?"

"The husband walked out to get a paper. He looks pissed."

"Yeah, DeLozier said to watch him close." Then, "Son-of-a-bitch!" yelled Wukich, shaking out the paper. "Look at this!" Burky leaned over to read a headline Wukich was pointing at. "That's the lady. Son-of-a-bitch."

Burky shook his head. "Fuckin' lawyers don't miss a chance. How much?"

"Eight million." Wukich was silent for a moment as he read. "They say the resident, Dr. Gallagher, was working without appropriate staff supervision." He read some more. "And that Billie probably didn't get the attention she deserved because she didn't have insurance. Well, that may be. The lady who checked her in was a real bitch. Holy shit. I wonder what's gonna happen now."

"Nothin'. The hospital will settle out of court. They don't want that publicity."

"I don't know. That's a lot of money."

"Time's up, Wuk. Get your ass out of here."

It was only a half hour before his morning schedule began, but it was the time of day Richard Ashton most cherished. It was time totally his, time free of husbandly duties, children, paperwork, patients. Normally he read the paper while savoring his coffee. Occasionally, before difficult or unusual cases, he would review pertinent articles or finer points of anatomy that had slipped away with the years.

The last few weeks had been different, though: the fear wouldn't go away. He didn't know how or when the news would come, but he knew it was coming. It might be a phone call, maybe a letter. He had dreamed one night it was the newspaper, and ever since it had been harder and harder to pick it up. That so much time had passed without more than passing questions from inside his own institution was surprising in itself. No pregnant patient had ever before walked away from the institute.

He had just managed to remove the newspaper from its plastic sheath and see that the front page was clear when there was a knock on the door, followed by the entrance of his secretary, Valerie.

"Dr. Fernandez called after you left last night," she said. "Nothing urgent, but he wanted you to call him today. At his house."

"Okay. Thanks, Valerie."

Her head retracted, then reappeared. "It's funny how things have a way of working out."

"What do you mean?"

"That surrogate-mother case. I mean, I know what happened to her is awful, and I know you would have preferred they didn't leave, but still, it could have happened here."

Her tone cautioned him to nod absently, and as soon as she closed the door, he flipped through the paper. On the front page of the local section he found it. Christ, and of all doctors for her to die on, it had to be that cocky little shit Brendan Gallagher. But the baby was okay, thank God, and there was no mention of him or the Fertility Institute. Well, the Moricks probably didn't want that particular piece of publicity any more than he did.

Ashton glanced at his watch—it was only an hour earlier in Mexico City. Carlos would be eating breakfast in the sun room.

"Ah, Richard," Fernandez said with the sound of Ashton's voice. "It has been much too long. But we are both to blame, so let us put that behind us. I called to make amends. Rachel and I want to go to Europe, and we would love for you to join us. Arlene too, if she can stand me."

"When?"

"Now! As soon as possible." Fernandez laughed. "But later this week or next week will do. I have a friend in France with a new chateau who would be delighted to have us. Come with us, Richard. It will be just like the old days."

"I have patients every day next week, Carlos. I can't just take off."

"Cancel them. Let Valerie do it."

"I can't."

"Just think about it. Okay?"

"I'll think about it, but there are too many things going on right now."

"One day you'll be dying, Richard, and there will still be too many things going on."

Ashton hesitated, then said, "Mrs. Williams died."

"Mrs. Williams?"

"The surrogate gestational mother."

"Madre de Dios!"

"Apparently she developed DIC after the delivery."

"And the baby?"

"She's fine."

"I'm sorry. I know you must feel awful. But these things . . . they sometimes happen, no?"

"It's not so simple."

"No? Why?"

"Because there's a big lawsuit, and . . . it's just not. You don't understand."

"I really am—did you say lawsuit? Why in the name of God would there be a lawsuit? What does this have to do with the law?"

"You know the way it is here."

"Well, that is one madness we do not have in Mexico. Who is this lawyer? So I can light candles for his soul."

"I don't know. I didn't read the article that closely."

"It's in the paper?"

"All over it."

"Madre de Dios. I'm sorry for you, Richard. I hope they leave you alone. And I'm sorry for the family. They seemed to be close to her. As a matter of fact, I was thinking about the Moricks the other day. Since they had asked for me to be consulted on their case, I wanted to send them a follow-up note. You know, just to minimize any hard feelings. Are they still in the area?"

"I don't know. I haven't heard from them."

"You'd think they would at least have the courtesy to let you know about the baby. You did put the damn kid there in the first place."

"We'll see. Maybe they will. I have to go now, Carlos. Don't count on me for France."

"I'll tell my friend we'll be four. If it doesn't work out, we'll go in the spring. But don't flog yourself. It's not your fault. Remember that, my friend."

Ashton was silent. "Richard?" Fernandez was saying. "Richard . . . are you there?"

"Sure," he said finally. "I'm here, Carlos. What is it?"

"I may be a bit sensitive about this matter, but surely you don't think—"

"Forget it, Carlos. It's just on my mind, to say the least. I'll talk to you later."

"I see. Well . . . try to relax. It'll blow over."

"Good-bye, Carlos."

"*Adios, amigo*. Be good to yourself. Okay?"

Ashton put the receiver down. He glanced at the article, then forced himself to read it straight through. Christ, Billie Williams's name was all over it, as well as the fact of her surrogate-mother role. It was a damn short trail back to him, back to those meetings with the Moricks. But who, except Susan, had had anything to do with the ultrasound? And Susan was as loyal as they came . . . wasn't she? For a moment he stared at the silver-framed photograph of himself with his two children on his desk. There he was—smiling, they were all three smiling. Then he went to his bookshelves, withdrew Sarah Morick's file from a locked cabinet, and locked it in his desk. Billie Williams had not died of an obstetrical oversight or accident, he thought. Brendan Gallagher was the best resident he had seen in years. But if that was true, then why . . . He shook his head, put the desk key in his pocket, and stood up. That he didn't even want to think about.

THIRTEEN

Wayne Masterson paged Gallagher a little after eight from the university hospital's emergency room. "Where the hell are you?" he said.

"In the residents' lounge."

"You okay?"

"Oh, just fine. Couldn't be better."

"Hey, man. We both know it's all crap."

"Jesus Christ, Wayne, I'm so sick of all this. Let 'em deliver their own babies I've had it. Fuck 'em. I'll work in a damn VD clinic."

"Hang in there, guy. Tonight we'll go out and get shit-faced. Okay?"

"See you tonight, Wayne." For a minute Gallagher stayed in the chair. Then forcing himself up, he kicked a trash can across the room and went back to the ward where a nurse had first given him the news.

It took all of his energy to finish with the patient he had been seeing. He worked automatically, answering questions and writing without thought. It was a process so ingrained that even on good days his mind was often elsewhere, and now it raced wildly in all directions. When he was done, he stayed for a minute, asking the woman casual questions about her work, her children. What would she think when she read the paper, or heard it on the news? Or would it be her husband who, knowing his hands had roamed inside her, would gently inform her of the incompetent she'd called "Dr. Gallagher"? He looked directly into the woman's eyes, and she looked away, unnerved by his frank gaze. So this is the way it will be, he thought. With every patient, every doctor, every one that knew him.

The page came a few minutes later. "Tell Dr. Lee you won't be available today," Coretti said, "and meet me in Kirby's office at nine o'clock."

At nine Coretti was already there; Danielle Parker was going to be a few minutes late. He, Coretti, and Kirby spent most of the next ten minutes in cold silence, until Parker finally swished through the office door, diffusely apologetic.

She was all motion as she spoke, pulling folders out of her briefcase, moving her chair into a more strategic position, flipping the pleats of her skirt into their proper place. "I'm telling you," she said, "this guy doesn't have anything. I mean *nothing*. I think they're trying to scare us into settling out of court."

"Fine," said Coretti, "but the most distressing concern still remains."

"You're referring to your professional reputations and the reputation of the hospital."

Coretti smirked, "What remains of them."

"I am very much aware of that. I intend to file a countersuit against this attorney and plaintiff for libel. I also hope to get some newspaper coverage from a *very* different perspective." There was silence as she looked around the room. "Now, let's get down to business. The list of—"

"Before you begin," said Gallagher, "I think I need to fill you in on a few developments."

"What are you referring to, Brendan?" said Coretti. "I certainly hope you haven't been sitting here for the last—"

"Let him finish, Joe," Parker said. "This is hard for all of us."

"I'm not quite sure where to begin," said Gallagher after a moment. "I suppose with the lab results." He got up and handed each of them a photocopy of the computer printout. Coretti didn't look at it. Parker studied it closely. Having attended medical school prior to law school, she was one of the new breed of medical-malpractice attorneys. She would know what she was looking at.

Finally, she said "From what I remember, this doesn't look like DIC to me."

"DIC can look like anything, Danielle," said Coretti. "I saw the results the next day, Brendan. What's the point?"

"Is there anything it does remind you of?" said Gallagher. "Look at the PT and PTT, and try to imagine how she was bleeding."

"Well, the PTT is affected much more than the PT during anticoagulation with heparin." She paused, frowning. "But she wouldn't have been getting heparin. You said she didn't have any medical problems."

Gallagher nodded.

Parker studied the printout again, then shook her head in disbelief. "Shit," she said. "You're telling me there was a mistake. Somebody hung the wrong IV fluid."

"Don't be ridiculous, Danielle," said Coretti. "For Christ's sake, they don't even keep heparin in the delivery suite." Turning toward Gallagher, "Do you have any idea what you're insinuating? We have enough problems as it is."

"Joe's right," said Parker. "There are a lot of other factors to consider here. Lab accuracy and preexisting medical problems, particularly hematological ones, just to name two."

"I've been working with the lab. All the tests were repeated several times. And I showed these results to a hematology fellow. She doesn't know of any hematological disorders that fit this picture. Joe," he said, look at her PTT. And her antithrombin three is normal.

"Look at her *PT*! I don't care what the damn lab says—the PTT in part is a lab error. They even told me that the machines aren't calibrated for values in that range. Have you *ever* seen one that high?"

"No," said Gallagher. "But neither have I ever seen anybody overdosed with heparin. She had heparin in her blood, Joe. *Before* we gave her any."

Parker was squinting as she watched him. When he stopped, she opened a notebook and took out a pen. "Go on," she said.

"You better have a damn good reason for this crazy idea," said Coretti. "A lot better reason than *one* lab test."

"I asked the toxicologist to assay the tube of blood they did the type and cross match from. The blood bank had frozen it."

"It contained heparin?" said Parker.

"The toxicologist thinks there's heparin in it."

"How do you know what he found wasn't already in the tube?" asked Parker. "The blood they do the cross match on has to be coagulated."

"They use EDTA as an anticoagulant in the test tube. He also extracted that, and it gives a different pattern than the heparin."

"This doesn't sound very standardized."

"It's not. But this guy was pretty complete. He made a positive control by taking a tube of normal blood and adding heparin to it. The extraction pattern from Billie Williams's blood matched the pattern from that tube. Except for one difference."

Parker's frown deepened. "Was he able to quantitate the amount of heparin?"

"That's the difference," said Gallagher, glancing at Coretti. "Yes and no. First of all, working with the sample was difficult because he didn't want to let it all thaw at once. In an hour whatever heparin was left would have been gone. Second, he's never been asked to determine a heparin *level* before. Patients on heparin are followed by their clotting studies, not by the level of heparin in their blood. He can tell us if it's there or not, but he can't tell us exactly how much. The only quantitative assay he knows of is the one that the drug companies use when they make it. There's not much blood left, but he thinks there's enough for one of their labs to work on it."

"They'll be pretty touchy about that," said Parker.

"That's what I figured, but just in case, what's left of the blood is still frozen." Gallagher paused, then said, "He did try to give me an idea of the amount by putting a normal therapeutic dose of heparin in the positive control. Judging from the intensity of the extraction pattern, Billie Williams's sample appeared to contain much more."

"I'm lost," interjected Kirby. "What's the bottom, line here? Are you saying somebody in the hospital messed up?"

Gallagher took a deep breath. "Not necessarily. I went over all the pharmacy 'records' with the pharmacist for that day and the day before. There were some patients in the hospital getting heparin, but the pharmacy wasn't aware of any missed doses. I also checked the patients' hospital records and the nursing medication records. And as Joe said they don't keep heparin in the delivery room or recovery room, so I don't think heparin was put in her IV fluid instead of oxytocin by mistake."

Coretti's eyes narrowed. "What are you getting at, Brendan?"

Gallagher held the other man's gaze. "Joe, besides the lawsuit being filed so quickly, there are a few unusual problems in this case."

Coretti stared at him.

"Beginning with the way Mrs. Williams arrived."

"They explained that to me."

"Would you mind explaining it to me? For heaven's sake, this was an in vitro baby. And knowing the guy who did it, I'm sure he isn't too pleased about her delivering here."

"That's confidential. Suffice it to say there were personality conflicts."

"Yeah, well *I* had to do the delivery without any history to go by."

"You should have called me."

"I did. Twice. And I paged you three times."

"My telephone was working, as well as my pager."

"If you hadn't—" Gallagher stopped himself.

"Come on guys," Parker said. "I was going to ask you later, Dr. Gallagher, but since the subject has come up, was anybody else around when you paged Joe? A nurse, a student, anybody that you can remember?"

Calm down, Gallagher said to himself. He gripped the chair. "No. I was in the doctors' lounge by myself."

Parker nodded and made a note on her pad. "Now, what—"

"How do *you* know about their doctor?" Coretti broke in.

"I worked with him."

"At the Washington Fertility Institute?"

"That's right."

"And who, pray God, were the Moricks working with?" Coretti said sarcastically.

Gallagher smirked. "If they didn't want to tell you, Joe, I'm not sure I should violate their confidentiality."

"Dr. Gallagher," said Parker firmly. "This is not a time to play games. The name of the physician they were—"

"They were working with Richard Ashton."

Parker made a note, then said, "You were there for an elective?"

"Yes."

"When? And who were the physicians you worked with the most?"

The lawyer continued to write for several seconds after he answered. Looking up, she said, "That would have been about the time of fertilization."

Gallagher nodded. "I watched Mrs. Morick's egg retrieval. It was a difficult case because of some scarring she had from an accident. That's why I think it's so strange they showed up here as they did. They should have been kissing Ashton's feet all the way into the delivery room, not avoiding him. I think we need to talk to him."

"Don't worry, Dr. Gallagher, I'll talk to him. That's my job." She paused. "Before we move on, are there any more surprises in that regard? Do you know of anything that might have driven them away?"

Gallagher took himself back once more to that February morning. For the most part all he remembered was feeling embarrassed and angry with himself for questioning Ashton. The rest was fragmented: Alice and Dr. Barton exchanging looks at his expense over the table; Ashton skillfully gathering the eggs; Fred taking them away in plastic dishes;

the radiant face of Sarah Morick when she had awakened to the news of a successful retrieval.

"No," he said, shaking his head. "But I still would like to know—"

"We'll talk about the institute later, Dr. Gallagher," said Parker. "I promise. Now, what were you saying before about 'unusual problems' in this case?"

"Mrs. Williams's first blood tests are missing, as well as the technician who was supposed to have drawn them. And there *was* a problem on the ward."

"We're well aware of the problem on the ward," said Coretti. Then to Parker: "We think that cardiologist I was telling you about was a reporter from one of the trash magazines. Apparently he was hanging around the delivery room also. They're big on the surrogate-mother stories. I'll fill you in more on that later."

"Surrogate *gestational* mother," Gallagher said to no one in particular.

"Yes," said Coretti. "She was a surrogate gestational mother. That's why we think they're trying to get a story out of it. It's a rather infrequent situation."

"Just the kind to make you walk away from your doctor," said Gallagher.

"There was a problem, Brendan," said Coretti. "That happens."

Gallagher nodded.

Coretti sat back in his chair. "Please finish what you were saying, Brendan."

"I did."

"I'm not sure you did, but I hope it's because you're beginning to realize the implications of *everything* you say. Generally, we, or anybody else, has some reasonable evidence before implying that someone in our hospital died as a result of anything other than a natural or disease-related cause. And I don't really think a court of law would consider a nonstandardized, behind-the-back test reasonable evidence. Do you, Danielle?"

"The standardization issue is a problem," said Parker after a moment.

"Why do you think she died, Joe?" said Gallagher.

Coretti was silent for a moment. "I think you were right the first time you thought about it. I think she had DIC. And if her husband had given us permission for the autopsy, we might have been able to prove it. But he didn't. Why she had DIC, I don't know. That happens, and not all that infrequently. I just wish I had seen her before she was almost dead in the ICU."

"And what would you—"

"Hey, guys," Parker interrupted, "we need to work together."

Coretti got up and glanced at Kirby, then at Parker. "I have to get to work, Danielle. Let's talk later today." He turned to Gallagher. "Brendan, we think it would be best for you to take a few days off and let things settle out a bit. It's going to be hard for you to concentrate with the paper playing this up."

"You have to be kidding me."

"No, Brendan, I'm not kidding you. we want you to take a few days off."

"'A *few*'?"

"Plan on a week."

Gallagher got to his feet. "I can't just walk out on the patients I'm taking care of," he said, fighting to control his voice. "There are some things I need to finish up."

"Do what you need to do today," said Coretti. "Then give the rest to Michael Curry. You can call me in a couple of days. I'll let you know what's happening. And we'll check the pharmacy and ward records again. If there was a mistake, we'll find it." Apparently finished, he paused, then looked at Gallagher again. "You know, Brendan, I've seen very good doctors professionally and emotionally devastate by lawsuits with less substance than this one might have. We all need to be very careful. We may never know why she got DIC and died, and why it happened really doesn't matter any more. It was no fault of ours. What matters right now is the *eight-million-dollar* lawsuit that's been filed against you and this hospital. And the rest of us by inference. We have a reputation, we have bills, we have debts to meet. This hospital *loses* money on the patients we take care of, Brendan. The only way we stay solvent is by donations. And that is directly proportional to how we are perceived by the public. Now if there was a problem like the one you're suggesting, then we'll most certainly address it. Just as we're addressing the Moricks' concerns. But until we know for sure that there was—there *wasn't*. Do you understand?"

"Yes, Dr. Coretti, I understand."

"And please don't voice your thoughts to anybody else," added Parker. "Every word you say is important. Don't forget that."

"May I go know?"

"Keep in touch," nodded Coretti.

By noon he had turned over his patients to Michael Curry, checked his mailbox, and cleaned his books out of his locker. In the eighth-floor residents' lounge, he picked up the phone and dialed the first number on the list. I'll be damned if I'm going to get fried alone, he said to himself as he listened to it ring. Finally he hung up. Wherever Mr. Williams was, he wasn't waiting by the phone for further instructions from his shyster lawyer. He was about to hang up on the second call when an answering machine with the voice of Nathan Morick clicked on: "The Moricks are not available at the moment. If you wish to leave a message, please do so after the tone."

He hung up and dialed information. The computerized voice issued a number, and this time, after multiple rings, a man answered without identifying himself.

"Mr. DeLozier?"

"May I ask who's calling?"

"Dr. Gallagher."

"May I help you?" The voice was not cold. If anything, it contained a trace of compassion.

"I'm trying to reach your daughter and son-in law. I'm sorry to bother you, but I wasn't sure when they would get the message I left on their answering machine."

"They maybe temporarily unavailable."

"This isn't in reference to the lawsuit, Mr. DeLozier. There was a problem in the hospital the other day that you may or may not be aware of. I believe it's within reason to speak to them about that incident. Since I was the first doctor to arrive after whatever happened, I'm being asked to make a statement about it."

"I agree. I'm not keeping them from you. They're just unable to speak with you now. I'm sorry. I can't tell you anything more than that at the moment."

"I can get a subpoena, Mr. DeLozier. One of the nurses is on the verge of filing an assault charge."

"As I said, I'm not keeping them from you."

"Well, just how do you propose I reach them?"

"Leave a message, as you did. If I speak with them before they receive it, I will relay your desire to talk with them."

"So you will be in contact with them?"

"I'm not sure. Listen, Dr. Gallagher, I can't tell you how much I sympathize with you in this regard. Please believe me, this recent development has nothing to do with any of us. In the future we'll cooperate with you and your lawyers to whatever degree it takes. But I cannot discuss the matter any further at the moment. My lawyer's been out of town, and I haven't yet had the opportunity to go over this lawsuit with him."

"Look, Mr. DeLozier, I really don't give a . . . hoot about your lawyer. I'm getting sued over a young woman who died under my care only hours after I met her. Not only was your family involved with this woman, but they, or their guard, were involved in a rather unusual incident the next day. I want to talk to them!"

"I'm not sure that's necessary, Dr. Gallagher. Have you spoken with Dr. Kirby or Dr. Coretti? They know what happened.

"I . . . yes, I have. But we're all a little confused."

"Please, Dr. Gallagher, try to understand our situation. I promise we'll help you as soon as possible."

"No, Mr. DeLozier, I don't understand."

"Dr. Gallagher—"

"It's all right, Mr. DeLozier. Please have your daughter or son-in-law contact me as soon as possible."

"I want to emphasize that we had *nothing* to do with this lawsuit."

"I understand that. but it doesn't change anything."

"I haven't finished. I presume your lawyer is quite interested in speaking with Mr. Williams."

"Why would you presume that?"

"Dr. Gallagher, I'm trying to help you. *Have* you spoken with your superiors about the incident on the ward?"

Gallagher paused, then said, "Briefly."

"I see. Well then, I'm not an expert in these matters, but it seems to me this lawsuit was filed pretty quickly. I suppose I would wonder why somebody's so money hungry. She's not even buried yet. I also suggest that someone on your end contact Mr. Williams rather promptly. I tried calling him a little while ago. He didn't answer, so I called the apartment building's manager to leave a message. She said he'd just paid his rent. Apparently he's moving out—and fast."

"What do you mean he's moving? He just filed an eight-million-dollar lawsuit."

"I don't know what's going on. Look, Dr. Gallagher, let me give you Mr. Williams's address in the event you or your lawyer decide to visit him." DeLozier read off an address and apartment number, then said: "He goes by 'Buck,' and he drives an old red pickup that's usually in the side lot. Whoever goes, be careful. He's big and mean."

"Thanks," said Gallagher grudgingly. "We'll look into it." He was about to hang up when he heard DeLozier speaking and brought the phone back to his ear.

". . . you want to talk to me, I should be home all afternoon and evening. Now I must say good-bye, Dr. Gallagher."

FOURTEEN

Gallagher zipped up his windbreaker and leaned into the wind that was cartwheeling leaves across the staff parking lot. It was one of the first fall days in which the cold overshadowed the brilliance of the autumn foliage, and the afternoon was full of winter warning. In his car he turned on the heater while he studied a map of the city.

The early-afternoon beltway traffic was light, and in twenty minutes he exited toward Hyattsville. A mile from the highway he began a series of quick turns through the neighborhoods, each block of row houses and apartments more run-down than the next, each in some way—the cracked, bumpy sidewalks, the old brick steps leading up to the porches, the seemingly contagious sense of defeat emanating from the opaque windows—disturbingly familiar. At a stop sign he watched a group of teenage boys coming down the sidewalk. One had a book under his arm, the others old basketballs or radios. They passed two girls sitting on a porch, and for ten yards they walk backward, shouting at them. When they turned around in unison, they were close to his car, the biggest of them holding his crotch and moaning into the air. Gallagher sat up straight, glanced at his unlocked doors, and took off his tie. Easing out into the small intersection, he was aware of the group's stares, then of several obscenities directed his way. A car pulled up beside him, startlingly close, and his hands rose in self-defense as if he had been walking home from his grade school and had been confronted by the older boys. "Get the fuck out of the way," yelled the driver, and Gallagher picked up speed. Minutes later he turned onto Crawford Street and parked across from the apartment.

The front entrance was deserted. The side parking lot was half-full, with a red pickup near the closest side of the building. It was overflowing with furniture, a box spring resting on top of the cab. With the truck in clear view, Gallagher decided to wait in the car. Two men soon exited from the front door, but neither were very large, and he sat back. Then a man wearing a hooded gray sweatshirt suddenly appeared from the back of the apartments. A mattress was pinned under one arm, a lamp under the other. Easily over six feet tall, and thick in his chest and thighs, the man loped toward the truck as if his arms were empty.

Gallagher got out and headed across the parking lot. When he was close to the man, he stopped and waited for him to finish lashing a rope over the mattress. The man tied the rope tight, then picked up another length and threw it over the top of the truck.

"Mr. Williams?"

No answer.

"Mr. Williams, I'm Dr. Gallagher. From St. Joseph Hospital." Williams worked without looking up. "Mr. Williams, I'd like to talk with you about your wife."

"Don't got one."

Gallagher stepped closer, "I know all of this is hard for you, but try to understand that we are very concerned about what happened. It won't bring her back, but if we can understand why she died, perhaps we can prevent it from happening to someone else."

"I already talked about Billie. She's dead. You killed her. There ain't nothin' else to talk about." His voice was flat, his face expressionless.

"I was hoping you would reconsider giving us permission to do the autopsy. Particularly since we have some new information that might help us understand what happened."

Williams turned. His mouth hung partly open, revealing several gaps in his teeth. What remained of them were a grayish yellow. "Listen, mister, doctor, whoever the fuck you are. You and all the other assholes, are really starting to piss me off. You just finished killin' my wife, and all you keep talkin' about is messin' her up some more. Now, I told you no once, and that should have been enough. Get out of here before I hurt you."

Gallagher looked at him. Then he glanced into the back of the truck. "I don't understand why you're moving. How are we going to proceed with this rather large lawsuit?"

Williams seemed to stiffen. Turning back to the mattress, he said, "Ain't none of your fuckin' business."

"I don't know about that, Mr. Williams. We also have certain rights in this matter. You need to be available to our attorneys."

"I ain't talking to no more assholes."

Gallagher cocked his head and stared at the big man, whose back was to him. "Some of the pretrial proceedings just can't be done long-distance," he said in the nicest tone he could muster.

Williams yanked a knot tight and turned around. "Maybe there won't be no need for that."

"Why not?"

"'Cuz maybe you're goin' to own up."

"To what?"

Williams studied him, then said, "Got me." He spat and turned back to the truck.

Gallagher watched him tie another knot. Finally he said: "I don't understand what you think we might 'own up to,' or why you're leaving. I think we need to talk, Mr. Williams."

"*We* don't need to do shit. Get the fuck out of here."

"Do the police know you're leaving?"

Williams stared at him.

"Maybe I'll go ahead and let them know."

"Maybe I'll beat your little fuckin' ass."

"Maybe, but I don't think that will help the situation much."

"Call the motherfuckers. They didn't say I couldn't."

"Why don't you just let us do an autopsy?"

Williams glared at him for several seconds. "Fuck you and your autopsy." Turning, he headed for the back of the apartments, his hands shoved into the pockets of his dirty jeans.

Gallagher watched the man disappear around the corner, then hurried after him. The back door was propped open with a rock, the stairwell empty but for the sounds of boots several flights above. Starting up the stairs, he took in the pockmarked cement walls, the peeling paint covered with graffiti, the cigarette butts and paper cups strewn in every corner. He smiled to himself. When he had said good-bye to some of his high-school friends at graduation, he had hoped never to set foot in such a building again. Above him a door opened. He exited on the third floor and looked down an empty, dim hallway. On the fourth there was an apartment, wide open.

Treading lightly down the hall, he waited in the open doorway. The apartment looked empty except for some wooden boxes strewn across the living area. Williams came into view, his face instantly turning an ugly mien, and started for him.

"Don't," said Gallagher. "You can't leave if you're in jail."

The man stopped two feet away and put his face up close. His breath was a disgusting mixture of cigarette smoke, beer, and fried meat. "You're asking for big trouble, buddy," he said. "Don't you hear nothing?"

"Mr. Williams, there are several things you ought to know. Number one, if you think St. Joseph's has any intention of settling out of court, you're mistaken. I can't tell you exactly why your wife died, but I can tell you we weren't at fault."

Williams pulled down the hood of his sweatshirt and shook out a long ponytail of black hair that matched his eyes. His face was a rich, natural brown, but marked with acne scars.

"Number two, if we can't do an autopsy in the normal fashion, I'll have to call the medical examiner. If I do that, then not only will we *have* to do an autopsy, but the police will want to talk to you."

Williams laughed. "Call whoever the fuck you want. I already talked to 'em."

"Not about why you beat your wife."

The Indian lunged and grabbed Gallagher by the jacket. Pinning him against the wall, he said, "What did you say, motherfucker?"

"I said you'll have to explain the bruises that were all over your wife. Which may have caused—"

Williams pushed Gallagher harder into the wall. "Listen, you little cocksucker! I never hit Billie once in three fucking years. So you go tell the cops to talk to the asshole who started all this. Goddamn—I hadn't even *seen* her in the last six months."

"If you didn't hit her, then let go of me and we'll talk." Williams didn't move. "I'm telling you, if you don't let go of me, you're going to end up in jail." Looking at the man's eyes, and at the burnt glass bowls and the little alcohol burner he could see through the kitchen door, Gallagher added, "And you know what you'll feel like come nighttime and no crack."

Williams pushed one more time, then let go and walked into the living area. There he rummaged in the front pocket of his sweatshirt, withdrew a pack of Marlboros, and lit one. "Whadda you want?"

Gallagher moved into the room a few feet. "To know why your wife died. And why she showed up at our hospital as she did."

"You tell me. You're the fucking doctor."

"What did you mean you said you hadn't seen your wife in the last six months?"

"Just what I said."

"Where was she?"

"Fuck if I know. And I wasn't the only one who would've . . ." Williams dragged on his cigarette, then began to study one of his fingernails.

"Who would've what?"

"Just would've been nice to know where she was, that's all." he looked up. "Seeing how she was my wife."

"You don't have any idea where she was?"

"All I know is she called, one day and said she'd be back after the baby, was born." He inhaled deeply and blew out a long stream of smoke. "Ask that asshole old man. I bet it ain't no coincidence I didn't see him no more after she left."

"What 'asshole old man'?"

"Jesus, man, that messed-up lady's father. The one that used to bug the shit out of us."

"Mr. DeLozier?"

"Yeah."

"Why'd he used to 'bug' you?"

"'Cause he thought we were scum. Why else? He even had some private pecker watching us."

Gallagher hesitated, then said: "Do you know why the doctors from the Fertility Institute didn't deliver the baby?"

Williams shrugged. "Ask the asshole."

"What did you mean when you said maybe we're going to own up? Are you thinking the hospital might settle out of court?"

Another shrug.

"Mr. Williams?"

"Screw you, buddy."

"How'd you pick your lawyers? Maybe he's jerking you around."

Williams grunted. "I didn't pick nobody. Three of 'em called the next day. Every damn one of 'em told me you did her in. they ain't all wrong, that's for goddamn sure." He was silent for a moment, looking at his hands. "And I'm damn well gonna get some money."

Gallagher snorted. "From whom? We're not settling out of court."

"Got me," said the Indian, looking at Gallagher with disdain. He stood up and lit another cigarette.

Gallagher stayed put. "One more question. You don't have to answer, but if you don't, our lawyer will find you to ask you again. why did your wife want to be a surrogate mother?"

Williams's eyes filled with anger, and Gallagher reflexively stepped back. "Because she had more inside of her than any fuckin' one of you. Because some asshole like you knocked her up when she believed his lies. Then he ran away with his tail between his legs. So you tell me, asshole—what's a sixteen-year-old girl with a preacher for a father supposed to do?"

"I'm sorry, Mr. Williams—"

"I'll tell you just so you know what kind of person you want to cut up. She had an abortion, and for four fuckin' years it near about killed her. That's why she wanted to have that goddamn baby. She wouldn't have one of her own until she made up to somebody for the first one. There was more in that woman than you'll ever know in your whole fuckin' life."

"They don't usually let a woman, who hasn't delivered a baby be a surrogate mother," Gallagher said softly.

Williams stiffened again. "Billie knew what she could do."

"It wasn't for the money?"

"Shit, I had to make her take the money Billie was going to give that lady a baby if it—" He stopped, his anger seeming to leak out of him. Then: "All she cared about was doing what was right. She didn't care about no money. Shit, we could've had a whole lot more if she'd only listened to me." He turned his head toward the ceiling. "And goddamn it, Billie, it did kill you. I ought to kick your old man's ass."

Gallagher moved for the door. "I can't tell you how sorry I am about your wife," he said, stopping in the doorway. "Really." He looked at Williams for a moment. "What about the autopsy?"

Williams ground his cigarette out on the worn carpet. "Fuck you and your autopsy."

*   *   *

The Moricks had left the Ramada at one o'clock, with Burky Jones instructed to stay behind them as far as the Chesapeake Bay Bridge. Wukich had peeled off at the beltway and headed for his next assignment.

But in Potomac Falls, there was no place for him to sit inconspicuously in his car. Cars were not parked on the street there. They weren't even parked in the driveways. Cars in Potomac Falls were parked where expensive automobiles belonged—in the garage. And no matter where he sat, the house and grounds were much too large for adequate surveillance. Certainly he could not patrol on foot. Strangers on foot were even rarer than parked cars. So for the last two hours he'd been driving in circles, feeling like the whole goddamn neighborhood was watching him.

At the moment he was on the back loop, getting only intermittent glimpses of DeLozier's backyard, and thinking again that he would call his boss as soon as possible. Not only was it ludicrous to make laps through this neighborhood, but there was no way he could watch this house by himself. And he wasn't about to have another incident pinned on him that wasn't his fault. He pulled onto the grass under a stand of oak trees near the DeLozier driveway. The trees were at the bottom of a slope so that approaching vehicles could appear relatively unannounced over the hill. This had bothered him from the beginning, and now he hardly had time to straighten up before the van was there, right next to him, blocking his view. He had one hand on his gun, one hand on the door handle, when he took it in that the van belonged to a swimming-pool maintenance company, and the man in its front seat was asking him if he knew where the "Brichta family" lived.

"No. I'm just waiting for somebody."

"Can't hear you," said the man, sticking his head out the window and cocking it to one side. He wore a baseball hat and sunglasses that covered much of his face. Thinking that the man was opening his door, Wukich pushed his door handle down, but he was too late. The van door had slammed into the side of his car.

"You fucking asshole!" he said, looking at the door wedged in his car. The man laughed and was about to yank the door back when Wukich swiped at him. He was off balance with one arm out the window when his front passenger door opened.

"You are not so smart," said a man with a gun barrel twelve inches from Wukich's face. Pulling the door closed, the man nodded to his friend in the van, who was still grinning. The van moved forward, the door still embedded in the side of the car. For a couple of yards it stayed that way, gouging and tearing, until it swung free at the front. The man waved as he closed the door and the van picked up speed.

"Follow him!" Wukich hesitated, and the gun barrel slammed into his forehead. "Move!" the man grunted.

A warm trickle of blood reached Wukich's eye brow, ran down the bridge of his nose, dripped into his lap. Catching up to the truck, he thought first of DeLozier in his big house, and then of his eight-year-old son, Eddie, whom he had told Carla he would pick up that afternoon. Eddie would be sitting on his football helmet, waiting, as darkness enveloped the field.

FIFTEEN

A row of crabapple trees lined each side of the driveway from the street to the house. Wrapped around the bases of the trees were well-manicured beds of low-growing shrubs, or the brown remnants of annuals. Larger beds broke up the yard into gentle curves of rich fall grass, speckled with the red-and-brown droppings of oak trees. The nearest house Gallagher could see was at least a hundred yards away, and almost completely hidden by two of the large oaks that flanked the west side of DeLozier's property. He stopped halfway down the driveway and took a deep breath of the damp air. The silence around the place was startling. No airplanes, trucks, horns. Nothing.

Seeing only the encroaching dusk, Gallagher headed up the flagstone walkway to the front door. Somewhere on the first floor, there was light.

The doorbell chimed clearly in the entry hall. Then again. After a third time Gallagher put his face to the narrow vertical windows beside the door. The curtains were opaque. Once more he rang the doorbell. Finally he grasped the door knocker and rapped out sharp cracks of brass on brass. No response. He hopped down behind a row of boxwoods and peered through a full-sized window. There *was* light coming from the back.

Moving to the other side of the doorstep, he tried another window. The mild breeze picked up, rustling the leaves of a Japanese maple right next to his head. Suddenly he had an urge to spin and run for his car.

But maybe DeLozier was watching television and couldn't hear the bell. Gallagher looked around one final time and headed for the side of the house, hoping DeLozier didn't own a dog. He turned the first corner and entered a dark alley formed by a string of junipers. Thirty yards ahead a faint light illuminated part of the backyard, and he hurried toward it as if he were emerging from a tunnel. A foot from the light, still in shadow, he stopped. Whatever room opened onto the large wooden deck jutting out from the house was the source of the light. He studied the yard. Close to the house the grass was yellow in the light, coming through the windows. But beyond that it was dark, almost impenetrable, until at the end of the yard only the suggestion of a white rail fence was visible.

Gallagher started up the stairs of the deck, then stopped short. The back door was ajar, the strike plate dangling from a single screw. Forcing himself to stay rooted, he studied what he could of the kitchen, the deck, the yard. There was no movement, nothing unusual that he could see. He took the last step up to the deck. Two more, and he was close enough to the bay window to see into the room. After the mangled strike plate, it was no surprise. Kitchen drawers, papers, and utensils were strewn over the countertops and floor. The phone, its plastic shell cracked into pieces, hung from the wall by eviscerated wires. He stepped closer to the window and cupped his hands against the cold glass.

In the bay of the window was a cluttered table. There were spots on the blue tablecloth, larger and darker near the end farthest into the kitchen. A sudden clanking noise broke the silence like a gunshot, and he wheeled, blood pounding in his ears. It was an automatic garage-door opener, doing its job somewhere in the neighborhood. Then everything was still. He turned and pulled on the doorknob. The door popped free, the strike plate and remaining screw clinking onto the wooden deck. For a minute he stood motionless, straining for any sound from within. Although he couldn't hear anything to suggest activity, he knew he had to move. Through the window he had seen a knife partially covered by papers on the kitchen table. He was only ten steps from it, and he moved for the table unconsciously, searching for the handle beneath the papers. In seconds he was back in the shadow of the door, ready to slash at anything that moved.

The weapon was more than he expected—a butcher's cleaver with a sturdy handle and a wide, gleaming rectangular blade. He hefted its comforting weight and turned it over in the light coming from the kitchen. He was about to let it drop to his side when his head moved an inch closer. Then right up to the blade. Specks of blood dotted the side, and the cutting edge was dark red. But it was not the blood he studied: it was the little nubbins of skin and cartilage stuck to the steel like fish scales.

Gallagher straightened. Still, there was no noise from the house. Stepping into the kitchen, he scanned the counters, the table, the floor. It seemed that it was mainly the drawers containing paperwork that had been emptied out, their contents everywhere on the floor. He moved closer to the table, under the bright light from the kitchen ceiling, and the specks of dried blood he had seen from the window turned to drops, then puddles. At one end of the table, mostly covered by papers, was a cutting block. The folds of the tablecloth next to it held a burgundy pool, the center of which was not yet completely coagulated. In front of the pool was a chair speckled with reed, as was the floor beneath it. A trail of maroon led and disappeared into a dark room off the kitchen.

For a moment he stayed put. Then he stepped forward and bent over the cutting block. The wells on the edges were full, as if a piece of beef had been carved several hours before and the juice left to sit. But not only was this coagulated, narrow pool too thick for juice, it was with evidence of its source. Peering at the block as he had on that day when he was introduced to his medical-school cadaver, he studied the inch-long tubes of now blue gray meat. There were three, their tapered ends and varying lengths sickening symmetrical. He knew quite well what they were before he saw the fourth, tucked partly under a book of coupons, the nail—as if it had a life of its own—cleanly reflecting the kitchen light.

He was still bent over the table when his head jerked toward the dark room. It was a desperate, guttural sound, part groan and part cry. He had heard it once as a boy, when he had stumbled across a man in the woods who had accidentally shot himself, and again on occasion in the emergency room. He peered into the darkness. The sound came again, and he gripped the knife. Warren DeLozier was moaning for his life.

PART THREE

Sixteen

Perched up on its pilings like a pelican, the stilted house creaked and groaned in mild protest to the wet gusts of wind swaying the edifice in a gentle rhythm. From a couch in the family room Nathan Morick could see through a window to the main part of town. Only a few stores were open this time of year, and cars were sparse. In the distance the red lights of the water tower had just been turned on. A sudden blast of air shook the walls, and he looked out to the ocean. Rolls of spray jumped off the tops of the waves. Closer, sand swirled in puffs from the beach and dunes. He'd better bring in more wood for the fire, he thought.

Sarah's face was relaxed, her body curled into the curve of his side. For the moment she had succeeded in slipping away. She had often talked of spending hours in front of just such a cheerful blaze with her children.

She looked up and met his gaze. "I don't know how else to tell you, Nathan. I don't understand either. All I know is that I trust my father, and I'm not going to push him. We have a beautiful little girl—that's what matters."

The anger was rising again. Keeping his voice down, he said "Dammit, Sarah, *we're* the ones hiding out like fugitives—not him. How long does he expect—"

"He said he'd call tonight, honey. Come on. Please. We *have* to do what he says right now."

"But this is crazy! Why can't they lock the guy up?"

Sarah pushed his arm away, "They can't *prove* anything, Nathan! This is America." She got up and walked to the sliding glass doors facing the ocean. With the sun about to set over the horizon behind the house, the ocean was dark, only a sliver of gray separating it from the sky. "And to be honest with you," she added, crossing her arms and hugging herself, "I'm beginning to think the whole thing was a mistake."

"Don't say that, honey." Nathan went to her and put an arm around her shoulder. "We have a beautiful baby. I'm sorry I'm such a mess. It's just so frustrating. It seems like the only thing that's gone right is Lauren."

Her voice rose. "You *know* I don't want to be here! You know I *want* to go home!" She opened the blinds the rest of the way. In the dusk they could barely make out two people at the end of the weathered boardwalk. They were leaning on the last set of rails, facing the ocean. "Look at them," she said softly. "It must be beautiful out there with the spray and the wind. That's what the ocean's all about."

"Why don't we take a walk? Your mother's okay with Lauren."

Footsteps came from the rear of the house, then Dorothy DeLozier with Lauren on her shoulder. The baby was stirring, and Dorothy was rubbing her back.

"She just woke up." Mrs. DeLozier passed the infant to Sarah.

Nathan went back to the couch.

"The storms coming from the east," said his mother-in-law. "The bay's still clear. It's always so pretty right as the sun's going down."

"I've never seen it in October before," said Nathan.

Sarah went over and sat down next to him. "Hold your daughter and be quiet."

Lauren was now wide awake. Nathan held her on his knees facing him, one side of her face streaked with the last rays of the waning sunlight. With each hour her scalp and face had lost more of the swelling from the delivery, though there was still a little bruise on her forehead. With each hour she looked more like Sarah, her cheeks retracting over her sharp cheekbones, her little chin narrowing to a gentle curve. Sarah's mother had pointed out all of this without fail for the past three days, but Nathan had kept what *he* saw—the gentle, pliant Morick eyes; the quick smiles; the stubby little fingers so much like his own—to himself. Lauren gripped his fingers as he rocked her up and down. When he grinned and tickled her, she gurgled and smiled back.

"Where's the camera?" said Sarah. "I do believe he's smiling."

"Oh, now I see," said nathan, suddenly bending hid head down close to Lauren's diaper. "You have a little poopy in there."

Sarah got up and tossed him the diaper bag. "It's part of bonding."

Nathan moved Lauren down onto the carpet and knelt over her. He unsnapped her yellow one-piece jumpsuit, adorned with an embroidered white-and-blue duck, then the two layers of cotton underclothes. By the time he got to her diaper, she was kicking, and he had to hold her feet together with one hand. As he let go to remove the soiled diaper, she put a foot into it, then back up in the air, flinging little spots of brown onto his leg. "Hold still, Lauren!" he pleaded. *"Please!"*

Sarah giggled, then began to laugh. She looked at her mother and rolled her eyes. "Why are men so incompetent?" she managed between breaths.

"Oh, for heaven's sake," said her mother, moving toward them on the floor.

"I'm okay, Dorothy."

She stood over him for a moment before returning to the window. When Nathan had a fresh diaper in place, Sarah turned on a lamp and walked into the kitchen.

"Well," she said, "I guess we need to think about dinner."

"I was thinking you and Nathan could go out," said Mrs. DeLozier. "I'll stay here with Lauren. The Rehoboth Crab House is open in the off season. Why don't you two go up there and have a nice dinner?"

"That's okay, Mom, we—"

"Why don't we *all* go?" said Nathan. Still on the floor, he was holding Lauren on his chest, her head listing to the right. "It'll be good to get out. We have the infant seat. I'm sure it won't be crowded."

Sarah looked at Dorothy. "Yeah, let's do that. And if it's not too cold, we can go out on the boardwalk. Come on, Mom."

"Are you sure?"

"Absolutely," said Nathan. He looked at Sarah for confirmation. "Let's get out of here. We can put the answering machine on in case Warren calls."

"I'll never forget the look on Nathan's face that first day," Sarah was saying. She looked at him and smiled. "You know, when that lady with the blond showed you the men's room." She glanced coyly her mother, who took a sip of iced tea.

"Is nothing sacred?"

"Don't be silly, Nathan," said Sarah. "There's nothing *wrong* with that. It's just . . . funny when I think about you and that receptionist. I thought you were going to stuff that brown bag right into her mouth."

"Over her face would have been better."

Sarah began to recount another of their trips through the Fertility Institute. Nathan glanced down at Lauren, asleep in the infant seat beside him, then out into the warm, well-lit room. Narrow aisles for the waiters and waitresses wound their way between the red-checkered tables. Virtually every inch of wall space was filled with buoys, mounted fish, and lobster pots. There were only a few other patrons, mostly older couples. Lauren was the only person he had seen all night under twenty. He stroked her cheek, watching her lips pucker.

When he looked up, Sarah was crying. He reached over to take her hand. "Everything's going to be all right, honey. We'll be home soon."

"That's *not* it." She pulled her hand back and looked away, fighting more tears.

"I know it's not. But we can only do our best now with Lauren. With what Billie gave us."

Sarah nodded and wiped her eyes. Then, looking at Lauren, she said, "I think we should give her another middle name. Either Billie or Leanna. That was Billie's middle name."

"We can think about that." Nathan motioned to the waitress and ordered beer for Sarah and himself, wine for Dorothy. "I've heard the oysters here are great," he said.

"They're wonderful," said Mrs. DeLozier. "Remember how much you loved them as a kid, Sarah? Before you turned into a teenager." She winked at her son-in-law. "Then you wouldn't come here with us anymore. Were we really *that* bad?"

"Of course not, Mom. You were better than most."

Nathan watched her, marveling at how these childhood memories, invoked over and over among Sarah and her parents, could wash any sadness from her face.

"Gosh," she was saying, "I remember one night I was on the boardwalk, with Ellen and Tricia, and you and Dad . . ."

"Those were the best oysters I've ever had." Nathan took off his jacket and threw it on the couch.

"If you were a *really* good husband, you'd go get some wood and get the fire going," said Sarah. "Lauren's still asleep. If I can put her down without her waking up, we can relax."

"Do you want me to call Warren?" said her mother.

"Cheek the answering machine first," said Sarah. "I'll put Lauren down."

Nathan was closer to the telephone. He started the tape, turned back for his coat, then stopped as the message filled the room: "This is Dr. Gallagher calling for Sarah Morick. Your father can't come to the phone right now, but he wanted me to give you a message. He wants you to leave for New York tonight—as soon as you can. He said to go to the Holiday Inn just outside John F. Kennedy Airport. Then he wants you to call him. If you can't reach him at the house, try his car phone." For a moment after the tape cut off, neither Nathan nor his mother-in-law spoke. Then she whispered. "I'll get Sarah."

"Goddamn it, Dorothy—"

"Now you listen here, Nathan." She whirled to face him. I'm sick and tired of your whining. None of this is my fault, and don't you even *think* of starting in on me. And you're so . . . so damn self-centered that you probably haven't even stopped to think of why Warren didn't call himself. *Have you?*"

Sarah came out from the back bedrooms. "What's going on?" she said, looking from Nathan to her mother.

Mrs. DeLozier wiped her eyes and went into the kitchen. "Ask your husband."

Nathan went over to the answering machine and rewound the tape. While it played again, he opened the curtains and looked out the sliding glass doors. When it was over, he said, "This is really getting crazy, Sarah."

Sarah nodded, sucking her lower lip into her mouth.

"If your father can't do anything about that lunatic, then somebody else has to. I'll go back myself. You can go to New York."

"I'm worried about Warren." said Mrs. DeLozier.

Sarah moved to her mother. "Don't be ridiculous, Nathan! What do you think my father's doing, ignoring him?"

"No, but Jesus Christ, *this* is ludicrous! I'm going to call—"

"Nathan! Can't you see that my mother's worried? And so am I. Why didn't my father call himself?"

He watched them for a moment. Then he turned and began to pick up some of their things from the family room. Shortly he said: "Gallagher would have said something if there was a problem with Warren, Dorothy. I'm sure there's a good reason he didn't call himself. We'll call him as soon as we can. Now let's get packed. I want to be out of here in ten minutes."

SEVENTEEN

"Why didn't you let the surgeon at least try to put them back on?" said Gallagher. The stoplight ahead turned red, and he checked his rearview mirror. They were alone on River Road, still a few miles from the house, and he eased to a stop.

"I told you—I don't have 'six to eight hours' to spend in an operating room."

"Why not?" said Gallagher firmly.

"Because I don't, goddamn it!" DeLozier rummaged in the pocket of his sport coat and swore under his breath.

"What are you looking for? Maybe I can help."

"My address book. I'm sure I put it in this coat. The phone number of the beach house is tucked right inside it."

"Look, Mr. DeLozier, I really think we should call the police. Especially if you're worried about your family."

The older man's voice took on a sudden firmness: "You don't get it, do you? Look at this—it's very simple." He lifted his white paw out of the sling. "This is only the beginning of what they'll do to my wife and my family if I go to the police. They were very clear about that."

"*Who* was very clear? And why the hell did they cut off your fingers? Why are they threatening your family?"

"Those men, goddammit! And don't worry about why. This is my problem."

"That's just the point, Mr. DeLozier. Not only am I being negligent in *not* calling the police, but this *isn't* just your problem. If what happened to you has anything to do with everything else you and your family have managed to get me involved in, it's *my* problem too. Besides, you know I can't leave you in the house alone."

"Sure you can. They won't be back. Not if they found that address book." The older man looked out the window for a moment, then said grudgingly: "Maybe you can help me look for it. I'm feeling a little woozy."

They crossed over the beltway, and Gallagher glanced in his mirrors. A car was cresting a hill behind him, and he sped through the yellow light at Seven Locks Road. At the Potomac Village stoplight he turned to speak to DeLozier, but the man's head was back against the seat, his eyes closed. The codeine was kicking in.

The light turned, and with the intersection clear and nobody behind him, he turned onto Falls Road and found the entrance to Potomac Falls. When they pulled into the driveway and up to the house, it was after midnight. DeLozier was able to walk to the front door on his own accord, but Gallagher stayed right next to him, ready to catch him if he fell. Under the porch light he studied the older man's face as he fumbled for his keys with his good hand. Though some of the color was returning, and with it the determined set to his mouth, he looked as if he were about to drop.

Inside, DeLozier headed straight for his library and walnut gun rack. He opened the glass doors, studied the array of weapons for several seconds, then methodically took down and loaded a Winchester 30-06 rifle and a Browning semiautomatic twelve-gauge shotgun. From a desk drawer he took out a handful of rifle shells and shoved them into his jacket pocket. Slinging the rifle over his shoulder, he handed the shotgun to Gallagher. "All you have to do is take off the safety pull the trigger," he said, clicking the safety on and off. Then walking past the younger man, he went into the kitchen, set the rifle across the arms of a chair, and began rummaging in the papers on the and counters.

"Sit down, Mr. DeLozier. You need to rest. What color is it?"

"Dark green. About so big."

Gallagher looked through the mess piece by piece.

"Damn!" DeLozier said when he was done. "Maybe it's upstairs. But"—he looked about to keel over—"I'm not sure I can make it. Can you . . . ?"

"Sure."

"Check my dresser first. Then check the telephones in the master bedroom and in Sarah's old room. Hers is the one with all the stuffed animals. Call her again if the phones aren't out." Gallagher turned for the stairs, and DeLozier added: "There's a handgun on a little shelf beneath the side of the bed closest to the door. Get it, but be careful. It's loaded."

Gallagher flicked on the upstairs hall light from the entry hall. Then, slowly, the Browning held firmly front of him, one finger on the safety, he ascended to the upper landing and stopped. All the rooms were dark. The only noise coming from them was the creaking of the air ducts. He headed for what looked to be the largest room, ready to move the safety with the slightest sound or movement. There was none. Flick, and the master bedroom was flooded with light. Drawers and clothes were everywhere; the phone was in pieces next to a nightstand. He moved for the handgun—for a split second admiring its handsome gunmetal gray sheen—and tested the safety. Then on to the closets and bathroom, his stomach fluttering with the image of some crazed, bloodied figure about to jump out any moment. Only after those rooms were lit did he look on the dresser, then through the articles on the floor. No green book. He moved down the hall, leaving open doors and lit rooms in his wake.

Downstairs he said, "They missed the phone in Sarah's room. There's still no answer." He handed the Beretta nine-millimeter pistol to DeLozier, who put it in the side pocket of his jacket.

"What about the answering machine?"

"Still off."

DeLozier closed his eyes and shook his head. "I need to call the Holiday Inn and leave a message for them to go to another hotel." Then a moment later, "What does it look like up there?"

"Your room's a mess, but otherwise okay."

"May I impose on you to make some coffee while I call?"

"You need to rest."

"After I call."

"Rest for a few minutes. They won't get to the Holiday Inn for a few hours."

DeLozier grunted and sat back. By the time the coffee was brewed, he was out, his chin resting on the barrel of the Winchester rise.

Gallagher watched him for a moment, then picked up the Browning and checked every lock, window, and closet on the ground floor. Creeping down the basement stairs, he turned on all the lights in the storage and recreation rooms, then looked behind every box and piece of furniture. Back in the kitchen he leaned against a counter and studied DeLozier while he drank his coffee. Although the man's face looked almost peaceful in sleep, his right arm was draped across the rifle, his hand clenched, the fingers tight against his palm.

Shortly he went upstairs and went through every room one more time. He called the Holiday Inn, left a message for the Moricks to go to another hotel, gathered some pillows and blankets, and returned to the kitchen. Gently slipping the rifle out of DeLozier's arms, he carried the slim older man to the living-room couch and set the Winchester on the floor within his reach. Then, moving into the family room, he stretched out on the couch with the Beretta in one hand, and the Browning on the floor next to him.

Fifty miles into New Jersey, the pavement suddenly dried, the sky partially cleared, and the rain stopped. Nathan Morick looked in his rearview mirror. The only headlights were those of the little Honda he had passed a minute ago. His hands lightened on the wheel, and he picked up speed. For the next few miles, he watched the road ahead and behind mindlessly, letting himself wander with the barely audible voice of Stevie Nicks coming from the front speakers. When he realized he was mouthing the words to her throaty ballad, he sat up in the seat with a little shake of his head.

Sarah and Dorothy were still asleep. Behind him Lauren stirred, and he reached back to stroke her leg. A moment later he craned his head around to look at her. Most of her face was in the shadow of the car seat. One of her hands rested on her chest, the tiny fingers slowly opening and closing in some vestigial neurological rhythm. As he turned back, the speedometer crept from sixty-five to sixty-eight. He checked the odometer. Another hundred and fifty miles at least, he figured. But at this point he would wait until they got to the hotel to call Warren again. Sarah and

Dorothy needed to sleep. The second time he had called, about two hours into the drive, he had lied about there being no answer. "It's busy," he had said. "I'll try again later. We have to keep moving."

Nathan checked his mirrors. With no headlights visible, he picked up a little more speed and set the cruise control. There was no other answer, he thought. And the more he pondered it, the more he could imagine it, the more he knew it must be true. It wasn't Billie's husband after all. It was *Ashton*. The desertion had been intolerable, and the superscientist had cracked. He imagined emissaries from the Fertility Institute hunting for Billie, perhaps even the psychotic Ashton himself. So Warren had hidden her. And now . . . but where the hell was Warren? A car entered the interstate, sped past him. One thing was sure: when they arrived at the hotel, he was going to get some answers.

Lauren started to move again, and Nathan resumed his stroking. Two hours later they passed through the Holland Tunnel and into New York. When he began seeing signs for the airport, he squeezed Sarah's leg.

"Oh my," she said, sitting up. "I'm sorry. I didn't mean to sleep so long. I wanted to keep you company."

"You owe me one."

She woke her mother, then combed her hair in the mirror on the windshield visor. "God, I look like the scag woman from Alcatraz. You check in. I'll scare them."

Nathan patted her leg as he pulled into the hotel driveway. "You look fine. Why don't you get Lauren ready while I go in?"

The clerk was on the phone and pushed a registration form across the desk. Nathan was working on the third line when he hung up.

"Do you have reservations?" he asked.

"Somebody may have called ahead for us. The name's Morick."

The man tapped on his computer keyboard and frowned. "Hold on a second." He walked to the end of the desk and picked up a telephone. Then he disappeared into a back office. When he returned, he said, "Our night manager's been expecting you. You have a message." The clerk handed Nathan an envelope. "She said it was called in around one."

Nathan opened the envelope and read the note at the desk. Then he reread it. "Did she take this?"

"No, Mr. Shelton did. But he's gone. Is there a problem?"

Nathan turned and looked through the front window at the car. Sarah was leaning over the seat doing something with Lauren. Dorothy was putting lipstick on with the aid of a hand mirror. He read the note one more time, swore, and headed for the row of pay telephones.

Dawn was still an hour away when a relentless, fiery pounding in Warren DeLozier's hand woke him. He opened his eyes and stayed still for a moment, feeling his bandaged hand, listening, letting his vision unblur. He heard the upstairs telephone ringing faintly in beat with the throbbing in his hand.

Sitting up, his vision darkened and his head spun. He regained himself and managed to get upright and walking for the stairs. Upstairs he hurried to Sarah's room, expecting each ring to be the last.

It was Nathan—and the hysteria in his son-in-law's voice brought DeLozier to his senses. He broke in sharply: "Calm down, Nathan. There are reasons for everything . . . . Because I couldn't . . . I was doing something with Wukich.

Don't worry about that—I'm fine . . . Yes, but not now . . . You must go to another hotel . . . No. Now! If you didn't erase the tape or turn off the answering machine, then you have to go *now* . . . . All right, goddammit! I'll talk to you for one minute. But if something happens to Sarah, Dorothy, or the baby, I'll never forgive you. Do you understand that? *I'll never forgive you!* . . . Okay, you're right—it's not Buck Williams . . . . Ashton? Christ, Nathan . . . . Okay, I'll look into it. Look, we can't discuss this now. You've got to get out of there . . . . All I can say is that these people are desperate . . . . I know it's a nightmare . . . . No, you can't come here . . . . Nathan, listen to me. All I can tell you is to get out of there—now! Go to another hotel and call me back . . . . No! You're *not* to call the police, got that? *No* police! They'll only make it worse, Okay? . . . Now, do you think anybody followed you? . . . Well, be careful—very careful. Call me from another hotel. I'll wire you money and a passport for Lauren. We'll work out the details later. Now get going. And remember, they're in your hands. Go out there smiling—and *move!*"

He hung up and his knees buckled. He made it to the bed—Sarah's old bed with its frilly canopy—and lowered himself onto it, breathing heavily, almost choking from the pain in his mutilated hand. Closing his eyes, he played the whole thing over again—the flash of red coming at them from the dirt road off to the right, the scream of his wife next to him, the blackness after the crunch of metal tearing into the Cadillac's rear door, the Cadillac spinning and spinning out of his control, and Sarah asleep in the backseat, who would never really know, never really remember, thank God for that, what had hit her. And then the hospitals. The years of hospitals and examinations. The hopes raised, the inevitable bad news. Until it was definite, over: his

Sarah: perfect in every other way, would never have the joy of childbirth, never be able to deliver her own child, his grandchild. Never . . . His head settled into one of Sarah's stuffed bears, and he closed his eyes.

When he awoke, the sun was pouring in from the garden, and Gallagher was standing over him.

"How're you feeling?"

DeLozier got himself up on one elbow. "All right," he grunted. "You spend the night here?"

"Of course. You think I'd leave you alone like this? How's the hand?"

"Did my son-in-law call?"

"Yeah, they're fine. How's the hand?"

"Fine, goddammit. I want to know about my son-in-law. Why didn't you wake me up?"

"Because they're at another hotel, they're fine, and you needed to sleep."

"Christ, I know about them *going* to another hotel! Which one is it? What's the number? And don't tell me what I need."

"I know you know about the hotel. I heard you on the phone. And I'll be damned if *you're* going to get sick and die on me." DeLozier attempted to stand, but Gallagher put a hand on his shoulder and held him down. "Look, Mr. DeLozier. This really is a matter for the police. This is much too big for you or your son-in-law to handle. Let me call them."

The old man's eyes blazed, and with a ferocious effort he got to his feet. Pointing a finger of his uninjured hand at Gallagher's chest he nearly bellowed: "Get this straight, Gallagher. I'm in charge here. No cops! My family will be out of the country in twenty-four hours. We won't need any cops!"

Gallagher took a step back, feeling his own blood rise. The old guy was losing it. And already the adrenaline of his rage had drained out of him, leaving him pale and gray.

"Relax," said Gallagher, handing the older man a slip of paper. "Here's the name of the hotel and the number. Your son-in-law said he'd call back at nine." Glancing at his watch, he added, "That's twenty minutes from now. Come on, let's get some coffee. It's just made. The phone's plugged in downstairs." Gently he took the older man by the arm, expecting to be shaken off. But DeLozier smiled.

"You're some fella, aren't you?" he said. "You've got thick skin."

"That's right," said Gallagher, smiling. "And I can give it back too. So watch out."

Downstairs DeLozier retrieved the rifle from the living room, the shotgun from the farnily and set them both on a counter. He put his hand out for the Beretta and placed it in a pocket of the robe he had put on. Sitting at the kitchen table, he said, "Don't you have to go to work?"

"No. I was laid off, so to speak."

"You're kidding."

Gallagher brought him a cup of coffee. "That's what I said. Are you hungry?"

"Starving. I could use one of those pain pills too."

Gallagher brought him his bottle of pills, then took out a frying pan and a carton of eggs.

"You married?" said DeLozier.

"No."

"Any family here?"

"Boston."

"I thought so. Are you going back after your training?"

"I had been planning on staying here. It's a little depressing where I grew up. The only people working are the parole officers."

DeLozier nodded. "We didn't even have 'em. Goddamn thugs ran everything. Western Pennsylvania coal town," he added. "Mean as a damn black snake and poor as fill dirt." He watched Gallagher for a bit, then said, "Did your family help you with school?"

Gallagher flipped an egg and smiled. "Are you kidding? I *send* money home. My father lost his job a year ago, and my mother can only get part-time sewing work. She prays instead." He looked around the large, open kitchen. "But I don't think he's listening."

"I worked my way through school too," DeLozier said softly. "I know how hard it is. And everything else. I'm sorry."

Gallagher shrugged. "It's just different." He carried plates of eggs and toast to the table and sat down.

The phone rang. DeLozier stood to answer it. At first he was quiet. Then, "No, I haven't," he said. He paused, then added: "Yesterday afternoon I told him I didn't need him anymore. Why? Is there a problem? . . . Well, I haven't seen him. I'll call you if I do." Hanging up, he found Gallagher's gaze on him. "Wukich's agency is looking for him. Apparently he didn't pick up his kid last night."

"Who's Wukich?"

"The detective that was with Sarah in St. Joseph's. I thought you met him."

Gallagher nodded. "Not formally. Is he the one who was watching the Williamses' apartment?"

DeLozier looked at him warily. "Yeah."

"Well, *was* he out here yesterday?"

"For a while." DeLozier glanced out the window. "I sent him home not much longer after I talked to you." The older man returned to the table and began to adjust his sling. When he was done, he said, "What else did you find out from Williams?"

"Not much. He wouldn't say why he's moving. I think he's getting money from someone."

DeLozier nodded.

"That doesn't surprise you?"

"That somebody doesn't want him around?" He shrugged nebulously. "Did you get an autopsy on Billie?"

"He refused. Why do you ask?"

"Just curious. She's kind of young to die like that, isn't she?"

"Depends on what was the matter with her." Gallagher refilled his coffee cup and looked at DeLozier. "Do you know something about that?"

"No."

"Look, Mr. DeLozier, Williams was *more* than happy to tell me what he knows about you and his wife. If you don't want to tell me the rest now, then you can do it in court. For Christ's sake—*you're* the one who sent me out there. I'll be damned if—"

"Listen here, young man. If I knew anything about what happened to Billie, I'd be the first damn person to do something about it."

"Then tell me what's going on. Maybe *I* know something about her that you can help me with. Like I do about your daughter."

"What do *you* know about Sarah?" said DeLozier belligerently.

Gallagher shrugged and sat down. After a bite of toast, he said, "I watched her egg retrieval."

"You what?"

"I was working at the institute in February."

DeLozier's face hardened, then softened into a wry smile. "You can be a son-of-a-bitch, can't you?"

"I guess. Like father, like son."

"Yeah, I know that one."

Gallagher was staring at him. "Mr. DeLozier, what happened to Mrs. Williams wasn't my fault. Even so, my career might be over. Everything that I've worked so hard for."

DeLozier held his gaze for a long moment, then looked out the bay window. Finally he spoke: "It was like a bad dream at first," he said softly. "The one who spoke English would ask me where Lauren was. I'd say, 'I don't know—then *wham*. I could see a finger lying there, and I knew I should be feeling something, but I must have blocked it out. Then it started to burn like crazy, and I guess I passed out, because I remember they were about to start on the other hand."

"They're looking for Lauren?" said Gallagher incredulously. "Is that what the cardiologist business was about?"

DeLozier shook his head wearily. "Apparently the guy these creeps work for saw Billie when she was pregnant and thought she was beautiful. Simple, right? They think it is. We can even name our price. That's why they didn't finish me off—so I could pass on the terms. Give up the baby for whatever we want, or"—he pointed to his hand—"this and more."

"Wait a minute. The baby's not even hers. I mean, she delivered it, but . . ."

"I *tried*. Believe me, it's hard enough to explain this baby to most people. I think the men who were here do understand now that Williams isn't the father. It's the concept of the egg coming from Sarah that's the problem."

"This is crazy. Why doesn't he adopt a baby?"

"I asked the same question. They laughed. Dr. Gallagher, they even *kidnapped* Billie. Right about the end of May. At least I guess it was them, he finished more to himself.

Gallagher' eyes narrowed. "Williams said he hadn't seen her for six months. Is that what he was talking about?"

"More or less. She got away the same day—just before they were going to examine her. I hid her the rest of the time.

"Examine her?"

Nodding, DeLozier watched the younger man.

Gallagher was quiet for a moment. Why were they going to examine her?"

DeLozier snorted. You tell me. I've been trying to figure that out for the last six months."

"She didn't have any idea?" Then hesitantly, "Did she think they knew what they were doing?"

"All she remembered was that they were speaking a foreign language—Spanish, she thought—and that it seemed as if they were going to examine her. She was drugged the whole time." The older man paused reflectively. "She might have recognized one of the voices, but she wasn't a hundred percent sure. Over the months I think more was coming back to her. When we last talked on the phone, she said she had a funny feeling about that voice and wanted to talk to me in private. We never had the chance."

"Why didn't you go to the police then?"

A louder snort came from DeLozier. "I did. As soon as we got back here. I don't think they believed Billie because of her husband. He's no stranger to them."

"They wouldn't protect her?"

"Hell, no. At least not the way I wanted her protected. And that's why I sent them all away now. Although the police and the hospital say they're working on it . . . that's not good enough."

Fiddling with his spoon, Gallagher was quiet for a moment. Then: "Why were you worried before she was kidnapped? Why Wukich?"

"I was just trying to make sure everything went all right. You saw that shithole she lived in. She even had the surrogate agency come to a friend's house when they checked her out. She explained why later, so I didn't hold it against her. But I still hated her being there."

"You hid her the whole time after she was kidnapped?"

DeLozier nodded. "Wukich moved her up and down the East Coast. Everywhere they went, she saw an obstetrician—we didn't lie to you about that. The pregnancy had been normal. But we didn't want her to deliver in a small town. And after all that time away, I had thought coming straight to St. Joseph's would be safe. Once the baby was born . . . I don't know. I guess I thought Buck, or whoever, would have given up by then. What the hell else were we supposed to do, move?"

Gallagher looked at him questioningly. "But if you thought it was okay to come back, why didn't you let one of the obstetricians from the Fertility Institute do the delivery?"

DeLozier shook his head in disgust. "Because that son-of a-bitch Ashton told us the baby was anencephalic. We wouldn't have let him near her with a ten-foot pole."

Gallagher forced himself to finish chewing before he swallowed. "He told you what?"

"He said he thought the baby was anencephalic."

"That's what I thought you said. I, uh, I guess you did have a problem. When did that happen?"

"Around mid-May he first thought the ultrasound was abnormal. Billie had an amniocentesis soon after that. Then at the next visit—on a Saturday so the son-of-a-bitch didn't have to 'rush'—they used a better ultrasound machine, and he was more definite. The alphafetoprotein levels were also back by then. In light of the ultrasound, he said they were high enough to say that the baby was probably anencephalic. And some other doctor agreed with him."

"Probably?"

"Yes, 'probably.' Nice, huh? He threw out some statistics and wanted Sarah and Nathan to make the decision. Either way, then, he wouldn't lose. Christ, on the phone this morning Nathan actually asked me if *Ashton* was behind this."

"Well, that's a little farfetched, but what happened there certainly isn't the norm. at least for Ashton. He's good—real good." Gallagher felt DeLozier's stare and looked up to find the older man studying him intently. "You too? Come on, the man's a medical superstar. Don't be ridiculous."

DeLozier shrugged. "What those goons told me is ridiculous. What were you just getting at?"

Gallagher shrugged. "I don't know. Just that I can't believe he'd . . ."

"Make a mistake like that? A medical superstar?"

"Well . . ."

"Well, he did. And ever since then . . ." DeLozier took out the slip of paper with the hotel name and number and looked at it. "Ever since then all we've had is trouble."

Gallagher watched him for a moment. Then, "I'll try once more," he said. "Maybe it's time to talk to the police.

They could get the FBI or whoever involved to protect Lauren."

DeLozier shook his head, his face drawn and tired in the morning light. "They'll give up soon. Either on their own, or I'll send Sarah and Nathan so far away it won't be worth their while. There are lots of other babies around."

"Do you really believe that?"

DeLozier stood and took his plate to the sink. When he came back to the table, except for the metered ticking of the kitchen clock, they sat in silence.

EIGHTEEN

Valerie's voice came clearly through the intercom on Richard Ashton's desk. "Dr. Gallagher's on the phone," she said. "Do you want to speak with him?"

Ashton hesitated. But the little mick would only get angry if he put him off, he thought. And he was probably more than suspicious of the Moricks' defection as it was. "Put him through," he said. Then, "Hello, Brendan. What can I do for you? By the way—hang in there. It'll all blow over, and you'll be fine."

"I'd like to see you. Can I come over today?"

"I don't think that's a good idea, Brendan. You know how people are."

"Dr. Ashton, I need to see you."

"I'm very busy today, Brendan. What is it?"

"For heaven's sake—you know what it is. I want to talk to you about the Moricks. But not on the phone."

"Does Danielle Parker know you're making this call?"

Gallagher was silent.

"Listen, Brendan. I know you're in an awful situation, but try to be patient. Parker is the best in town. If she thinks that what the Moricks did to me has any bearing on this case, believe me, she'll call herself." He paused. "But between you and me, they were a difficult couple. You know that. Enough said. Try to forget it. You've got a great career ahead of you. That's all you need to be concerned with. Now, I have to go. Take care."

Nathan Morick opened the minirefrigerator, took out a candy bar, the next-to-the-last soda, and shook his head. "We've got to eat a real meal sometime to day," he said, straightening and looking at Sarah on the bed. Lauren was holding onto one of her mother's fingers, her feet waving in the air.

"Maybe we can stop at a drive-through on the way to the airport," Sarah offered.

"That'll be *hours* from now. Jesus Christ, all I want to do is go downstairs. Or get room service."

The sound of a hair dryer came from the bathroom, and Sarah looked up. "Dammit, Nathan, you heard him just as well as I did. He said not to leave the room. For *anything*. Are you deaf? Or is it that you just don't care?"

"You are so fucking brainwashed. Lauren is *our* child, Sarah. This is *our* life. We don't—"

"Shh!" said Sarah as the hair dryer cut off. "Come on, try to relax. We'll probably be here most of the day."

Nathan turned on the television and sat in an armchair near the window.

Mrs. DeLozier came out of the bathroom, brushing her hair. "How are we for diapers, Sarah?"

"We're down to two."

"What about formula?"

"We'll be okay until early afternoon. She just ate."

Sarah's mother leaned over Lauren and cooed at her. "I swear, Sarah, she's going to look just like you."

Sarah picked up Lauren and hugged her. "You're going to be the best little girl," she whispered.

Mrs. DeLozier began folding some clothes on the bed. When she was done, she looked at Nathan and said, "Why don't you try to get some sleep? It's going to be a long day."

"I can't sleep when I'm hungry."

"We're all hungry, Nathan." She turned back to Sarah, gently lifted her daughter's chin, and smiled. "It can only get easier, honey. Trust him. He knows what he's doing. And he loves you so much. He feels so—"

"Goddamn omnipotent," broke in Nathan. "For Christ's sake, Dorothy, what do you mean 'he knows what he's doing'? Why doesn't he call the police then? There's somebody after our baby! As a matter of fact, I'm about to—"

"Let's not make things more difficult than they are, Nathan," broke in his mother-in-law with a glare. "Please sit back down. He said *no* police. *None.* I don't know why, either, but we *have* to trust him."

"The shit we do." Nathan walked to the door, then back. "Goddammit, I can't even walk in the goddamn hall," He looked at Sarah, his eyes glazing.

"Come here, honey," she said.

He moved toward the door.

"Where are you going? Don't do this to me, Nathan!"

The bathroom door opened and closed.

Gallagher slipped into the stairwell, unseen. Peering around the next door leading into the hallway, he found the corridor clear and hurried toward the visiting doctors' dressing room. It was one of six places in the institute where he knew the day's operating-room schedule would be posted, as well as the area he was least likely to run into Ashton. Ashton's schedule, he noted with satisfaction, was full of artificial inseminations. They were relatively simple procedures not requiring ultrasound guidance; which meant that Susan would either be in her office or in the ultrasound lab.

Susan Arnette was at her desk, a pile of multicolored folders beside her. When she, saw him, her eyes narrowed, and she seemed to retract as though he were carrying some communicable disease. She waited for him to speak.

"Hello, Susan. Remember me?"

"Sure, Dr. Gallagher. What can I do for you?"

"I've decided to apply for a fertility fellowship, and I'm trying to tidy up the documentation on some of my cases. The Fertility Board is getting real picky. I was pretty good about keeping records while I was here, but I'm missing a few ultrasound reports from the first two weeks. Could you possibly—"

Susan was shaking her head, "Any patient information has to be released through our records office. *After* the staff on the case says it's okay. You worked mainly with Dr. Ashton, didn't you? I'll call him."

"That's okay." He backed out of the office as she picked up the phone. "I'll just go down to his office myself. Thanks." Outside her door he paused long enough to hear her say, "Valerie," then he turned and ran for the stairwell. On the second-floor landing he glanced at his watch. Ashton should be in the middle of a case. And if not, well, what could he do to him?

The young woman in archives heard his request with a pleasant-enough smile. "Dr. Simpson's tied up in a case right now," he added. "Otherwise he would have come up himself. It'll only take me a second to get what he needs. I don't even need to check them out."

She returned with two patient records—two of the three cases on which he had scrubbed the morning of February 10. "The other one's checked out to Dr. Ashton," she said.

Gallagher flipped through them, then headed for the payroll desk. Next he went to the back of the records department. A woman he didn't recognize was typing reports into the institute's computer system. "Hi, I'm one of the residents," he said. "Can you tell me the name of the lab that does our amniocentesis assays? All the doctors are tied up right now, and I have to check on a result."

"Bio Lab," said the woman, taking a headset off her ears. "I think they do pretty much everything we don't do. I should buy stock in them for all the money they get from us."

"Anybody there in particular I should talk to?" said Gallagher after a moment.

"Depends on what kind of test it is. Did you say amniocentesis?"

"Right."

"Well, that depends too. We only send them what we don't do here. That's not very much as far as amniocentesis goes. What is it exactly that you want to know about?"

"Alphafetoprotein."

"Is that the one to check for the brain problem?"

"Right."

"Yeah, they do that." She reached in a drawer and pulled out an index card filled with handwriting. On a notepad she wrote down a name and number. "Talk to Chris."

Turning to leave, Gallagher added, trying to sound as casual as possible: "I know Bio Lab does preadmission chemistries and things like that. what else do they do for us? Who knows," he said with a smile, "I could be looking for an investment."

"Research type stuff. Mainly samples from Dr. Ashton's projects."

"Right. I forgot about that."

"Do you want me to call Chris for you? I talk to her almost every day."

"No thanks. I've gotta few minutes."

At a pay telephone inside a Hardee's a block away, Chris from Bio Lab came promptly on the line. She could find no amniocentesis results for a patient named Billie Williams. There was nothing filed under Morick, either.

Hanging up, Gallagher called the institute and managed to get Lindsey Baines to come to the phone. Saying he was in the area for an interview, he asked her out to lunch. She declined. Ashton had gotten tied up earlier in the morning, and they were behind schedule. But at least she was not cold. "Maybe some other time," she added.

Gallagher found himself thinking about where he would take her, and smiling. Then, forcing his thoughts back to Ashton and the Moricks, he decided he'd better get something to eat. It would be a long afternoon in the institute waiting for the boss to leave.

Sarah answered the phone on the first ring. "Are you all right?" she said. "I keep worrying about why that doctor had to spend the night with you."

"I'm fine. Everybody there okay? . . . Good. Now listen up. I got yours and Nathan's passports from your house, but Lauren's is a problem. I'm outside the State Department right now. I have a friend there who'll get me an emergency passport, but even he needs a copy of her birth certificate. So I have to run over to the goddamn hospital." DeLozier looked at his watch—it was almost one o'clock. "The bottom line is, I don't know if I can get all the passports to you in time for a flight out of JFK today. I think we need to plan on you taking a shuttle down here and leaving from Dulles."

"Whatever, Dad. Just tell me what you want us to do."

"That's my girl. Now here's the plan: take an evening shuttle from La Guardia to National. As soon as you're in the terminal, get a security guard to stay with you. Tell him you're sick or something. I may have somebody else there with you too, so don't be surprised. I'll tell him to carry a magazine in his right hand. After you get your luggage, go straight to the main entrance. There'll be a car there to take you to Dulles. I'll put your tickets and passports in a security box and leave the key with a British Airways executive. I'm going to book you on the last flight to London. It leaves at ten-fifty. Got that?"

"Got it."

"Make sure you have Nathan repeat everything to you. And don't leave La Guardia too late. You know how those shuttles can get messed up. You need to be at Dulles by ten at the latest."

"Gotcha."

"Then call me from Heathrow, and I'll tell you what to do from there. I have lots of friends in London. Now, one more thing. Have Nathan buy the shuttle tickets with my corporate credit card. Your mother has one. Then have him buy return shuttle tickets to JFK in time for the last flight to Rome with one of *your* credit cards. And go ahead and have him buy the tickets for that Rome flight with the same card. Okay?"

"Got it. You don't want us to talk to you until we get to Heathrow?"

"Not unless there's a problem. It's too risky. Don't worry—I'll have people watching out for you. And I'll have everything you need—diapers, formula, whatever—waiting for you at the airport. Is Nathan all right?"

"Yes," she said, looking at her husband lying next to their daughter on the bed. Nathan lifted his head and motioned for the phone. "He wants to talk to you."

"Put him on. I love you, Sarah. Tell your mother the same."

"Warren?"

"*You* can do it, Nathan. If you can get Lauren out of the country for a while, I think she'll be safe."

"I *know* what I can do."

"Calm down. This isn't the time for that. Just do what I say. Sarah knows all the details . . . Nathan?"

"I *am* going to call the police."

"Nathan—if you call the police, you will bury your wife, my wife, and your daughter. *Do you understand?*"

Nathan hung up, and DeLozier slammed down the phone. The little gutless fucker, he thought. Goddamn him for marrying . . . The phone was ringing and he grabbed it.

"Nathan!" he barked.

"It's Brendan, Mr. DeLozier. You okay?"

"Dr. Gallagher, uh, Brendan. Fine, just fine. Look, we haven't got much time, goddammit. What did you find out about Ashton? Maybe Nathan's right. Maybe the son-of-a-bitch is crazy. Not only did every damn bit of this start after we left him, but Billie was up in goddamn stirrups. Maybe *he's* the one who hired those goons."

"Listen, Mr. DeLozier, I'm checking into it. I just left the institute, and I'm going back soon. Tell me, you said the ultrasound that really showed the alleged problem was done on a Saturday. Do you know who did it?"

"No, but I can find out from Sarah."

"Well, the payroll clerk told me Ashton's main technician doesn't work on Saturdays. And another thing, did you have the alphafetoprotein tests sent somewhere special? There's no record of them anywhere that I can find."

"No. That son-of-a—"

"Hold on. Give me a couple of hours and I'll find them. They're probably in the record. I'm going to try again to see it."

"They wouldn't let you see her record?"

"Just a few hours, Mr. DeLozier. I'll call you."

DeLozier hesitated. "Call me as soon as you can. Same thing—try the car phone if I'm not at the house."

Gallagher rose from the toilet seat. His buttocks and back ached, and he stretched, ready to hop back on with the first squeak of the door. He pressed up against the window and peered down at the sidewalk. It was five-thirty and Ashton still hadn't emerged into the parking lot. But he shouldn't be much longer, he thought. Thursdays the surgeon generally went to the hospital for a staff meeting. Valerie invariably left several minutes after him.

He glanced at his watch. The cleaning crew would be arriving between five-thirty and six, starting on the third floor, at the opposite end from where he was now. And from the evenings he had spent studying in the institute's library, he knew that they didn't get down to the first floor until after eight. If all went well—if Ashton left, and soon—he would have plenty of time.

The shadows near the exit were deepening, and he almost missed Ashton striding toward his Jaguar. Gallagher watched him drive away, followed a few minutes later by Valerie and two nurses. Then he put on his white coat, picked up the stack of medical textbooks on the ledge next to him, and opened the bathroom door. Seeing no one, he slipped out and headed for the sound of the vacuum cleaner far down the hall.

From kitchen to sun room to loft, the blinds were closed, the rooms were dark. There were few sounds: the raps of his shoes on the hardwood of the formal dining room and the marble of the foyer; the soft padding on the plush carpet of the stairs and bedrooms; the faint street noise filtering through the windows.

He hadn't slept for two days. Not since Roberto had left the gringo on the floor, the baby still in the gringo's arms. And then his mother had called. He's getting worse, she had said. He won't eat. You must come.

Soon, he had said. I will come soon.

Now he poured a shot of whiskey and drank it straight. He walked to the sun room, looked at the telephone, threw it against the wall. It hit with a ringing crash and bounced to the floor. He picked it up and threw it at a large vase. The vase split open like a dropped melon. He laughed. He took the largest piece and flung it at the framed photograph of Benito on the mantle. The glass shattered; the photograph fell to the floor. He picked up a shard of glass and ran it down his arm, watching and laughing at the thin red line that followed. He wrapped the shard in a handkerchief and put it in his briefcase. With one swipe he would sever Roberto's carotids. He looked around. Still, the other telephones in the house were silent.

So let him die, he thought for the thousandth time. Let the bastard die. He felt his hands shaking and took another shot of whiskey. But then what? Who would lead the way? Who would show the flaws, and the ways to fix them? Some blameless soul in the States, in Sweden, in France? No! No! No! *He* would. The bastard, right here, in Mexico, so that they all could watch. And then when it was perfect, they would watch again. It was the only way. It was both salvation and penance. It was perfect.

Fernandez strode into the kitchen. He opened the freezer and took out the last empty test tube in the rack of ten. He turned his head toward the ceiling, closed his eyes, fumbled with his pants, and masturbated. He put the warm tube in the rack. Yes! If he had to fertilize a *thousand* eggs to get a match, then a thousand eggs it was. Damn Roberto.

The phone was ringing. One more day, Roberto said.

NINETEEN

The ticketing lines were long with the rush for commuter flights. Nathan took a step as the line moved, his eyes flicking from face to face like a drug runner's. Finally the man behind the counter took his credit cards.

"Let's run through this one more time," said the agent, typing on his computer terminal at an agonizing pace. "You want to take the shuttle from La Guardia to National in D.C. Then you want a flight back to JFK in time for the last flight to Rome."

"Correct," Nathan lied.

The agent rapped several keys and paused to study the screen. "You're going to have a busy evening."

"It's a long story."

"Sounds like it." The agent stuffed the tickets into their respective envelopes, handed them to Nathan, and looked sharply at him. "You feeling okay? You're a little pale for . . ." But the young man had turned and was hurrying away.

Halfway to the coffee shop where he was to meet the hotel bellboy who would check their luggage, a sudden sourness filled his mouth, and he veered off for a bathroom. Lunging for an empty stall, he leaned over the toilet, his forehead clammy, his stomach aching to contract and heave. Yet the thought of being in there alone was just as sickening, the room already reeked of vomit, the toilet seat was smeared with yellow fluid, and he was standing in a grimy puddle. He rushed out, looking for an exit.

Outside, the nausea quickly receded, and he reentered the terminal. He found the bellboy, slipped him the tickets, and met him again at a book stand. Then with a clear view of the boarding gate, he waited in a niche in the wall between a row of telephones and a bathroom.

At precisely quarter to six, he saw his mother-in-law stride through a USAir door and head for the boarding gate. When she was thirty yards from him, he started in her direction with the tickets hidden in a folded newspaper. Twenty yards from each other, their eyes met, and she looked right through him. At a counter he set the newspaper down, fumbled in his coat and pockets, swore, and headed back down the terminal lobby, not looking back to see whether she had idly picked up the newspaper as planned.

The taxi discharge and pickup areas were well lit and crammed with vehicles and people yelling for luggage and porters. But beyond the congestion it was dark, the evening moonless, the streetlights seeming feeble. Nathan searched in the light for a glimpse of Sarah. Suddenly she was there, grabbing his arm, with Lauren bundled in a blanket beneath her coat.

"Have you seen anybody?" she whispered as they hurried through the lobby.

"Only two or three hundred. What about the hotel? Did anybody see you leaving?"

"No."

"Well, this is just fucking great. We're going to pop in on some strangers in London as if we had nothing better to do. I'm sure they won't mind a whole family. Oh, and don't mind us looking out in the street all the time. We're just a little nervous. Great, Sarah. This is fucking great."

Ahead Dorothy DeLozier was waving at them. "So much for being inconspicuous," said Nathan, as his mother-in-law stopped the flight attendant from letting the first passenger through the gate.

Their boarding passes were taken, and they hurried onto the plane. Passengers began to slide by them as they settled in their row of seats near the front of the cabin. Sarah sat next to the window with her mother beside her. Nathan took the aisle. There was nothing to do but wait.

Two young girls approached. They looked nervous —most likely their first plane trip. The man and woman behind them kept up a steady stream of encouragement, all the while looking into the rows with contented smiles. As they passed, Nathan leaned over and rubbed Lauren's leg. Next Christmas, he decided, imagining his parents' beaming faces at the arrival gate. Lauren would be up on his shoulder, beautiful in a new dress. Gosh, he thought, feeling her chubby thigh, she might even be walking by then. Next Christmas for sure. They could put away a little money each month to save up the airfare. And Sarah could hit up her father. He'd owe them for a long time after this was over.

Several dark-skinned men entered. Nathan sat up, stiffened, then relaxed as two more made their way into the cabin. They were Asian, wearing Toshiba name tags, and looking everywhere but at him. For a moment he closed his eyes. He was seven years old and striding John Wayne-style into the midst of a rock fight. His face and eyes were fearless—as hard as the pieces of quartz and shale flying by harmlessly. Then the barrage stopped altogether, his second-grade enemies paralyzed by the brazen act. Opening his eyes, he firmed his face and stared straight ahead.

Ten minutes later passengers were still boarding, the line continually held up by somebody taking off his coat or loading handbags and briefcases in the overhead storage space. Several arrivals caused Nathan to look two, three, four times at their faces. So far, he decided, so good.

A flight attendant removed an oxygen mask from the wall and began her routine. Nathan clenched his fist, wanting to raise it over his head and shake it. He turned and smiled at Sarah, who was feeding Lauren. Sarah met his gaze, then her eyes shifted forward, and she turned toward the window. Nathan glanced up. Behind the stewardess two Hispanic men and a woman were slowly making their way into the cabin. The men were dressed in suits and gripped leather carry-on bags; the woman wore a silk raincoat.

They came abreast, and Nathan gripped the elbow rests, ready to spring to his feet. The shorter man and the woman passed, the taller man seemed to slow. Nathan counted to five. The man moved past them; the plane backed away from the boarding ramp. He leaned back into his seat and closed his eyes. His father-in-law had said to be wary of any Latin-looking men, but he had said nothing about a woman. And four or five other Latinos had boarded. Stay calm, he told himself. Everybody's okay.

Gallagher entered the office where the vacuum noise was coming from and set the books down. An elderly Asian man smiled at him, quieted the machine with a deft kick, and in broken English said something to the effect of Gallagher having gone away. Gallagher rattled off an explanation and then pointed in frustration to the stack of books. Moments later he left with the man's keys.

The library and the physicians' offices were on the first floor. Gallagher went to the library, where he unlocked the door, reset the automatic lock, and set his stack of books on a table. Then making sure nobody else was around, he went to Ashton's door, on a diagonal across from the library, and sequentially inserted keys from the ring. The tenth key turned, and the door opened. Pushing the little steel button on the strike plate, he closed the door and turned the handle back and forth.

After returning the keys, he walked to each end of the first-floor corridor, then back to Ashton's office. He looked around one more time and stepped in.

It was black outside, and blacker in the office. For a moment he stayed motionless, listening. Hearing nothing, he turned on the lights and went over to one of the bookshelves. Ashton was a medical-history buff and had many textbooks Gallagher had never heard of. He withdrew two books on reproductive endocrinology, and opened them to a topic on which he was, in fact, writing a paper. Setting them within easy reach of the files, he rehearsed his reason for being in the institute at this time of evening, for needing the books. He walked to the door to listen. Taking a deep breath, he looked at his watch. It was a few minutes before six o'clock.

The files were in three rows of built-in cabinets. They were locked, but twice in March he head come to get Ashton for surgery and had watched him replace a patient's record he'd been studying. Ashton had then stopped by his row of vases, his back to the door, and lifted one. Gallagher lifted the largest Chinese vase and smiled. Underneath the hollow base was a key ring with six small brass keys, each with a tiny numbered piece of paper taped to it. He opened a cabinet and began to flip through the files. Then he skipped to the last cabinet and worked backward from the end. There was nothing under Morick. You can't be that stupid, he thought. An anencephalic baby was the stuff malpractice lawyers dreamed about. The documentation *had* to be in the original case record. Which was undoubtedly somewhere in the office, but apparently under better lock and key than these records.

Maybe it was under DeLozier. After all, the man had said he paid for everything. It was not.

There was no place else to search but Ashton's desk. He went to it and stopped, focusing on the wall directly behind the surgeon's leather armchair. From a gold-framed portrait Ashton was smirking—subtly—just as he did when an underling was floundering, one way or another. Gallagher studied the photograph, feeling the man's gaze as if he were indeed standing only feet away. Then he lightly tested the desk drawers—all were locked. Turning back to the cabinets, he pulled out a file at random.

The top sheet was all basic information, the same sheet that was stapled to the left side of the folders in the records office. Beneath it were Ashton's handwritten notes from the office visits, followed by the operative report, ultrasound interpretations, lab results, and the final narrative summary. All were photocopies. Two sheets—the operative report and one of the lab reports—had additional written entries in black ink. Gallagher flipped back to the front of the record and studied it more carefully. Again he saw nothing unusual until he reached the operative report. There in the margin was some type of shorthand around two blackened circles and two open circles. The open ones had lines, or semicircles, around them; one blackened circle had a diagonal line through it, the other a circle around it. Turning to the lab sheet, he studied the other handwritten entry: "7/13—typed." The operative report was from August 20, 1986, so he presumed the numbers meant July 13. But what did "typed" mean? The lab results beneath the written entry were standard hormone studies. He closed the folder and checked his watch.

He pulled out four more records. Each had a similar entry on the lab sheet; each had similar cryptic symbols in the margin of the operative report. Closing his notebook, he replaced the files and keys and returned Ashton's books. Then, reaching for the lights, he stopped, his eyes landing once again on the wall behind the desk. The two doctors looked at each other. "What are you hiding?" said Gallagher under his breath. A moment later he turned out the lights, set the lock, and shut the door.

The pilot announced their descent, and he opened his eyes. Sarah, Lauren, and Dorothy all seemed to be asleep. He jostled Dorothy's leg. Her eyes still closed, she said in the conciliatory DeLozier tone: "I'm awake. Why don't you let Sarah sleep as long as she can? She's exhausted."

Nathan watched her for a moment, then looked down into the aisle, exhorting himself to calm down. In minutes they would be—the airplane hit the runway with a thud that pressed him into his seat. Skipping twice, it rapidly decelerated to a smooth roll. When it stopped at the connecting ramp, he stood to retrieve their coats and bags. Sarah was awake and bundling up Lauren on the seat. "One thing at a time," he said. "First we have to get off the plane. Then we'll get out of here. Do you want me to carry Lauren?"

Sarah shook her head as she wrapped and buttoned her coat around her daughter.

Huddled together, they exited the plane without looking back. Nathan approached the first security guard he saw and, telling him that his wife was sick, asked him to stay with them a few minutes. Not until they were seated in a corner of the baggage waiting area did he scan the faces crowded three deep around the conveyer belts. The trio from the plane were nowhere to be seen, nor was there anybody who seemed unduly interested in them. Their bags appeared, and with the security guard and a porter in tow, they began the trek to the main entrance. One thing at a time, he told himself: door, taxi, Dulles, London.

Sarah stayed wedged between her mother and him as they pressed through the noisy crowd. After ten yards Nathan noticed a red-faced man who had been at the luggage area staying right behind them. The man seemed to wink at him—but had he?—and Nathan gripped Sarah tighter. He knew the man was following.

As soon as they reached the main lobby, the porter picked up his pace. Nathan called him back. The man who had been behind them was right on their heels. Coming alongside, he muttered something: "Wait," was all Nathan heard. Then he remembered: the magazine in the right hand. He saw it just before the man disappeared through the front doors, and he stopped them in a close group near the exit. The guard had agreed to stay with them until Sarah got into a taxi, and for a moment, somehow feeling safe, Nathan envisioned them pausing in this exact place on some other day, with hundreds of people scurrying past and a little girl clutching his hand for comfort. Then the man with the magazine was back, holding the door open, and they were moving again, moving toward the open air.

A four-door gray BMW sedan was waiting at the curb. Instinctively they ran for it, Nathan pushing Sarah the final few yards and into the backseat. Throwing money at the porter as he tossed the last of their bags into the trunk, Nathan yelled to the driver and slammed the door. The driver gunned the engine, and soon they were speeding down the George Washington Parkway toward Virginia.

The drive went quickly. Only one other car, a taxi, passed them as they turned onto the Dulles toll road, too fast for Nathan to see who might be in the passenger's seat. Before they knew it, they were stopped in front of the big international airport and the car door was open.

Horns and voices filled the air. Taking Sarah and her mother by the arm, Nathan steered them through the crowd. He saw the man with the magazine again, whispering now to an airport official at the front doors. The official turned to them, and as they drew close Nathan could see a British Airways name tag pinned to his wool blazer.

"Good evening," he said, looking at their disheveled clothes and the fatigue in their faces. "Please come with me, I will arrange your boarding and anything else you might need. The flight is a touch delayed, so please be patient. I'll make sure you're comfortable," Looking at Sarah, he said, "Do you desire assistance, madam?"

"No, thank you. I'm fine."

The airline executive turned and entered the airport without looking back. The man who had spoken to him winked at Nathan once more, then disappeared in the crowd.

They passed the British Airways counter, continued a little farther down the terminal lobby, and passed through a door into a quiet hall. Opening the door to the VIP lounge, the BA official saith "I think you'll find everything you need in here. Please help yourself to the food and beverages. Your personal belongs—diapers I believe—are in a bag in the corner." The man grinned. "Anything else but that, I can help you with."

Nathan smiled at Sarah and looked around the plush, empty lounge,

"Mr. Morick," said their host, "please come with me. I have something for you in my office."

"Well, two calls in one day. What's the occasion, Gallagher? Is that nursing student out of town? You know, the one who still wears her high-school ring?"

"We haven't been going out for a while, *Baines*."

"I'm sorry."

"I'm not."

"Oh. Well, what's up? I heard you were over in our neck of the woods today. So did Ashton. He was looking for you."

"I called him before I went. He said he didn't want to see me."

"I'm sorry about that lawsuit. You don't deserve it."

"I'm not sure that'll be one of the jury's criteria."

"You'll be okay, Gallagher." Her voice was empathetic. "Really. Don't worry about it."

"Would you *please* quit calling me Gallagher? For Christ's sake, I—"

"Okay, *Dr.* Gallagher."

"Lindsey," Gallagher said plaintively.

"Okay, *Brendan*. I didn't realize one ride home and two months of washing powder off your gloves entitled me to such familiarity."

"Do you think you could meet me tonight? How about a drink?"

"I don't know. I have to work tomorrow. And this is rather . . . sudden."

"It's important."

Lindsey Baines didn't respond.

"It's about Mrs. Williams, the woman who died at St. Joseph's. Do you remember her?"

"Should I?"

"You prepped her."

"I did what?"

"You prepped her. For her implantation."

"Then why . . . I never heard anything about one of our patients leaving. To say the least about dying in another hospital."

"I'm sure you didn't. And I'm sure Ashton would like to keep it that way."

"Where are you?"

"Two blocks from your apartment."

Lindsey laughed. "Okay, Gallagher. How about Garret's? In a half hour."

"What do you drink?"

"Beer. No umbrella drinks."

His next call was to Warren DeLozier.

"How's your family?" Gallagher said.

"Fine. They should leave Dulles within the hour. Tell me about Ashton."

"I still can't find the record. He's hiding it."

"Well, I'll make the son-of-a-bitch cough it up. I'll go to his house tonight if I have to. Listen, the more I think about it, the more I think he is crazy. Maybe he's trying to get rid of his mistake. Dammit, I am going to see him tonight. I—"

"Hold on, Mr. DeLozier. I agree with you—we need to talk to him. Something happened that he doesn't want anybody to know about. But we don't have anything right now to force him to talk. And I'd bet whatever records he has have been doctored up. We need something else on him. But I need a little more time. Let me tell you what I saw in his office . . ."

"Well, try to get her to talk," said DeLozier, "but make sure she doesn't warn Ashton. I don't want him on guard."

"Don't worry. But don't you do anything before I have time to talk to Lindsey Baines and work on these symbols. We can see him first thing in the morning."

"Call me," said DeLozier.

At eleven o'clock an announcement that Flight 325 to London would board in fifteen minutes came through a speaker in the VIP lounge. The Moricks and Mrs DeLozier were gathering their belongings when the British Airways executive returned and urged them to relax.

"They're being optimistic," he said. "There's still ice on the wings. The plane came down from Montreal." He set another plate of garnished sandwiches on the glass coffee table by the couches. Pouring fresh champagne into the women's glasses, he said to Nathan "Would you care for a brandy? It's a rather good night for it."

"Sure, why not?"

Setting a snifter of Courvoisier in front of Nathan, the man said he would take them to the first-class cabin himself when it was time to board. At the door he stopped and looked at Lauren. She was wide awake and starting to cry.

"Madam," he said with a trace of a smile, "I happen to know one of the best-kept nannies' secrets."

Sarah smiled at him.

The executive brought her another glass of champagne and looked at the pacifier in her hand. "Just a few dips. That's all. It makes for a much more pleasant trip." Then, asking if there was anything else he could get for them, he backed out the door.

Sarah looked at the glass, then her mother.

"You're no worse for it," said Mrs. DeLozier.

185

"*Mom*, you didn't."

"Ah-hah," said Nathan. "Now we have the truth. Your social development was arrested in infancy. That's your problem."

"Oh, be quiet. Are you serious, Mom?"

"Sarah, that's *no* nanny secret."

Lauren's crying was more insistent, and Sarah looked at Nathan. When he shrugged, she dipped the pacifier in the champagne. "Just one little taste, honey. That's all you're getting."

Nathan sipped his brandy and sighed. "One day, Sarah, we'll always travel like this."

"And there are so many places I want to go," she said excitedly. "Just wait until you see London, Nathan. You're going to love it." Sarah leaned back with her champagne glass. Lauren, who had quieted enough to take a bottle, was resting comfortably in the crook of her mother's arm. "We can see Buckingham Palace and take Lauren into Hyde Park. Maybe we can even see a show. Since we have a babysitter," she added coyly.

Nathan nodded. "Maybe I can get some work done too. Our firm has a big client there I can look up."

"That's a good idea, honey." Sarah winked at her mother. "Mom and I will meet you at Harrods."

"I can't believe he would make a mistake like that." Lindsey Baines gazed into her glass of beer. When she looked up, Gallagher thought her eyes were moist. "And he certainly wouldn't . . . do that to Mrs. Williams."

"I tend to agree. And if it weren't for the baby, I might just let things come out on their own. But . . ."

"You really think he has something to do with that?"

Gallagher shrugged. "I've told you what I know."

"But kidnapping a baby? Murder? Come on."

"Lindsey, when I go to court, he's going to court. His career, and the institute, may never recover. We both know what that would do to him."

"Why are you telling me all this? What do you want me to do?"

In the back of the bar, the light dim, Lindsey's soft brown eyes were full of empathy one moment, wary the next. Trying to read them, Gallagher felt as though he were seeing her face for the first time. When they had been together at the institute, she had almost always been masked; or in the lounge with a surgical cap over her shoulder-length mahogany hair.

"I want you to save my ass," he said, smiling.

She laughed, and he leaned closer to her.

"Let me tell you what I found out today. Then you decide what you want to do." She was still grinning, so he began with his visit to Susan. When he came to the amniocentesis results, he asked her about the clerk's offhanded remark in regard to the blood samples.

Most of what we send to Bio Lab is from the project Ashton's been working on for the last few years," she said. "You know, the one where he's trying to prove that most fertility disorders are genetic."

"I never talked with him about his research."

"You're lucky. It's usually the first thing he talks to students and residents about. So they can do his scut work. Anyway, he's trying to match HLA types—which, as I understand them, are basically genetic fingerprints—with infertility disorders. All he needs to do the HLA typing is a blood sample, so its a simple study design. We used to do the sperm donors too. For controls."

Typing, typed, Gallagher thought. "Maybe that's what the 'typed' entry means," he said to himself.

"What?"

"Never mind. I'll get to that in a minute." Frowning, he said "That kind of immunologic typing is a little disturbing in his line of work. Especially with as many people as he's typing. These aren't chicken eggs he's dealing with."

"No, but the guys *are* cocks. Sorry," she added, watching him blush. "I couldn't help it—I have to deal with them. But I understand what you mean. All I can say is the protocol did go through all those committees."

"DeLozier didn't say anything to me about HLA typing. And he's pretty aware of everything that happened there. Do the patients know about it?"

"I guess. They sign a release form giving Ashton permission to use them in his publications."

"But do they know about that *specifically?*"

Lindsey studied him. "I don't know. If you want, I'll look at one of the forms in the morning. And I know the guy who does the HLA typing over at Bio Lab. He can tell us if the Moricks were typed."

Gallagher nodded. "If they were, and they didn't know exactly what it entailed, it might give us some ammo. Can you check with Bio Lab early? DeLozier's really hot to talk to Ashton."

"Sure."

"Now," said Gallagher, taking out his notebook, "let me tell you about what I saw in his office."

When he was done, Lindsey said, "I don't know what to say about the records. I mean, most of us know they're there." Their eyes met for several seconds before she looked away.

Gallagher moved his leg so that their pants were touching. "Why does he keep so many in his office? That's what the records department is for."

"For publications. He gets statistics and other information from them instead of having to bug the clerks."

"He's going to need another office if he keeps a copy of all his patients' records in there."

"He doesn't do it with all of them. Mainly the in-vitros. They're more complicated."

"Hmm. Come to think of it, they were all in-vitros."

Robert Veracruz watched the same British Airways official who had led the Americans through the door two hours before come out again. Walking quickly, the man was soon out of sight. For a moment there was no one else in the main lobby of the terminal, and it was totally quiet. Almost too quiet. Then several mechanics, laughing, came out through a side door. Soon a flight attendant and a janitor appeared from the opposite direction. Roberto looked for Josefina. It was time. But they would have to be very careful. If they missed her now, his name would be ruined.

Josefina Ortiz came from the direction of the British Airways waiting area. The flight was about to board, she related softly in Spanish. Roberto nodded once, then signaled to Manuel, his shorter companion, across the lobby. Manuel began to walk, staying on the opposite side. Roberto stayed abreast, the heels of his custom-made Italian loafers clicking on the gleaming linoleum. Josefina waited until a passenger coming toward them passed, then she followed Roberto.

At the door through which he had seen the official emerge, Roberto paused, glancing about. There were no airport employees in sight. Then, casually, he opened it. Manuel and Josefina were now right behind him. Josefina reached into her large purse, making sure the baby blanket and bottle were easily reachable.

The first four rooms, dark behind the glass insets in their doors, were locked. Roberto moved faster. Five yards from the VIP lounge, he saw the sign, stopped, and whispered briefly to the other two.

The older lady was sitting on one couch, her head back on a cushion, her feet up, a champagne glass in her hand. The mother was feeding the baby on a different couch. The man—now wide-eyed—was beside her. Roberto had planned on a casual entry, then minutes later the bombs. But they were alone, and the man, now clearly frightened and panicking, was getting to his feet. The mother too was sensing trouble. He reached into his pocket, pulled a pin, and as the man looked straight at Manuel, threw the first bomb into the far corner.

Nathan Morick thought he was going to vomit. Rising to his feet, he knew he had somehow to get to the taller man. But the shorter one was looking right at him, and he couldn't help but meet his gaze. Beyond that moment he was never again sure what happened. A billowing plume of gray smoke came from behind him. He started to reach for his wife and baby, but a second cloud almost next to him, denser than the first, turned him in confusion, and he fell to the ground several feet from the couch. Dense smoke filled the room, choking them. He heard the rush of bodies, the struggle, the shouts from his mother-in-law. And then he heard himself screaming as he groped for Sarah and Lauren on the floor, all the while acutely aware that there had been no noise with this smoke, that there were no sounds of physical pain. He heard the door, to the lounge close, then the shrill blasts of smoke alarms. But as he ran to the door and pulled futilely on the locked handle, it was not the smoke alarms that filled his ears. It was the other scream of anguish that was piercing the air in resonant, sickening waves, and it was Sarah's.

PART FOUR

TWENTY

Although it was still dark outside, from the full-length window in the kitchen Richard Ashton could see most of the backyard in the glow of the floodlights. The leaves needed to be raked. The deck, five years old this spring, the weathered rails splintering, needed to be sanded and sealed. He was going to have to find a handyman, he thought. Or even better, move. A new house would occupy Arlene, maybe make her happier. This one was all used up.

The coffee finished dripping—enough for each of them to have a cup with breakfast, and one in the car. He heard the shower go on above him, glanced at the clock, and filled his cup to the top. Arlene was running late. He would probably be gone before she came down for her breakfast—the single oat-bran muffin that would often last her until dinner. All part of the routine that kept her within a few pounds of the weight at which she had married.

Ashton sat down at the table in the breakfast nook, a bowl of cereal and a medical journal in front of him. He was halfway through his cereal when Arlene came into the kitchen. She was in her robe, her hair wet.

"Aren't you going to get dressed first? It'll throw you off all day."

Arlene poured herself coffee without answering. Looking at the pot, she poured another half a cup into her husband's car mug, capped it, then put the pot back on the burner.

"I've decided to change my routine. Otherwise we'll never see each other." She put a frozen muffin into the microwave. While it warmed, she studied her face in the reflection from the glass door of the oven. It was long and oval, the skin, forty years old, remarkably free of the early wrinkling and blemishes that plagued so many of her friends.

"I'm sorry I was late last night. The staff meeting just went on and on."

"They seem to do that rather regularly." The microwave dinged, and she took the muffin out. "But not as regularly for Jim Baxter. Marla says she sees him most Thursday nights."

"That's because he pages himself out of the meeting. I can't help it if I was asked to chair two of the committees. Do me a favor—call the head administrator. Tell him I have to be home at a reasonable hour."

Arlene shrugged. "The kids were expecting you."

"I thought you might have taken them out."

She sat do at the table. "I wasn't up to it. Derek's team lost, so he was moping. And Sandra was being a real pain."

"Did he score?"

"Do you really want to know? No—he didn't."

Ashton was quiet for a moment. Then, "I'll take him to the next one."

"Oh, great. That will really help."

"My, you're in a good mood this morning."

"I work too, Richard. I realize selling houses isn't quite as glamorous as saving the world, but . . ."

"It'll be better soon. I'm going to hire another staff before Christmas."

"Will you be home tonight? It's been a week since we've eaten together."

"Yes and I'm sorry. Maybe we can let the kids eat first and have a quiet dinner. I'll get the wine."

Arlene nodded and picked at her muffin. Watching him read his journal, she said: "I was thinking we all might go away this weekend. Did you decide about Carlos?"

"What do you mean?"

"You said he asked you to go to France. With . . . whatever her name is."

"Rachel. And I said he asked both of us to go."

"Well?"

"I also said I had patients scheduled all next week."

Arlene shrugged. "I'm sure you could work it out if you wanted to."

"I don't *want* to go." Ashton closed his journal. "I presumed you didn't, either."

"I thought you might be waiting for Rachel to drop out. Then the two of you could be alone." She smiled and kicked his foot under the table when he didn't respond. "Come on, Richard, lighten up. They do have a two—or three-month-old baby, don't they?"

"What's the matter, Arlene?"

"Nothing. I just want to know you're up to. If you do go with him, I might take the kids somewhere."

"Do you *want* me to go with Carlos?"

Arlene took a sip of coffee. "No, I don't *want* you to go. I'm just trying to make it easier for you. maybe if you can get away with him for a while—for whatever it is the two of you do—then you'll have some more time for us."

Ashton put his spoon in his bowl and pushed ft away. "We can go away this weekend. That's fine."

"Or maybe you *want* her to go," said Arlene, a caustic twinkle in her eyes. "Does he share that with you too?"

Ashton stared at his wife, then past her to the front door. A string of construction-paper pumpkins ringed the door frame. A witch hung from the entry-hall chandelier.

"Well, if you do go," Arlene was saying, "he can pay for it. In case you haven't noticed, some idiot put a big dent in my car. It's not worth fixing. I want to get a new one."

"So get one. What's the money problem? Last week you were upset because you thought we were *spoiling* the kids."

"It's *not* a problem. It's just . . . I don't know."

"What?"

"Picking up and flying off to some chateau in France. It must be nice."

"That's old-family money, Arlene."

"Hmmm."

Ashton went to the sink. "Is the maid coming today?"

"Yes."

He set his bowl and cup down noisily and retreated into the hall.

Arlene watched him put on his coat and come back into the kitchen. "I didn't see anything in the paper yesterday," she said.

Ashton glared at her.

"About the lawsuit. You don't *really* think they're not going to find out where that lady had her in vitro, do you?"

"No, but what difference does it make?" His stomach burned despite the coating of milk. Each of the last two days he had drunk a whole bottle of antacid.

"None, I suppose. But you know that lawyer's going to want to know why *you* didn't deliver that baby."

"I made a mistake. It happens. They were a very difficult couple to work with."

"I'm sure they were, judging from how they showed up at St. Joseph's. But you'll still have to say so in court."

"It's not a big deal. I don't know anybody in town who hasn't been to court." Ashton glanced out the window. The sky was gray now, the trees beginning to take shape. But all he saw was the indistinct figure of a lawyer, summoning the young doctor who had looked over his shoulder to the witness stand.

The fire was raging in his stomach, and he looked back to Arlene. She was saying "That resident you didn't like—Gallagher—I hope you were at least civil to him. He's going to be fighting for his life." She watched his blank face. "And I hope you kept your comments about his accent and his clothes to your self." Standing to clear her plate from the table, she added, "Not that *you* owned a suit before Carlos bought you one in Paris."

"I'm beginning to think you're looking forward to seeing me in court."

Arlene's tone was serious. "Don't be an ass, Richard. Your patient left you, and then she died in another hospital. That resident and everybody else are going to want to know why."

Picking up his car mug and briefcase, Ashton shrugged. "It's not a big deal. They would have left anybody. As you said, look at how they showed up at St. Joseph's. Obviously they *never* found an obstetrician they could work with."

He was opening the door to the garage when Arlene, her voice trembling, called after him.

"So tell me, Richard—what's her name? Which one of your little bimbos are you meeting after work?"

He stopped, his back to her.

"At least Fernandez has the guts to come out and marry them," she added bitterly.

Turning, he saw her eyes filling with tears. "Arlene, this is a difficult time. I'm not—"

"Damn, you, Richard!" she stammered between sobs. "I curse the day I ever met you."

In the windowless, unfinished storage room that spread out under half of the house, Warren DeLozier wheeled toward a cinder-block wall almost forty feet away and planted his feet. The white paw came up to steady the butt of the Beretta, and three rounds crashed into the cement, spraying out splinters of concrete and leaving ragged holes in the partially hollow blocks. The noise echoed, built in his ears like a drum-roll, and he dropped to the floor. Rolling once, he stabilized his forearm with his paw. Lauren was gone—*crash*. Gone—*crash*. Lauren—most likely the only child his daughter would ever have, the only grandchild he would ever have—was gone. *Crash*. Three more rounds slammed into an area the size of a softball. Breathing heavily, little drops of spittle on his chin, he got to his knees, then to his feet.

The wall—after thirty-plus rounds—looked like a grenade had gone off five feet from it. Ten had gone in after Sarah had called at one, crying so hard he had barely been able to understand her. There hadn't been much to say. They had set off smoke bombs. They were too strong. Whatever. Nathan, *fucking Nathan*—DeLozier dropped to one knee and fired—had failed. Now the airport had roadblocks up. Roadblocks—*crash*. He struggled to his feet, his arm, weary from the weight of the pistol, falling to his side.

Ten rounds had gone in after Gallagher called. More time, the young doctor had said. He was still working on the symbols. The nurse, first thing in the morning, would make some calls and talk to the ultrasound technician. This is Ashton's career, Gallagher had said. This is his life. He won't go down easy. We need something firm, something he can't get around. Then the doctor had asked about some blood-typing that DeLozier had never heard of. Sarah would know, he had said. But Sarah—his arm came back up, and he fired—was in a fucking hotel room full of police. First thing in the morning, my ass.

Ten rounds after he had gotten himself ready for the morning and his exit from the house. They want to talk to you, Sarah had also said. She had made the call from another room, alone. The FBI, the local police, the airport authorities. They want to know about the hospital, the beach, New York. They don't want you doing anything else. They want you with us."

Tell them I'm not home, he had instructed her. And don't worry about me. I'll be there soon. But he had known Sarah could put them off only so long, and at some point the police would be wanting to know more about the disappearance of Wukich. The poor bastard. He'd hated lying about him, but it would've only meant more questions, and cops. So he had packed a lightweight bag, most of its weight from ammunition. He had sharpened the butcher's cleaver and cleaned and oiled the Beretta. The cleaver and Beretta he had kept with him. The bag had gone into the trunk of his Lincoln with the other necessities: sleeping bag; cooler with food, ice, and sodas; Winchester 30-06 rifle; Browning semiautomatic twelve-gauge shotgun.

Now he went back upstairs and finished preparing the house for his absence. He looked out the kitchen window. The first sign of light was showing over the tree line. It was time to leave. He filled a glass of water, took a pain pill, and went into the garage.

In the Lincoln he sat for a minute with the garage door closed. Gallagher was wrong. Yes, the Fertility Institute was a temple in its on right, and one did not visit the shrine, nor its gowned keepers, without more than intuition. But if the young doctor didn't call back, and soon, he would get to Ashton himself. *His* way.

DeLozier's phone rang, and he smiled. Together they would nail the son-of-a-bitch.

But it was Sarah. The airport had removed the roadblocks.

TWENTY-ONE

With his head on his arms, the pencil still between his fingers, Gallagher drifted into the fringes of sleep, where one dreamy image after another assaulted him in rapid succession. Yet no matter how distorted the figures, how bizarre the faces and the words, there seemed to be a focus: Richard Ashton was everywhere. One moment he was gowned and masked in the operating room; suddenly he was translocated in his white coat to the laboratory; next he was whisked to the conference room, over which he presided with military precision. Now he was lecturing. With big swings of his arm, he carved circles into the wall, a long, attentive row of them. Then, suddenly, two were dark—their centers blackened—and they were coming at Gallagher like bug eyes. But Ashton inexplicably saved him. With a slash of his pointer, the circles were still, fixed in midair with some type of spear running through them.

Gallagher stirred, almost awoke. As he slipped back, the circles were gone, and Ashton was looking at him with his portrait smirk. You were there, he was saying. Where? Where was I? There. You were there. *Where? There!* With me and Lindsey and . . . Ashton laughed and turned away. Then the room lightened, and somewhere it was morning. Now DeLozier appeared, sitting at his kitchen table in his robe. Gallagher saw himself gliding around the kitchen, taking down cups and plates, pouring coffee. DeLozier was talking, but he couldn't hear him. He was busy with breakfast: melting butter in the pan, making toast. The oily smell of eggs frying filled the room, and little drops of grease pricked him as they leapt out from the pan. He looked down at the eggs spread out like is lands, each with its own symmetrical orange mountain curving up as if it were a perfect—

"Son-of-a-bitch," said Gallagher, rising up from his folded arms. He looked at his own refrigerator. "They're not circles—they're spheres. They're fucking *spheres!*" He looked at his notebook. Then he reached for the telephone to call Lindsey. But he stopped with his hand on the receiver, his mind filling with the early-morning images of February 10; Dr. Barton, Lindsey, Alice, Susan, Ashton, himself—all around the operating table. He, still in his first week, nervous, but challenging Ashton just the same. Ashton, sharp and defensive until the case had been over. Until Fred . . . Until Fred from the lab had come in for the eggs and Ashton . . . Jesus-fucking-Christ. He had to talk to Fred.

DeLozier parked on the street fronting the Fertility Institute, within view of the main entrance and the staff parking lot. He had just turned off the engine when the car phone rang.

"One more hour," said Gallagher. "Then I think I can make him talk. Whether he can tell us anything about Lauren, I don't know."

"What do you know?"

Gallagher hesitated.

"What do you know?"

"I'm not exactly sure yet. I have to talk to Fred—the reproductive biologist. He won't be in until eight." He paused for a long second. Then, "I think Ashton's taking eggs."

"What?"

"I think Ashton's taking eggs. Either right from the egg retrievals, or if they're left over after the fertilization."

DeLozier was silent.

"I know—I don't know what it means either. But it's something. Right now it's all we have. And if I can prove it, then he's up a creek." DeLozier was still quiet. "I'll call you as soon as I can . . . Mr. DeLozier?"

"Yes."

"Where are you?"

"On the way out of the airport."

"Wait for me. I think we should see him together."

Gallagher hung up, and DeLozier dialed the Fertility Institute, expecting to get a tape. After the voice finished, he left a message for Ashton's secretary. Then he sat, waiting for the man he had seen only briefly from the waiting room on the day of his daughter's egg retrieval.

At seven-thirty he saw Ashton arrive, in a Jaguar no less. Then car after car pulled into the staff lot, including a Toyota, from which a plump black-haired woman emerged. He thought she was the woman Nathan had pointed out as Ashton's secretary, but he couldn't say for sure.

At eight o'clock Valerie called.

"Yes, you may," he said in answer to her greeting. "My daughter was one of Dr. Ashton's patients, and I'd like to speak with Dr. Ashton about her. I know this is short notice, but I'd like to see him today. Early this morning if can; I have to go back to Florida this afternoon."

"I'm sorry, Reverend Owen, but I just don't think that's possible. He's operating now, and he has meetings scheduled for the rest of the day. His schedule is usually booked weeks in advance." Valerie paused, trying to match the name with a face. "If you like, I'll schedule you the first available appointment. I'm sure Dr. Ashton would like to talk with you."

"I understand he's a very busy man, but I flew up from Florida for her funeral, and I really do have to get back." He paused. "You know how it is. The more you know about these things, the easier it is to understand them."

"Oh, I'm so sorry. Was she in an accident?"

"No. She died in the hospital. Her married name was Williams. Billie Williams."

The young, sincere face flashed through Valerie's mind. "Why, yes, Reverend, I most certainly do understand. Let me talk to Dr. Ashton before he goes into the operating, room. I suspect he'll want to slip you in sometime this morning. Can I call you back at this number?

"Please, and thank you very much. You don't know how much I appreciate your help."

"Oh, don't be silly. I'm so sorry about your daughter."

"Yes, it was a tragedy. She's with the Lord—now, though. And I know she hears your prayers. Well, thank you again. I'll be waiting for your call."

DeLozier gently set the phone down, his gaze moving over the cars now turning into the Institute's main parking lot. As he watched, the barest perceptible trace of a smile creased his mouth. One way or another Ashton was going to talk.

The car phone rang. It was Valerie. Dr. Ashton had said he would see him between cases. Whenever he could get there.

Parking well down the street from the institute, Gallagher cut back through an adjacent building's parking lot to the rear service entrance. The door led to the shipping-and-receiving area in the basement, which was ground level in the back of the building. His first day's tour of the institute with Dr. Simpson had ended there, the purpose of the stop to see the banks of freezers from which the institute shipped specimens to other fertility centers. And next to the freezers, Gallagher remembered, was the office from which the shipping manager presided over such shipments. He hurried up the cement stairs and pulled against the locked steel door. A few minutes later one of the technicians who worked in the freezers pulled up. Climbing the stairs, she glanced at Gallagher's white coat with the university logo.

"Lost?" she said.

"No, I'm trying to retrace my steps from yesterday. Dr. Simpson brought me down to see the freezers, and then we stepped out here for a moment so he could talk to Mr . . . . the man who runs the shipping end of it."

"Mr. Wagner?"

"Right. Anyway, I dropped my pen somewhere along the way. If I don't find it, I'm gonna die one way or another. My mother gave it to me for my birthday."

The young woman opened the door. "Let's take a look in here."

For a minute they searched the floors. Then, "Oh, forget it," said Gallagher "She'll get over it. Let me just check with Mr. Wagner before I go to the OR."

"Hi, I'm Dr. Gallagher," he said to the older man sitting behind the desk. "After I finish working with Dr. Ashton, I'm going to be starting a fertility clinic out west. I was wondering about your shipping."

"No problem. Same day anywhere in the States."

"If I get a research protocol approved, can you supply a lab?"

The man shrugged. "Depends."

"On what?"

Grinning slyly, the man rubbed his thumb and Index finger together and said, "What else?"

Gallagher returned the grin and winked. "Nothing wrong with that. Thanks."

Taking the back stairs, then corridors away from Ashton's office and the main routes to the operating rooms, he headed for the surgical suite. In the back of it, he found Lindsey Baines in her office, in street clothes. She covered the mouthpiece of the phone. "I'm on hold. Sarah Morick was HLA-typed on the fifteenth of November. Nathan Morick on the twenty-second. The release form does mention HLA typing, but it's listed among a bunch of other things that 'might' be done at some point during the initial workup or after the fertilization."

Gallagher nodded but was silent.

"Bob's checking on something else. He's the guy who does the typing. Apparently Sarah Morick had some additional testing done." Lindsey took her hand away from the phone and said, "Okay." Hanging up, she looked at Gallagher. "It's going to take a few minutes."

"Can you wait?"

"I already told Ashton I was sick and couldn't scrub."

"Thanks, Lindsey. I—"

"You really think he's taking eggs?"

"Yes, but I want to talk to Fred."

"That bastard! I've been working with him almost every day for five years. If he's been using—"

"Hold on, Lindsey," said Gallagher, moving for the door. "Let me talk to Fred before we crucify him. I'll be right back." A step from the door he stopped.

"There's one more thing," Lindsey was saying. "I talked to Susan. She didn't do that ultrasound."

Gallagher stayed still, his back to her.

"She saw it, though. She said the print was in Spanish."

Valerie saw the man walking toward her, and for a brief moment wondered if it was Reverend Owen. But as he drew nearer, she recognized some part of his face and, knowing she had never seen Billie Williams's father, searched her memory for a name.

"Good morning," said DeLozier. "I'm Reverend Owen. I hope I can still have a moment with Dr. Ashton."

She looked up at him, but nothing else would come. Pushing a button on her desk, she said, "Reverend Owen's here. Do you want to see him now, or after your next case."

DeLozier moved for Ashton's office.

"*Sir*, Dr. Ashton will call for you when he's ready."

"He's ready," said DeLozier under his breath.

Ashton opened the door and looked at Valerie. She shrugged and made an exasperated face. "I'd like to see you after my next case, Reverend," said the surgeon. "We'll have more time."

"I need to talk to you about my daughter," DeLozier said softly. "It will only take a few minutes."

Ashton began a quick reply, then stopped. The reverend's face was deeply fatigued, his eyes red, the skin around them sunken and bluish. Opening the door, he said: "I'm sorry. I can only imagine how you must feel. My case can wait for a few minutes."

"Thank you. I do feel as if I'm at the end of my rope."

Ashton led DeLozier to one of the armchairs, then sat down behind his desk. "Were you in an accident?" he said, looking at the green sling covering the man's arm and hand.

"No, I just sprained it."

"I'm sorry. You don't need that now." Ashton paused. "I'm afraid I don't have a lot to tell you. As I presume you know; I hadn't seen your daughter since May."

DeLozier nodded. "She didn't want to leave you. Actually, she was very upset about it. But she said the parents were getting hysterical."

Leaning forward, Ashton folded his hands on top of the desk and lowered his voice. "Between you and me, Reverend Owen, they weren't the most pleasant couple to work with. Quite frankly, I've never before had a couple leave me at that stage."

"It surprised me too. That's one of the reasons I wanted to talk to you. I can't help but think that this never would have happened if they had stayed with you. Who knows what doctors Billie was seeing, if any? And then"—DeLozier shook his head in remorse—" she got dumped on that doctor who's barely out of medical school. I'm tempted to file my own suit against him. He ought to be bared for life."

"I understand your concerns, Reverend. Although I can't speak for any doctor she saw before the delivery, if it makes you feel any better, I happen know Dr. Gallagher, the resident who did the delivery. He's a fine young man. I don't believe what happened to your daughter was his fault."

"Then *whose* was it?" DeLozier looked as if he were about to cry. "Why did my baby die?"

Ashton sat back, his hands in his lap. "I know how frustrating it is, but there may not be an answer to that. Sometimes these things happen. And I'm not sure another lawsuit will help matters at all."

"Oh, I don't care about the money." DeLozier wiped his eyes, aware of the surgeon purposefully glancing at his watch.

"Is there anything else I can help you with?" said Ashton.

"Can you tell me why the parents left you? That seems to be what started everything. Maybe I should talk to them too."

"I don't think you'll find them very receptive. They're rather angry people." Ashton stopped, apparently ready to end the conversation. But the man across from him was staring at him expectantly. "I'm afraid I can't go into details. That's confidential. Basically they wanted everything to be perfect, and at the first little problem, as your daughter said, they got hysterical."

DeLozier nodded. "Maybe I ought to sue them. I'm sure they didn't get Billie the proper care."

Sitting up straight, Ashton said: "I would think they did. That baby meant everything to them. And they truly cared for your daughter."

"But that doesn't make sense. Why would they leave you then? I've been told you're the best."

"Because," said the surgeon, his voice now hard, "they couldn't *tolerate* the thought of anything going wrong. At one point there was a *potential* problem. But even though I would have held their hand for the next six months, they only heard what they wanted to. Now, I'm sorry, but I do have to go to the operating room." Standing, Ashton moved to shake the man's hand.

"Billie told me you wanted her to get an abortion."

The surgeon's face visibly paled. He sat back down and gathered himself. "Reverend Owen, I don't even know what to say. That's just . . . preposterous. Is that why you're really here?"

"That's one reason. She said you told the family the baby had no brain."

"I would never—"

"She said you said it would be a vegetable, if it lived at all. I don't understand, Dr. Ashton. I was told the baby's normal."

"First of all, I never said one bit of that. In addition to everything else, that couple are a pair of *liars*. And secondly, I told you—there was a *question* of a problem that, if I had been given just a short period of time, I could have easily resolved."

"She said you were so angry when they left, that you used to call her and try to get her to come back."

Ashton smiled and shook his head.

"She even thought you were the one who had her kidnapped."

"What did you say?" said Ashton, his face growing serious.

"When she was kidnapped back in May. She thought maybe you had somebody do it."

"What in the name of God are you talking about?"

DeLozier looked at him. "You don't know about that?"

"Obviously not."

"I'm sorry. I thought you did. She was kidnapped in May. By somebody in the medical field. They had her up in stirrups before she got away."

Ashton stared at DeLozier, the color draining from his face as if he were hemorrhaging. "Reverend Owen," he said softly, "I categorically had nothing to do with whatever happened to your daughter. Yes, the last thing I ever wanted was for her to leave here, but after she did, I never saw her, nor spoke with her."

DeLozier rose to his feet. "Then why the hell did you scare the family away?" he almost yelled. "Why didn't you wait until the ultrasound *was* more definite?"

"Wait for what?"

"Before you counseled them."

"I never said the baby was definitely anencephalic, nor did I make any recommendations to the parents. I simply stated the facts as I saw them at the time. as a matter of fact, I *did* say we could wait!"

"Bull shit! You scared them, and you know it!"

"You obviously have a lot of misinformation, Reverend. And you're too upset to have a rational conversation. I think you should leave."

"I'm not going anywhere! You're going to explain why Billie died."

"I *don't know* why your daughter died. And I can't talk now. I have surgery to do." Ashton stood and looked from the door to DeLozier, focusing on the bandaged hand that was now protruding from the sling.

DeLozier approached the desk. "Please, Dr. Ashton, look at my hand. Would you like to know *why* it looks like this?"

"I'm afraid you'll have to—"

"Two men cut off my fingers."

"What?"

"That's right. Two men chopped off my fingers when I wouldn't tell them what *they* wanted to know." DeLozier reached into his sling and took out an object wrapped in a dish towel. Removing the dish towel, he brandished his butcher's cleaver. "With this. They put me in a chair, held a knife to my throat, and"—with a solid thud he embedded the knife in the edge of the desk—"cut off my fingers."

Ashton put his hand to the intercom. "Valerie, would you please call—"

The cleaver arced—the plastic box splintered into pieces across the desk. Ashton jumped back, his hand against his chest, and stared at DeLozier incredulously.

"Now," said DeLozier, "go to the door and tell your secretary that you'll be tied up for a while. Tell her to go have a cup of coffee." He put the cleaver in his sling, withdrew the Beretta from the shoulder holster under his suit jacket, and pointed it at Ashton's head. "And don't say *anything* else, or you'll be minus a face. I promise."

Ashton complied, and DeLozier waved him back to his chair. "Sit down," he ordered. "Put your hand on your desk, index finger out."

Ashton looked up at him fearfully. "Reverend Owen, please let me help you. I know how much your daughter's—"

"Put your hand out!" DeLozier pushed the safety off and moved the pistol close to the surgeon's face. "You don't know shit about that!"

Slowly Ashton put a clenched fist on the desk.

"Index finger out," grunted DeLozier, his eyes wild. He put the Beretta in the sling and took out the cleaver. "Now, tell me what happened to my daughter."

"I don't know. I swear to God. Maybe that resident did make a mistake."

"Why did you kidnap her?"

"I don't know anything about—"

The cleaver slammed down inches away from Ashton's hand. Recoiling, the surgeon looked up, sweat on his brow.

"What do you know? How could you make such a mistake with the Moricks?"

"I . . . I—"

"Put your hand back out and say it!"

"I told you. I—"

"Say it! The truth! Couldn't you steal enough eggs the first time? What did you want them to do—get an abortion so you could do it all over again?" The cleaver slammed into

the desk, this time only an inch from Ashton's index finger. "You did, didn't you? You stole some of *my* daughter's eggs! *Tell me!*"

Ashton nodded, looking as if he were about to get sick.

"Why, goddammit? Tell me! Now! Why'd you steal her eggs? Why do you want my granddaughter?"

For several second seconds they looked at each other: DeLozier with spittle on his lips; Ashton for the most part terrified, but then his face beginning to firm.

"What are you talking about?" managed the surgeon.

"My granddaughter, you son-of-a-bitch! Lauren Morick, the baby you said had no brain. She's gone! Do you understand? *Gone!* Somebody kidnapped her, and you're going to tell me why." DeLozier raised the cleaver, and the door burst open.

Gallagher and Lindsey Baines stepped in, Gallagher closing the door behind them Lindsey her eyes burning with anger, approached Ashton's desk with a piece of paper held up for him to see.

"Richard," she said, "why did you need *subtyping?* What in God's name have you been doing?"

Ashton started to speak, but Lindsey went on "So help me God, Richard, if you've used me to . . . to do any of this, I'll make sure you rot in hell."

DeLozier moved for Lindsey and the piece of paper, but Gallagher stepped between them. "I asked you to wait, Mr. DeLozier."

"For what?" DeLozier stopped short of the younger man, his eyes still on the paper. "We're wasting time. She's gone, and he knows why. Now what is that? What the hell's subtyping?"

"Why don't you sit down before I call the police? And give me that." He put his hand out for the cleaver.

"Don't threaten me, son. I'll . . ." DeLozier studied him hard for a moment, then wrapped the cleaver in the dish towel, put it in his sling, walked to the door, locked it, and returned to Ashton's desk. Taking out the Beretta, he pointed it at Ashton's face. "He's a goddamn criminal," he said to Gallagher. "Now say what you want to say. And hurry it up."

Gallagher started to object, then looked at Ashton. "Did you take some of Sarah Morick's eggs without her consent? You dissected her aspirates yourself. And I know you did too many aspirations."

Ashton straightened his tie and shirt and placed his hands on his desk.

"That was the only egg retrieval you dissected that day. I know what your circles mean."

A sudden flash of anger crossed Ashton's face.

"He took the eggs," said DeLozier. "Get to the point."

"Why?" said Gallagher.

Ashton just shook his head.

"Do you want to do this in court? We'll ruin you and your institute."

Ashton smiled. DeLozier stepped beside him and put the Beretta to his temple.

"Why did you take Sarah Morick's eggs?" said Gallagher. "Why were you so convinced the baby was anencephalic? Why is the print on the last ultrasound in Spanish?"

"*Talk,* you son-of-a-bitch, or I'm going to put a hole in your head." DeLozier pushed Ashton's head sideways with the muzzle. Softly, almost calmly, he added: "Look at the clock. You have twenty seconds."

216

Gallagher took a step forward, and DeLozier pushed Ashton's head another inch. "Don't, son." Then, "Ten seconds."

Ashton looked to Gallagher.

"Five."

"I'd already fertilized her for Christ's sake! She didn't want them!"

The muzzle didn't move.

"Why did you take them?" said Gallagher.

Although his head was still bent from the force of the gun, Ashton seemed to regain some composure. "Because there are many important fertility questions that can be answered only by doing research on eggs, sperm, and embryos. And we live in a country where the decisions about who can do what and when are made by imbeciles."

Gallagher snorted "You are crazy. That's illegal."

"That's science."

"That's bullshit. Why the HLA typing? And the subtyping?"

"Genetics is at the heart of many of the problems we see—the HLA genes are a critical component of genetics. I'm not the only one who feels that way. Read the international journals." He looked up at DeLozier. "I think this would be easier if you sat down."

DeLozier stared at him coldly, then moved a step away from the desk.

Ashton straightened his head. "Your daughter's HLA profile was in our computer network. It matched up with a type that . . . somebody was looking for."

"Who's somebody?" said DeLozier and Gallagher at the same time.

Ashton hesitated. DeLozier stepped to him.

"Carlos Fernandez."

Lindsey made a disgusted noise and sat down on the couch.

"The fertility specialist?" said Gallagher, remembering once more that early February morning, hearing Ashton say to Lindsey that Fernandez was in town.

"Yes."

"He was there the day of the egg retrieval. You intentionally retrieved more than enough."

"I did. Carlos was pressuring me after he saw her initial profile." He paused momentarily, gazing into his lap. "For what he was looking for, it was like matching the first five out of six numbers on a lottery ticket. I never before seen such a match in nonrelated persons. Then, if you will, the sixth number was matched." He looked at Gallagher. "The subtyping."

"What was he going to do with the eggs?"

"I didn't ask. I didn't know."

Silence. Then, "You do now."

Ashton stared past them, the only sounds the faint noise of traffic filtering through the window.

"*Richard*," said Lindsey, "there's no other choice. You have to help."

Ashton looked at her, then at some indiscernible spot on the wall. When he spoke, his voice was barely audible. "He was going to fertilize them. But something went wrong when they were transferred to the culture medium. They died."

"So?" said Gallagher. But a moment later he was staring at Ashton in disbelief. "You're kidding. He wanted more. You got another baby's ultrasound and phony amniocentesis results through Fernandez, and you told the Moricks the baby was anencephalic. You *wanted* them to abort so you could start all over again. You—"

"No!" cried Ashton, backing up in his chair as DeLozier jammed the Beretta against his head. "That was the last thing I would have *ever* wanted. But they were going to kill us!" Looking up at the man above him with frank fear in his eyes, he said: "*Please* sit down, Mr. DeLozier. I'll tell you what I know."

DeLozier's hand slowly dropped to his side. He moved back a step, then another as Ashton began to speak. Gallagher sat down in an armchair.

"There's a very prominent man in Mexico who has bad Parkinson's disease. Apparently he won't live much longer the way he is now. I don't all the details. I'm just telling you what Carlos has told me. Basically, this man's family is in a period of business and political transition for which the stakes are enormous, and they're just not ready for him to die."

Ashton moved his gaze to the wall. "When none of the standard medications were working, the family literally got hold of a neurosurgeon who does research in transplanting fetal brain tissue into patients with Parkinson's disease. It's still essentially an experimental procedure, but there have been some promising reports in humans. And because there's usually only a small area of degenerated brain tissue that has to be replaced, it's an attractive hypothesis. As with most transplantations, rejection of the graft by the recipient is the main problem. Fetal tissue eliminates some of that risk because it's not fully developed immunologically. To minimize it even further, the neurosurgeon also wanted the best HLA match he could find. As sick as this patient is, he'll die for sure if the tissue is rejected. But Sanchez, the neurosurgeon, couldn't find a good match in the usual sources. That's when he went to Carlos."

For a moment Ashton closed his eyes. Then with a little shake of his head, he went on. "Carlos, as usual, had a 'great' idea. Since Mrs. Morick and this man are almost identical HLA matches, he was going to take the man's sperm, which is still viable, and incubate it with one of Mrs. Morick's eggs. Then he was going to implant the embryo into a surrogate mother. It would have been an ideal tissue match under the circumstances. But he messed up the eggs."

"Are you implying they would have aborted the fetus to do the transplantation?" asked Gallagher, knowing the answer.

Ashton nodded. "So you did need more eggs. You did want them—"

"I did *not* want that! Listen to me: you know that if I had wanted that fetus, one way or another I could have caused Mrs. Williams to abort. I *didn't* want that. I *wanted* them to leave me." He turned to DeLozier. "You're right—I scared them away. But only because I knew your daughter would run in the right direction."

For a moment the room was quiet. Then Ashton deliberately went on: "When Carlos told them there were no more eggs, they threatened to kill his wife until he came up with a solution. He told them they could wait for fetal tissue from an accident or some other source. They said they couldn't wait, and they took one of his kids. They said they'd kill his kid and the both of us if we didn't do something. That was when he thought of the fetus."

"Wait a minute," said Gallagher. "The anencephaly bit wasn't so you could get more eggs?"

Ashton shook his head.

"You mean Fernandez wanted the Moricks' *fetus* for—" Gallagher was out of his chair and moving for Ashton. Yanking DeLozier off the surgeon, he pushed the older man, his face ashen and grotesque with rage, into a chair. Turning to Ashton, he said incredulously: "Is that why Billie Williams was kidnapped? So Fernandez could abort the fetus?"

"I suppose so."

"You just said—"

"I said that was what *Carlos* wanted. I did not want that. *I* told you—I scared them away. And I swear to God, I never knew anything about her being kidnapped."

"But you would have aborted the fetus if they hadn't left you."

"No I wouldn't have! I don't know what I would have done, but I wouldn't have done that. After the Moricks left my care, I presumed it was all over. Carlos went back to Mexico and told the neurosurgeon they weren't going to abort. I think he was going to try to fertilize some other eggs, but I didn't get into that at all. As far as I was concerned, it was over. It wasn't until Mrs. Williams died that . . . I started to wonder."

Gallagher looked at him with some relief. "Even if the Moricks had decided to abort, the fetus would have had half of Nathan Morick's genes."

"He also matched on several major HLA loci. It was a better match than any other donor tissue they had available."

"But what about now? Why do they want the baby?"

Ashton shrugged. "I guess they decided to take their chances with the baby since it's closely matched. The researchers don't really know how old is too old in regard to fetal tissue. All they know is that at some point as a fetus or baby matures, it becomes more capable of initiating a tissue rejection."

"But you've thought about it for days," said Lindsey Baines, stepping toward the desk. "You've at least wondered if they're after that baby's—God, I can't even say it—and you haven't said a word. You're sick! Goddamn you! You're—"

"They were going to kill him, Lindsey! They were going to kill me!" His voice dropped to a whisper: "Let me talk to Carlos and the neurosurgeon. It's all I can do."

PART FIVE

TWENTY-TWO

In the roadside café an hour from the hacienda, Carlos Fernandez ordered a big breakfast and a Bloody Mary. The waitress stayed for a while at his table, talking about the weather and the summer's crops. Her father was a farmer, she said, and had had a good harvest. He had just planted his fall crops. Fernandez agreed that it had been a decent summer, but he said he expected a better fall. He too would be planting, he added. He asked her what her father expected of the late growing season. One, maybe two very good months, she said. Then a mild winter. Fernandez toasted her father's seed, then his own. It was so good, he said, that before the first frost in the mountains, he would have a field that was tall and strong.

He drank, feeling the warmth spread out from his belly like an early spring sun lighting up the morning. Like the giver of strength that it was. He drank again, emptying the glass, and looked up to find the waitress watching him from the bar. He lifted the glass and pushed it toward her, then kept his hands together on the table. She nodded and turned away. While she worked, he studied his hands. They were good hands, he thought. They could sow and harvest as well as any that had gone before him. The bottom one pushed against the top, and he pushed it back. When the waitress returned, he put them in his lap.

Shortly he went out to his car. Every step was light and sure. He began to sing. In the road, though, with the

225

Mercedes pointed toward the hacienda, he lost his voice. Suddenly he felt empty, and for a moment frightened. He slowed. He started to pull off to the side, but then he remembered that his mother had said Felice would be arriving this morning. Felice, beloved Felice.

The Mercedes gained speed, and he felt his sister's soothing presence as if she were right there with him, as if she were holding him just as she had done the day of Benito's funeral. She had been twelve, Benito ten, he six. The day before the procession, when Don Rafael had drawn up the list of those to honor Benito by carrying him to his grave, he had hidden in the wine cellar. His father had come looking for him, and he, hearing the boots on the stone steps, had pretended to be searching for a rat he had spied in a corner. Don Rafael had lifted him from the floor with one hand, brushed the damp earth from his pants, and put two big brown hands on his skinny shoulders. "Tomorrow, Carlos," he had said solemnly, his eyes drawing a film, "I want you to help me bury my son, your brother. Then after we rest his body in the ground, I want you to come to me. I want you to come to me in front of all who will be there."

He turned onto the narrow one-lane road. The car felt warm, and he rolled down the windows. At the iron gates he stopped, studying the ornate heads on the two main posts. On the left was Demeter, goddess of the fields and everything that sprang from them. On the right, Apollo, god of the sun. Don Rafael's great-grandfather had carved them himself, a century ago. Fernandez bowed his head and moved on.

The paint on the fences had weathered since the spring. The fields, full of brown and yellowing cornstalks bending toward the ground, gave off an earthly-acrid scent of decay into the mild breeze. But it was that time of year. There would be another spring.

He passed the barns and drove up to the house. Caught off guard, one of the boys suddenly scrambled his way. Fernandez gave him the keys and a coin. The porch door swung open. His sister's voice floated down to him.

"Oh, Carlos," she said, embracing him. "How I've missed you. We should both come home more."

Fernandez hugged her and smiled. "Actually, Felice, I've been here quite a bit lately. I think it's you who's been remiss."

"You can't fool me." She looked around them. "You just don't want anybody to say you weren't here."

"'Weddings and deathbeds are invitations from God,' Felice. That's what Papa used to tell me. Except for mine, I suppose."

"Let's not go through that again, Carlos. You know I was going to bring Mama to your wedding. But . . ."

Fernandez put his arm around her and steered her toward the wide porch that wrapped around three sides of the house. "I know—I heard it too. 'God only comes to one of each.' And if God only comes to one, then Papa surely only comes to one. Anyway, how is Papa? Mama said he isn't eating. She said I *had* to come."

Felice's voice saddened. "He doesn't look well. I think that Mama knows that . . . he's going to die soon."

"Let me see him. I received good news last night."

They stepped in a side door, into the large kitchen full of the familiar odors. Senora Fernandez rose from the heavy wooden table where the Monsanos took their meals to embrace her son. When they parted, he greeted two of his uncles and their wives. Spaced between the relatives at the table were vases of freshly cut flowers and bowls of fruit. He turned back to his mother.

"Papa is not eating?" he said softly.

She started to cry, and he held her again. One of Don Rafael's brothers shook his head sadly in answer to the question.

When his mother had calmed, Fernandez pulled away and said he would see his father now. He stepped into the hall leading to the central staircase, passed the steps to the wine cellar, and paused in the doorway to the dining room with the long banquet table and the credenzas full of silver and linen. The hall, and the great room at its end, were as dim and still as the dining room. All around was the musty smell of old air. For a moment he saw the huge stone fireplace in the great room burning at Christmas, with all of them young and scampering around in nightshirts. Then everything was as still as he could ever remember. As still as when the priest had arrived for Benito's funeral. It was a stillness none of them could stand, and soon they had left for the graveyard.

They had walked in a slow, winding procession, the priest leading, his father at the head of the casket. The graveyard was past the first of the main coffee fields, nestled in a meadow looking down on a spring-fed pond. All he could remember now of the first hundred yards was breathing in dust and trying not to step on the backs of the shoes in front of him. But by the time they had reached the coffee field, he remembered, his aching arm had begun trembling uncontrollably. And with sweat dripping off his forehead and burning his eyes, all he had wanted was to lean on his father's wide back.

The service had lasted nearly an hour. Standing between his mother and Felice, he had daydreamed about Benito and his death, about the sight of him earlier that morning when the coffin was still open, with that gaping plow gash in his neck. But then he had begun to feel the heat and had gripped his sister's hand. There had been no breeze that day; the air was warm, heavy, perfectly still. With the sun high and clear, he had soon felt faint, and when they lowered the coffin into the grave, he had slipped on the loose dirt, sending a noisy avalanche onto the wooden box. Straightening up, he had brushed off his hands and looked at his father. Don Rafael had turned to him, his face a frightening mix of rage and hurt. He had looked for a moment to his mother, but she would not look at him. He remembered Felice looking as if she wanted to run to him and carry him away. He remembered the force of two hundred staring eyes, and feeling a six-year-old's sense of impending disaster. And he remembered that at that moment he had begun to walk toward his father.

Some of the sounds were familiar: the steady hum of the engines coming from somewhere off to the side and beneath her; the fairly constant background mix of voices, clinking utensils, the crackle of plastic. Some of the sensations—the feel of arms around her, the weight of the blanket on her back—were familiar too. But most of what was impinging on Lauren Morick from all directions was different, frighteningly different, and once again she started to cry. Once again the soft voice was in her ear, whispering unrecognizable sounds in tones and inflections she had never heard before. They only made her more uneasy, and she moved against the pressure around her. The pressure tightened, pressing her against the woman in the seat, her chest suffused with a sweet but foreign smell.

Lauren listen to the rhythmic beating of Josefina Ortiz's heart, indistinguishable to her from the thumping she had listened to for the first five days of her life, and she calmed. Then the dry rubber nipple was being pushed into her mouth. She turned her head. It came again, along with the prying fingers. She turned her head back the other way. Drops of formula dripped onto her lips and chin. Although she was hungry, its taste was strange, and she jerked again. She began to cry, louder and louder. The voice in her ear grew louder too, then harsh. Sharp pain shot through her thigh. One last cry, then a whimper. Then it was dark, the pressure lightening and lightening until it was gone.

The door to Don Rafael's room was slightly ajar, and Fernandez looked in for a moment. Don Rafael was on his back, apparently asleep. Next to his bed the nurse was reading in the faint light seeping in from the upstairs hall. When she saw him, she stood and came to the door.

"These last two days he is worse, Doctor," she said. "It is difficult for me to feed him."

Fernandez nodded. "He will go to the hospital soon."

The nurse quickly agreed it was for the best and offered to wait outside. Fernandez told her that one of them would stay with Don Rafael until he left, and she went back in for her belongings. On the way out she touched the sick man's shoulder and crossed herself.

Fernandez closed the door and turned on a lamp by the bed. His father's eyelids were closed and did not move. He pulled the nurse's chair up close and sat down only feet away from Don Rafael's head. Leaning over to stroke his forehead, he was distracted by the sheet moving up and down where it covered his hand. Quickly he reached out and gripped the closest hand, quieting most of the sheet. Then pulling away the white cotton cloth, he held the bony remnants of the big hand between his own. Now it was muddy gray, and crisscrossed by greenish blue veins covered by only a wafer of flesh. And with the normal neurohormonal control of so many of his movements eaten away by disease, his wrist wanted to bend, his thumb and index finger wanted to move, tremble, roll. Fernandez pinned them all still.

"Don Rafael," he said softly. "Papa."

The sick man's eyes opened, and for a moment he looked blankly at the ceiling. A narrow stream of drool had dried on one side of his chin; a fresh little rivulet was slipping down the other side. Slowly he focused on his son, his eyes warming, his hand returning what it could of the grip.

"Ca . . . Carlos," he said, his voice stale and stiff. "How . . . how—"

"Sad, Papa. You are not well."

"I . . . I am an old man, Carlos."

"Yes, but not that old. Only part of you is too old."

"The . . . part that counts."

"Only a small part of it. you can be well again."

Don Rafael attempted to smile, but his face was as stiff as his voice. "Ev . . . every man only wishes to be well again. But . . . so does the rabbit with claw in his neck."

"Do you feel claws, Papa?"

"No . . . no, Carlos. Not yet. He . . . is still diving."

"Then you can be well again. I do not see or hear any birds with claws. I hear only the winter birds. They'll be here soon."

"It is . . . that time of year?"

"Yes."

"The the . . . corn is gone.

"Yes."

"The coffee beans have . . . been picked?

231

"Yes."

A look of pleasure came over the old man, and he closed his eyes. "No . . . I see no claws."

"I am glad." Fernandez paused. "Because as I told you in the spring, I can make you well again."

Don Rafael's eyes opened. "My . . . my son. You . . . are still my dreamer. I should have let you be. I was wrong. I . . . I see that now. I . . . am sorry."

"No, Papa. I should have watched and listened. But this is not a dream. There has been a donation that can make you well. A very loving and a very perfect donation. All I need is for you to be strong. To want—"

"You . . . did watch. But you . . . never listened."

"I watched, but I did not see."

Don Rafael's forehead attempted to furrow, "You . . . did not *want* to see. You wa . . . wanted everything. You wa . . . wanted school . . . Europe . . . women. And . . . and then you wanted our—"

"No! I just wanted . . . one thing."

"Ah," he grunted. "But . . . that that does not grow like the mesquite in rock. It needs . . . soil and water. It needs . . . tending. Benito, and Felice, they—"

Fernandez squeezed his father's hand. "I do see now, Papa."

"Wha . . . what do you see?"

Fernandez smiled. "I see you and Mama. I see Felice and the men and the fields. I see Benito. I see what Benito saw."

Don Rafael closed his eyes and lightly squeezed his son's hand. Fernandez kissed his cheek and stood. At the foot of the bed, he paused, studying his father. Finally he whispered: "I see you, Papa. Every minute of every day. And now, one more time, you will be strong. Now, Papa, *you* will come to *me*. In front of any who will be there."

On the porch he said to Felice: "There is a pregnant woman in the city hospital who may not make it through the night. She has donated the fetus. Even though it's a little older than Dr. Sanchez would like, the mother is as good a match as we'll ever find outside the family. As good as the one in the spring that didn't work out. This is his last chance. I think we should go in the morning. Will you ride with him if I have to go back to the city?"

"Do you think he's well enough?"

Fernandez nodded. "I'll tell the hospital to expect you tomorrow noon."

Twenty-three

Fifteen minutes after DeLozier left the office, Ashton hung up the phone in frustration. "No one in his lab has seen him since early in the week," he said. "They think he's away. I'll try his office and house again, but he may have already left."

"Do you know where he was going in France?"

Ashton shook his head, his eyes still on the phone.

"What if you can't reach him?"

"Then I need to go to Mexico. I'll go this afternoon." He looked at Lindsey. "Maybe you can keep calling. He trusts you. You can tell him I had a fight with Arlene, and I'm trying to catch up with him."

"What good will going to Mexico do if he's in Europe?" said Gallagher.

Ashton met the younger man's irritated gaze. "If he hasn't left yet, I think I can find him. If he has, then I need to find the neurosurgeon."

"You're not alone."

"This isn't your problem."

"It most certainly is. What would you like me to do, go home and forget it? Or do you want me to call the police, or the local medical society, with the report of an ethics violations?"

Ashton turned towards the window. "I realize you're in a difficult situation."

"Well?"

Looking out through the blinds, the surgeon was silent. "I'd like you to help," he finally said. "From here."

Gallagher shook his head and looked to Lindsey. "Will you stay here? Besides trying to call Fernandez, you could keep in touch with DeLozier. He knows he has to stay if we go down there. I'll go with him," he finished looking at Ashton.

"I don't think that's a good idea," said Ashton.

"You've got to be kidding me. You—"

"*You* don't know Carlos. And I'm beginning to think he may be scared in ways I don't even know about. I think there's only—"

"What about the police or the FBI?" Lindsey broke in. "They must be working with the Moricks. You're really not going to tell them what's going on? For heaven's sake, why don't you call the State Department?" She looked at Gallagher. "What makes either of you think you can get the baby back when these guys kidnap and mutilate people?"

"What were you going to say?" Gallagher said to Ashton.

"First of all, I understand you're both in a very difficult situation. And regardless of what Mr. DeLozier thinks, if that's what you decide to do, I won't fight you. But I don't think that's our best chance of getting her back."

Lindsey shook her head and looked away.

"Let me try to get the surgery canceled. I think I can do that."

"Which conveniently protects you and your family," said Lindsey.

"And DeLozier's, but that's not the point. If this family in Mexico feels any pressure, I don't think we'll ever see the baby again."

Gallagher looked from Lindsey to Ashton. They were both right, they both knew it, and they were both waiting, staring at each other and waiting, for him. "How long do you think it will take us to find Fernandez?" he said.

"If he didn't go to Europe, I can find him."

"How long?"

"A day. From when I get to Mexico."

"I think he's right, Lindsey," Gallagher said a moment later. "And until Mr. DeLozier has the chance to talk it over with his daughter and son-in-law, that's what he wants too." He shrugged helplessly. "It's his family. I think he or they should have some say in it, if not all. So for the time being I think we need to plan on going to Fernandez."

Ashton shook his head.

"Do you *really* expect us to send you off alone to find the guy you couldn't control from day one of this?" said Gallagher

"It's different."

"Different! What's different? The only thing that's different is that we caught you in all your lies."

"Oh, don't be so goddamn righteous Brendan. One day you'll find that everything isn't as simple as it looks. Jesus Christ, you've told enough lies in the last week to last a lifetime."

"What's so difficult about deciding whether or not to steal eggs?"

"People like you! You don't—" Ashton stopped, and for a moment, the two men glaring at each other, the room was quiet. Then the surgeon said evenly: "Brendan, I can't change what's happened. All I can do is try to get her back. And at least to begin with, I think I have a better chance by myself. As soon as I find Carlos and get things rolling, if you still feel you need to, then you can come down."

"I'll stay here until Saturday," said Gallagher. "That's a day and a half." He wrote his telephone number on a piece of paper and tossed it onto the desk. Then turning to see if Lindsey was coming with him he headed for the door. "Keep in touch," he said over his shoulder. "If I'm not home, call Lindsey. I want to know where you are. Flight numbers, hotels, everything."

"Are you crazy?" said Lindsey in the hallway. "Carlos is insane. You'll never see that baby."

They walked down the hall and into the lobby in silence. Pushing through the front door, he said: "No, I'm not crazy. Stupid maybe but not crazy."

When they were beside his car, he stopped and glanced back at the institute. "I'm not waiting until Saturday," he said. "Actually, I'd like to beat him down there. All I need is a half hour to go to my apartment and to make a quick stop in the medical library." He looked at her. "I'm going to let him try to get the surgery canceled. But if I need to, I'll get to Sanchez myself. And it won't be alone." Getting into his car, he added: "You might want to get a few phone numbers together. Maybe the people you mentioned in the office, and the American embassy in Mexico City. Just in case we need to call someone in a hurry. Listen, Lindsey, I can't let Ashton screw it up again." He reached out the window and gently squeezed her arm. "I'll call you as soon as I get to Mexico City. If Ashton wants to talk to me, tell him I'm in the operating room. Tell him my mother died, tell him anything you want. And check on DeLozier. He's crazy too."

* * *

Flight 390 from Dallas-Forth Worth to Mexico City hit the runway and bounced. Lauren Morick opened her eyes. She sensed a change—instead of the steady pressure of the hands on her back, little jolts were now coming through her arms, shifting her more upright. Suddenly she was turned completely around, and bright light filled her eyes. She moved her head in search of dark, but all she found was brilliant squares of sunlight, and her eyes closed. Without the light she was drowsy, and she slipped into the blackness.

Moments later her eyes opened again. She was being moved upward, being shifted one way, then the other. The voice—melodious now—was murmuring in her ear. The pressure around her shifted, and she was moved higher onto a shoulder. All, around her was a myriad of gray shapes, some stationary, some in motion. One came right up to her face, touched her cheek, breathed on her, made vaguely familiar noises. From behind her came the deeper voice she had heard from time to time. It was close, almost next to her head. Then she was moving and bouncing against the hard point of the shoulder.

Inside the terminal the light changed. Not as bright, but endless in every direction. Shapes loomed, grew small. The jumble of sounds she had come to recognize was louder than ever before. She was moving faster, riding up and down on the shoulder, her arm bumping and brushing against the indistinct forms next to her. The pressure tightened, and she was moved to the other shoulder, a slightly different feel of bone sticking into her abdomen. The deep voice came, and she was moving even faster. Then sudden bright sunlight made her shut her eyes; a din of horns, doors slamming, and yelling voices reverberated in her ears. She felt as though she were falling, and instinctively she reached out. But the sensation abruptly stopped as she was settled into a new position on the familiar form beneath her. A heavy thud vibrated both of them. Then the soft hand was stroking her head, and the voice was in her ear, light and playful. In front of her an engine roared to life. The car jerked forward and accelerated, pressing her against the warm, scented flesh.

Gallagher passed through the doors of the Baltimore-Washington International Airport and stepped to the side. Looking around tentatively, he let the incoming crowd flow past him. Not that he was afraid of running into Ashton—Lindsey had said he would be leaving from Dulles, and not for an hour or two. He was just unfamiliar with the airport's lobbies and passageways, and he liked strange terminals about as much as fecal impactions. Spotting the Eastern ticket counter, he moved ahead with one of DeLozier's corporate credit cards in hand.

He bought his ticket, kept his carry-on bag with him, and went to a computer screen showing departures. While waiting for his own flight, he had hoped to watch the boarding areas of any flights heading in the direction of Mexico. Who knows? he had said to himself several times on the drive over. Maybe he could end this now, with plenty of policemen around. But what seemed like a relatively simple idea was in fact overwhelming. In addition to several direct flights, there were numerous departures to multiple airports that connected to Mexico. He glanced at his watch. All he could do was watch the most direct flights. There were three before he was due to take off, and he headed for the farthest from his own boarding gate.

Ten minutes later that flight boarded without incident. He checked his notes and headed for the next, studying every passing face, every bundle that could be an infant. But there were so many that barely did he have time to scrutinize one before the next was only yards away. He gave that up and found the boarding area, where a baby was crying in the far corner. The cry escalated to a shrill scream, and heads began to turn. A woman stood and faced the wall, her shoulders swaying in a gentle rhythm. He moved—he stopped. Although he could see part of the woman's cheek, brown enough to make him wonder, just what was it he was going to do? he asked himself. Ask to see the infant? Call the police? A man looking as if he belonged with them approached with a diaper bag, and the woman put the baby down on a chair. Gallagher turned and headed for his own gate.

A flight attendant informed him that they would board in twenty minutes. He glanced at his schedule of departures, shoved it into a back pocket of his jeans, and began to look for a place to eat. He found a lounge and ordered a sandwich at the bar. Looking up from the menu, he saw a head moving in the mirror, realized it was his, and laughed. Not wanting to take the chance of Ashton changing is plans and spotting him before he had even reached Mexico, he had shaved off his mustache, slicked his hair back, and donned an old black John Deere baseball hat. The T-shirt he wore was also black, with the name of a rock group emblazoned across the front. His jeans were old, a little tight in the waist and thighs, but not too uncomfortable. The cowboy boots he had pulled from the back of the closet were gray imitation snakeskin. He grinned again and shook his head. He looked like holy hell.

His sandwich came. He began to eat, gazing at the television suspended from the ceiling behind the bar. It was a local station, with a perfectly made-up young blond woman speaking in a perfect voice, her words rising and falling with just the right amount of inflection. She flashed a quick smile, then an even quicker glance at her notes. Looking back into the camera, her voice took on a slightly more serious tone.

The news came to Gallagher gradually: ". . . was found early this morning on the Maryland side of the falls by a hiker. A police officer on the scene estimated that it had been there for at least two days and also said there was evidence of foul play. Although the body has not yet been positively identified, it is presumed to be that of Russell Wukich, the Laurel man who has been missing since Tuesday evening."

TWENTY-FOUR

Ashton passed through the arrival gate and into the loud, hectic Mexico City terminal in the early evening. He paused momentarily in the first lobby he came to, then quickly moved on. At first Gallagher thought he was looking for someone. But then the surgeon headed directly for an empty telephone stall. He dialed from memory and turned partially toward the wall. Across the lobby, his hat pulled down almost to his eyes, Gallagher moved to a better angle and took off his sunglasses. Ashton's lips were motionless. The surgeon hung up and dialed again. This time he spoke, the call lasting fifteen or twenty seconds. When it was over, he turned and gazed absentmindedly into the congestion moving past him. Then picking up his brief case, he headed for the ramps leading to the baggage-claim areas.

Gallagher, sunglasses back in place, his hands shoved into the pockets of his jean jacket, stayed well behind him as he forged through the crowd. He surgeon turned, passed through the gates to the baggage area, looked up at a board with red flashing flight numbers, and moved into the crowd ringing a conveyor belt. Gallagher moved behind a column thirty yards away. When Ashton's bag appeared a few minutes later, he watched him sling it over his shoulder and head deliberately down another corridor toward the ticket counters. He followed, easily keeping him in sight.

In the main lobby Ashton went to a bank of wall telephones. Twice he dialed; twice he hung up without completing the call. Gallagher felt himself getting angry. "You're the one who wanted to come by yourself," he said under his breath, "and you can't even find him. Now what are you going to?"

The surgeon crossed the lobby, fell into line at the Aeromexico counter, purchased a ticket, and crossed back to a restaurant. Gallagher watched him sit down and take a menu before he went to the same clerk and, describing Ashton, told her he needed a seat on the flight that his boss had booked. She looked at him warily, but tapped on her computer nonetheless. When she asked him for his credit card, he hesitated and said on second thought he needed to check something with his boss, who was right across the lobby in the restaurant. He turned a corner and called Lindsey Baines.

"He hasn't called yet," she said.

"Well, he goddamn better well soon. He's been on the phone ever since he got down here."

Lindsey was silent.

"Did you get a hold of DeLozier?"

"He called and wanted to know what was happening. I told him both of you had left and you'd check in with me as soon as you got to Mexico City. He said he's call back later."

"Did he say anything about calling the police?"

"No."

More silence. Then, "Okay," said Gallagher. "Stay in touch with him."

At eight-thirty Ashton left the restaurant and made another unsuccessful telephone call. Shaking his head in apparent disgust, he then headed for the departure gates and checked in at Gate 34: Aeromexico's Flight 119 from Mexico City to Acapulco. After speaking briefly with the flight attendant, he crossed the narrow lobby to a wall telephone.

Gallagher watched him dial and stay on the phone for almost two minutes. When the surgeon crossed back to the waiting area, he called Lindsey, hoping the man had finally checked in with her.

He had. "He can't find Carlos anywhere in the city," she said, "but he doesn't think he went to France. He's going to his beach house tonight. Apparently Carlos's new bimbette went there earlier this week. He said he called the beach house once, and the line was busy. He doesn't want to call again. I think he's afraid Carlos might run off."

"How do I find the beach house?"

"It's about thirty miles north of Acapulco. In a little fishing village called Las Gaviotas."

For a while Gallagher studied the brightly lit coastline with interest. Then, as they headed farther north and the glow of the beach grew dimmer, the traffic lighter, his eyes fixed on the road in front of them. When they were near what he calculated to be thirty miles north of Acapulco, he saw the flash of a small white sign and felt the taxi slow. They swerved toward the ocean, dipped once, and crested a hill that poised them magnificently in view of the dark ocean and star-ridden sky. Below them was a cluster of lights.

"Las Gaviotas," grunted the driver. He stopped the car and asked Gallagher for instructions.

Gallagher asked the man to take him to the house of Dr. Carlos Fernandez. The man balked. One of DeLozier's twenty-dollar bills landed on the front seat, and the taxi dipped down toward the lights, the driver calling up another driver on the radio. By the time they reached the edge of town, the other driver had radioed back with an address.

They passed through the village proper seeing only a few cars and pedestrians. Lights were blinking out on every street. The driver brought them out onto a narrow road, then turned again onto an even narrow gravel driveway. Gallagher requested he stop well away from the house, and the man slowed, pointing ahead to a group of lights near the ocean. Looking around at the dark road and houses, Gallagher motioned for him to drive back up the loop of road they had just come down.

When they were a hundred yards above the house, they pulled off the road and sat in the dark, the meter running. Intermittently a shadow passed through the faint yellow rectangles of light below, but there was no other sign of activity from the house, or from the one car in the driveway. The driver turned on the radio and rolled down the front windows. For a while, with the meter running and the soothing smells of saltwater and tropical flowers filtering by, the man seemed content to listen to the music and drum his fingers on the steering wheel. Then he began to get restless. This Dr. Fernandez, he finally said, tapping the side of his head, must be a very smart man. Tito, the driver who had given them the address, had said the doctor makes babies. He then patted the left side of his chest and added that Tito had also said the doctor was a fine man. The best.

Gallagher nodded and asked the man to take him to the closest rental-car agency.

*   *   *

On the porch of the hacienda, Carlos Fernandez imagined Richard Ashton sitting on the guest-bedroom balcony, pondering their telephone call. It was Richard's favorite spot in the beach house. On many occasions he had told him that whenever he thought or dreamed of visiting, it was of that balcony, that view, whether in shade from the powerful sun, or as it would now be, open to the brilliant western stars and tiny lights of ships miles out to sea. It was only fitting that he should sit there one more time in the early blackness.

Fernandez imagined his friend soon going to bed, or more likely walking the beach, hoping for some answer from the waves. For Richard, though, the waves would be silent. For himself, even the lapping of the pond near the graveyard would be full of life this night. Roberto was in Mexico. Roberto was on his way to Santa Maria, and Don Rafael—the promise of the glory of salvation—would have his chance to live and show the way.

Fernandez listened to the far-off howl of a dog, wondering if perhaps this night he should let Emilio and the waves help his old friend. But Rachel would be expecting to see him in the morning. Although she was a late riser, she would get up to see him off. Better to wait. He stepped off the porch and headed down the hard dirt path.

The last light in the house finally went out in the early morning. Gallagher waited a while longer, then crept close to inspect the chocolate brown Mercedes in the driveway. No bags—no sign of an imminent departure. He walked back down the driveway and up the winding gravel road. Starting his rented Fiat, he drove away hurriedly, the noise of the engine and the crunch of gravel grating in his ears. At the top of the cliff, he stopped to watch the spot of black where he knew the house was. It was still dark, with no sounds from below but the steady pounding of the waves. He drove out to the highway to find a telephone and a place to eat.

TWENTY-FIVE

The dawn was gray with the first traces of light when Gallagher heard the engine of the Mercedes catch. From his vantage point he could hear intermittent voices, including a woman's, but the words were lost in the mist. He heard the trunk open and close, followed by the solid thud of a door. Minute by minute the mist was lifting. Soon it would be clear enough to follow them. The little Fiat, rented for its unobtrusiveness, was his only concern. If they headed for the airport, there weren't many places they could lose him. But if they went north or east, toward the mountains, the car might not be up to the task. Turning on the engine, he drove to a point where he could watch them leave.

When the mist had cleared, the brown sedan backed out and headed for the ocean road. Through his roommate's binoculars—the sole previous use of which had been to compile Masterson's guide to North American cheerleaders—he could see that there were two figures in the car. But as the sedan climbed the road, he also saw that the driver was young, much younger than Fernandez could possibly be. A surge of anger filled him, and he moved to block the car's exit. Then he stopped just as quickly. The beach house had only been Ashton's best guess. But surely it was to Fernandez that they were headed. He let the car turn and pull out after it, feeling his hands tight on the wheel. The son-of-a-bitch should have let Lindsey know what was going on when he got to the house.

At the ocean rode the Mercedes turned north and rapidly picked up speed. Gallagher pressed hard on the accelerator. For several miles he was able to stay a comfortable distance behind, losing the car only once on a steep hill. But then the first sign for the highway that led northeast toward Mexico City appeared. He sped up, only to watch the Mercedes turn onto the highway and shoot ahead of a truck. The Fiat's gas pedal went to the floor—seventy-five, seventy-eight, eighty. It wasn't going to be good enough. The brown sedan passed a car and seemed to pick up more speed. A minute later it disappeared around a curve.

Gallagher slammed his steering wheel, slowed, and finally pulled off to the side of the road. For a while he sat still, staring at the black trail of asphalt winding around the foothill. When the highway was clear of cars, he cut across the median and headed back to the ocean road.

In Las Gaviotas he found a telephone booth and called Lindsey. She said Ashton hadn't called, but DeLozier had called several times wanting to know where they were and what was happening. He asked her to put him off as she could until he called back. He hung up and opened the telephone directory. "Fernandez CL" was one of three "Fernandez" listings.

A woman answered. "I'm sorry to bother you," Gallagher said in broken Spanish, "but I need to speak with Dr. Ashton. I'm Dr. Simpson, one of his associates. Do you speak English?"

"I do," said Rachel

"Good," said Gallagher, sounding relieved, "My Spanish is awful. Anyway, Dr. Ashton told me I could call him if it was necessary. I hate to do it, but I have no choice. One of his patients is rather ill."

"I'm afraid you just missed him. Would you like me to have him call you?"

"Well, what I'd really like to do is fax him some information on the case. You're outside of Acapulco, right? Do you know of a place nearby where I could do that?"

Rachel hesitated. "I don't believe he'll be coming back here."

"Darn. This is one of his *special* patients, if you know what I mean." Gallagher thought he heard a soft laugh.

"Unfortunately, I do. Richard and my husband seem to attract them. She paused, then said: they're meeting in Santa Maria later this morning. I don't know if the hotel can handle the fax, but you can at least leave Richard a message. The name of the hotel is Posada Las Palmas. You'll have to call information in Santa Maria for the number."

"I can handle that. Listen . . ."

"Mrs. Fernandez."

"Thanks a lot, Mrs. Fernandez. I hope I get to meet your husband one day. Richard says he's the best."

"Don't tell him that."

Gallagher chuckled. "Okay. Thanks again." He hung up, quickly called Lindsey, and then hurried for his car. Santa Maria is what he had hoped he would learn. But—halfway between Acapulco and Mexico City—it was hours away.

*   *   *

The soft, muted hum coming from in front of her was for the most part steady. From time to time, as it was now, it would vary in intensity, her sense of motion then changing as well. Suddenly both stopped altogether, and her head pressed against the shoulder. The soft voice came, the hand rubbing her back. The deep voice sounded, faded, disappeared. From beside her came aloud noise, then a rush of warm air. She was being lifted upward; the searing bright light was all around. Larger, firmer hands took hold of her, the fingers digging into her ribs. She was held still. Then she was back on the familiar bony shoulder and moving, feeling each of the woman's steps.

She heard strange sounds, saw an upright rectangle of darkness. A moment later the brightness was gone, the air around her was cool. Lauren looked over the shoulder. Some of the shapes—the bed, the chairs—fit patterns she had seen before. But nowhere was the form or scent, of what she instinctively searched for. Her lips and mouth felt rough, dry. Her throat burned. She began to cry. The sharp pain came. The blackness.

The hotel was an old brick structure, its walls pale and mottled from the years of direct sunlight. Surrounding it was a wide array of shrubs and flowers; around the grounds was a stone wall. Shortly before noon Ashton stepped out from under the awning that stretched from the front door to the bottom of the steps and shielded his eyes. Right behind him was a burly Hispanic man who ushered him out to the street. The two men stood together, the heavier one gesturing in a direction behind the hotel. Gallagher studied the unknown man through his binoculars and smiled. Maybe Ashton was on track—the man fit Lindsey's description of Carlos Fernandez right to his wide, irritating grin.

The two men spoke for another minute or so before the heavier one put his arm around Ashton and, smiling, seemed to shake him. Again Gallagher felt a surge of anger. Then, this time, anxiousness. What cause was there for gaiety? What had they learned? What were they doing? He moved out from the shade of a storefront across the street.

A moment later he stepped out to the sidewalk. He couldn't believe it. They were splitting up. He took another step, wanting to yell to Ashton. He started after him, but Fernandez was moving as well, apparently for a car parked across the street. By the time Gallagher reached his Fiat, Ashton was already in Plaza de las Monjas, heading for the central fountain. Gallagher stood by the car for several seconds with an eye on both men. He had to decide—he had to move. He thought it unlikely that Ashton was going to the neurosurgeon by himself, and at some point it was through him—this Dr. Sanchez—that Lauren had to pass. But where was Ashton going? What was the man up to, alone, in Santa Maria?

Fernandez stopped next to a silver Mercedes. The Mexican surgeon, he presumed, was going to Sanchez, whom he already knew worked in Santa Maria. From his time in the university medical library the day before, he also knew the location of the neurosurgeon's office and the two hospitals where he operated. He didn't need Fernandez for that. But what if Fernandez was headed to Lauren? What if . . .

In his peripheral vision he saw Ashton stop near the fountain. Watching the man, he shook his head in disgust, climbed into the Fiat, started the engine, and moved out into the street. Ashton, though he appeared to be studying the fountain, also seemed to have an eye on the street.

The silver sedan pulled out and turned at the first corner it came to. Gallagher followed but slowed at the corner to watch Ashton through his rearview mirror. As soon as Fernandez had turned, the surgeon had approached an old man sitting on a bench. The old man was now standing and motioning across the plaza. Gallagher crept forward, then sped around the corner as Ashton started off in the direction the man had pointed him. Hitting the gas pedal hard, he caught up with the Mercedes. But whatever relief he had had upon seeing the two doctors together was gone. Following the Mercedes through the narrow streets that spread out from Plaza de las Monjas like a crazed spider's web, he felt lost. The only consolation was that Ashton had called Lindsey in the late morning to say where he was. There was no reason to think he wouldn't call again. And whenever he was going, it probably wouldn't be for long. Even in October the midday sun was hot, and the fool wasn't even wearing a hat.

Fernandez turned onto Rio Elba, then picked up Paseo Primera in the opposite direction of Dr. Sanchez's office. When he was a few minutes from the house of Dr. Leonidas Valdez, he pulled into a gas station, stopped next to the public telephone, and made three calls. The first was to Dr. Valdez, an old friend, to request a moment of his time for a favor he would ask. The second was to the nursing station that controlled Hospital San Pedro's operating rooms. He had operated there on several occasions as a visiting professor, and the nurse who answered the phone recognized his name.

"Yes, Dr. Fernandez," she said, "the neurosurgical room is open in the morning. Dr. Sanchez is out of town and isn't due back until Monday."

Fernandez said he was aware of that, that he and Dr. Sanchez had been keeping in close touch, and that he would be talking with him shortly. He asked her to schedule the room for an emergency case in the morning. "There's a transplantation Dr. Sanchez has been waiting to do," he explained, "and because of a tragic accident, the tissue has just become available." They spoke a little longer before he hung up and dialed again. Now he really did need to speak to Gustavo Sanchez.

Slouched in the Fiat, Gallagher watched Fernandez hang up for the third time. Smiling, the man climbed into his Mercedes and merged into the traffic on Paseo Primera. Gallagher let several cars go past before he pulled oat after him. Fernandez turned west on Paseo de Montejo and picked up speed. For the next several blocks, however, the traffic was impenetrable, and the Mercedes moved from lane to lane, searching for an opening. Suddenly it veered off down a side street. Gallagher accelerated but immediately had to slow as a truck ahead of him came to a stop. By the time he reached the side street, the Mercedes was almost out of sight. He gunned the engine and made up half the distance. The Mercedes turned again. Half a block behind he followed easily.

They passed Hospital San Pedro and crossed Avenida Santa Cecilia. Away from the major intersection, the traffic lightened, and Gallagher let the sedan creep ahead. A moment later he sped up as he saw a group of schoolchildren stop at the curb ahead of him. Fernandez raced past them. The woman leading the children shook her head at his car and stepped forward. The Mercedes turned at the same time, and Gallagher stopped short as the children filled into the street behind the woman. He backed up and cut around the block. The silver sedan was nowhere in sight.

At the next intersection he pulled over to the side. For a minute he stayed there, studying his map between quick glances up and down the street. Then when a disconcerted shake of his head, he turned and made a wide loop through the streets, hoping to catch Fernandez if he was doubling back. Fifteen minutes later he headed for Posada las Palmas.

The front of the hotel was deserted. The old man, still on the bench next to the fountain, was the only person he could see in the plaza. He parked, took off his hat and sunglasses, put on good shoes, and strode purposefully over to the old man. With hand motions and broken Spanish, he described Ashton and asked him if he had seen the doctor pass through the plaza.

"The professor?" said the man in Spanish.

"Yes," said Gallagher, "the professor."

"Ah," said the man, followed by a sentence Gallagher couldn't understand. After several repetitions he realized that the man was speaking about the local medical school. He thanked them, got the same directions that Ashton had, and headed that way.

As soon as he was out of the old man's sight, he doubled back to a small restaurant on a diagonal across from Posada las Palmas. He called Lindsey from the pay phone. She said Ashton had called twenty minutes before to say that Fernandez was meeting Sanchez that afternoon. She hadn't heard from DeLozier for several hours, since she had told him that Ashton was to meet Fernandez that morning and everything seemed to be on track. When DeLozier had wanted to know where they were, she had only said near the town where Sanchez works.

Gallagher took a seat at an outside table in the shade of the awning. The entrance to Posada las Palmas across the street was in full view, as was most of Plaza de las Monjas and several of the side streets that fed into the loop of asphalt encircling the plaza. The waiter came. He ordered a light lunch and waited, his binoculars in his lap.

In the midafternoon Ashton came out of a narrow street from the direction of the medical school. With out stopping the surgeon disappeared into the hotel. Gallagher called Lindsey. No new messages.

Three hours later he watched Ashton step outside. The surgeon looked up and down the street, then all around the plaza. He was nervous, Gallagher thought. Most likely because Fernandez should have been back by now. Or he had heard something about Lauren. His stomach tightened.

Ashton went back inside. Gallagher ordered another bottle of mineral water and debated his options. There weren't many. And most of them depended on whether Fernandez came back—on whether Ashton still seemed to be on track, or if the man was lost.

Which he was beginning to wonder about in light of the calls Fernandez could have just as easily made from the hotel. He decided at least to give Ashton the full day in Mexico that he had asked for. And which he himself had agreed to. The man knew that everything important in his life was at stake. At some point he would have to be trusted.

The sun had all but set, in its final minutes of descent splaying stripes of red and blue across the brick and gardens of the plaza, when he stood. A deep shade quickly enveloped the surrounding streets. As it progressed to dusk, he called Lindsey. Ashton had called at six and was supposed to call back between nine and ten, she said. He was waiting for Fernandez to return from his meeting with Sanchez. Gallagher was quiet for a moment, then hung up.

He moved for the deep shadow of the stone wall enclosing the hotel grounds. And as the night grew darker, the pedestrians fewer, the angrier he became. He was counting on Ashton, for so many things, and it infuriated him that the man had made this error in judgment. For if Fernandez was as scared as Ashton had said he was, the son-of-a-bitch should have never let him out alone. He glanced at his watch—it was five after ten. One more time he studied the front awning, the sidewalks, the street. Then he moved for the restaurant and the telephone, suspecting that Ashton had now left him no choice.

Several blocks from Posada las Palmas, Fernandez stepped into a bar and made a light supper of *antojitos*. Although he was not hungry, he forced himself to eat. With everything in place it was going to be a long night, most likely without time for a proper meal. The only problem was Richard. But neither he nor Roberto had the time this night to take care of him. Don Rafael was worse by the hour, and he could not be allowed to slip away. He must live! He must seize this opportunity to show the way, and to see how wrong he was. And if he could not, if he was not strong enough, or finally willing to see his second son, then, and only then, could he pay with his life. Fernandez looked at his hands. The bottle between them was moving uncontrollably. He drained it and ordered another.

Shortly he stepped to the telephone in the back of the bar. Richard could meet Emilio one more time, he'd decided. It was the least he could do for his friend. Although Emilio was good, he would be much kinder than his cousin, Roberto Veracruz.

"Where the hell have you been?" answered Ashton.

"This is not an easy task, my friend. The family will just as soon stake out Sanchez as you or me. But it's done."

"The surgery's canceled?"

"At last. You are a clever man. Sick, but clever. You should have seen his face when he realized the surrogate must have gotten infected when she was pregnant."

"What'd he say?"

"*Nada.* What's there to say? There's no point in trading one disease for another. He knows better than us that the AIDS virus often concentrates in neural tissue. It's a perfect story."

"So now what?"

"The baby will be returned to you tomorrow morning in Mexico City. Emilio will take you. You're to be in the parking lot of the café across from my office at seven. I need to stay with Sanchez. He's petrified."

Ashton was silent.

"What's the matter, Richard?" said Fernandez angrily. "I have risked my life for this . . . problem that I too was forced into, and now you have lost your tongue? *Madre de Dios!*"

"Everything's great, Carlos. Calm down. What do you want me to do?"

"Wait there. Emilio will come for you within the hour."

TWENTY-SIX

Gallagher hurried down Calle Quiroz, parallel to the short block that held Posada las Palmas. At the corner of Rio Balsas he turned and headed for the rear door of the hotel. It was ten-fifteen. Lindsey hadn't heard from Ashton, and they had both agreed it was time to check in with him. Now he was wondering what to do once he did. Other than taking the risk of scaring Fernandez or Sanchez, the choices were the same: keep on, or call the State Department or the FBI. The hotel came into sight, then Ashton on the sidewalk outside the rear gate, hands in his pockets, staring off at some point over the horizon. Gallagher stopped short in the wide shadow of a magnolia tree. A car passed. Ashton didn't move, didn't seem to notice it.

A minute later the surgeon began to walk slowly around the hotel. Near the front he cut through an alley, came out on the street that paralleled the west side of Posada las Palmas, and made his way into the plaza. For a while he stood at the foot of the fountain, staring at the rolls of water dripping into the lily pads. Then he moved to a bench and stared some more. Shortly he stood and headed for Calle Tercera, the side street he had come out of that afternoon. Halfway down the block he entered a restaurant.

Gallagher advanced close enough to the front window to see into the well-lit vestibule. Ashton was at a wall telephone, his head tilted down and toward the wall as though he were in the midst of a private conversation. Before long he hung up, and Gallagher backpedaled up the sidewalk to an alley. A minute later, with no sign of him, Gallagher returned to the window. Ashton was talking again, his back to the sidewalk. Gallagher watched him for a moment before stepping back and surveying the narrow, semi-residential street. Fifty yards away was the dark shadow of a recessed retaining wall. With one eye on the restaurant doorway, he moved for it until a dog barked, and he veered off to the other side of the street. The dog barked even louder, followed by a solid thud, a yelp, and then silence. Smiling, he walked up to the porch of a guest house, where he pretended to study a map.

Several minutes later Ashton exited and, glancing at his watch, paused on the brick sidewalk. Gallagher stepped back farther on the porch, the soft breeze bringing him the loosed scent of fried meat. He heard the car turn into the street. He heard it accelerate, and before he was conscious of moving, he was off the porch and running for the sidewalk. But after only few yards, realizing that he wasn't going to get to the street in time, he pulled up and turned in a frantic circle, searching for a throwable object. All he saw was a potted plant at the end of the walkway to the guest house. He ran for it, grabbed it, and with a big underhanded swing and a loud yell, let it fly for the street. The dark sedan—the one that Ashton had left in that morning?—was only twenty yards away when the pot landed, close enough that he could see the driver's silhouette. The car never slowed. Zeroed in on the sidewalk fronting the restaurant, it crunched the cracked pot into little pieces as though it were a twig. But with the noise Ashton had looked up, and after appearing to be rooted into the sidewalk, hew now leapt for the restaurant's steps and rolled. The car jumped the sidewalk, swerved, careened back down into the street, and bounced sideways. Screeching around the corner, the sounds of its exit filled the air for several long seconds. Then the street was quiet.

Staring at the motionless form on the steps, Gallagher was sure Ashton was dead. He took several steps toward him and stopped. Heads were poking out through windows and doors. He looked up and down the street, seeing himself as the locals must, and he had a sudden urge to run. When he looked back to the restaurant, Ashton was up and almost out of sight. A moment later the surgeon darted into the black opening of an alley.

Gallagher started to walk. Calmly at first, as though he were out for an evening stroll. Then faster and faster until he was running. After several blocks, his head pounding, he stopped and turned around to listen for voices or footsteps. He heard none and took off again, this time cutting back through the streets toward the hotel, the direction in which he thought Ashton had reflexively headed. Outside the front door of Posada Las Palmas he stopped to catch his breath and wipe the sweat from his face. When he thought he could talk without pausing, he went to the desk and asked for Ashton's room number. On the second floor he pounded on the door for a full minute. He waited for two more in the hall. Then once more he headed for the restaurant telephone.

*   *   *

The deep gnawing sensation in her stomach awakened her. Her lips puckered and sucked. All she felt was their dryness. She opened her eyes. All she saw was darkness, and she started to cry. Someone rose from a chair beside the bed and picked her up. In his arms she only cried more. He reached for a bottle and tried to put the nipple into her mouth. With each crying breath she spit it out. For another minute he tried to calm her. Then he carried her into the next room and put her into different arms.

Baby girl Lauren seemed to recognize the woman who walked her up and down the room, and for a while her cries slowed. But then the gnawing sensation grew stronger, and she started to scream. One short shrill burst after another filled the room. The woman took her into the bedroom and closed the door. Sitting on the edge of the bed, she rocked Lauren back and forth.

But Lauren wouldn't stop crying, and the man came in with a syringe. The woman shook her head.

She finally got the nipple into Lauren's mouth. Lauren sucked on it, her face red, her swollen eyes shut tight. The man watched them for a moment. Then he went into the other room and called the laboratory.

"Jesus, Brendan, I've been calling that restaurant every five minutes looking for you." Lindsey's voice was strained, almost ready to break.

"Why? Did he call? This is unbelievable. Somebody just tried to kill him."

"He called ten minutes ago. He said he wanted you to come right away. I didn't tell him where you were, but I did tell him that you had left this afternoon. He's expecting you—"

"What's going on, Lindsey? I don't think we have much time."

"Jesus, Brendan . . . I don't know what to tell you. First he says everything's okay and that he's going to get the baby in the morning. Apparently Carlos got Sanchez to cancel the surgery. Then he says you have to come because he's not sure he believes Carlos. He thinks Sanchez has him scared to death. *Then* he says the surgery really isn't canceled. At least not yet. He called the operating room, and as far as they know, it's still on for eight o'clock tomorrow morning. At Hospital San Pedro."

"Eight o'clock tomorrow morning," Gallagher said softly.

"Right. Which means—"

"They have to harvest the tissue tonight."

She was silent for a moment. Then: "Richard wants you to go to Sanchez's lab and watch it until he gets there. That's where he thinks they'll do it. Obviously they can't do it in the hospital. I have the address. He got it from one of Sanchez's research papers that he looked up this afternoon."

"Then what?"

"I don't know. He just said he'd meet you there after he goes to the hospital and makes sure the surgery's canceled. He said one way or another he'd take care of that."

"You've got to be fucking kidding me! Did he say anything about getting help?"

"He said you and DeLozier had to decide that."

"Where's DeLozier?"

"I don't know. He hasn't called back. I tried to reach him a little while ago, but he's not at any of the numbers he gave me."

Gallagher was quiet. Finally he said: "Look—call the State Department, the FBI, whoever. I don't care. Just get us some help as fast as you can. Send them to the lab. I don't have time to go to the police now, and I don't want them to hold me up while . . . she may be in there."

"I agree. I have all the numbers. I was just waiting to talk to you."

"Jesus Christ. Gimme the address of the lab."

"Be careful," she said a minute later. "I still want that lunch."

Ashton pushed out through the swinging double doors of the operating-room nursing station and found an elevator. In the thirty creaking seconds it took to climb four more floors, he removed the small canvas carrying case from his coat and prepared its contents. Then, in the order he hoped to choose one from, he replaced the syringes in an inner pocket. There were three: the first two with enough potassium to kill five men; the third, empty, but capped with a five-inch needle that would effortlessly slip between the man's ribs and puncture his heart.

The light blinked at number seven, and the doors opened. He was in a hall with only one way to go.

Turning a corner, he saw the sole entrance to a patient ward. "The ward reserved for dignitaries," the nurse at the operating-room desk had said. Moving back to gather himself, he heard the door to the ward open, followed by footsteps and the thud of the door closing. On the other side of the elevators, another door—probably a stairwell, he thought—opened, then clinked shut. He stepped to the door leading into the ward and opened it.

A desk in the hall blocked the entrance but for a narrow passageway. Empty coffee cups and magazines spoke of recent occupancy, but there was no one in the area. He took a step, then stopped as a woman's wail came from down the hall. A moment later several men and an old woman rushed out into the corridor. As the woman's wails deteriorated into sobs, the men turned to each other with escalating oaths and hand motions. Ashton inched closer, hoping to get down the hall in the confusion. But with one glimpse of his coat and bag, the old woman pointed inside the room and spoke to him pleadingly in Spanish.

He was quickly beside a nurse and a woman of middle age, who was holding the hand of what appeared to be a dead man. First he checked him for an intravenous catheter. There was one, but he doubted that this man would need any help from him. His face was gaunt and drawn stiff in the frozen fix of advanced Parkinson's disease; his arms were thin tubes of sagging flesh. He started to turn away, but then looked back. Something was awry. He studied the man more closely. The angle of his head was all wrong. It was arched back, as if caught irrevocably in a painful death gasp. And his eyes. Although they were clearly those of a sick man, they did not have the look of final acceptance common to the terminally ill. They were surprised, almost bug-eyed. They were also motionless.

He bent over the man's blue gray lips and turned his own cheek, waiting for a brush of air. Feeling none, he lifted a bony wrist. The nurse said she thought the patient had just died, and the old woman who had come back into the room sobbed harder. All Ashton could understand at the end was the name Sanchez.

"I think you should call Dr. Sanchez," he said. "I'm sure he will want to be here. This man has died."

The old woman threw herself over the end of the bed. Letting go of the sick man's hand, the other woman turned to comfort her. The nurse said she would notify Dr. Sanchez and turned to the phone.

Ashton removed one of the syringes and placed it in his side pocket. With all the distractions it had been hard to tell if there was still the barest trace of a pulse or not. He encircled the man's wrist again, was still unsure, and reached into his side pocket. But the nurse was suddenly beside him, saying that Dr. Sanchez was being called at home. The old woman rose from the bed and pleaded to him, then fell back down and prayed to God.

"No," said Ashton, shaking his head. And for the first time he saw the other woman face to face. He guessed she was a few years older than he, but none of the years had dimmed the beauty he somehow recognized. Unable to take his eyes off her face, he stared, feeling the anger and hurt rise up uncontrollably. It was. It was Felice, Carlos's beloved, indispensable older sister, whose younger face, in the photograph on his desk, had accompanied her brother from Paris to Mexico City. He stared at her a moment longer, the fact that it had all been lies slowly sinking in. *Everything was lies.* The "dignitary" who had to be saved, the threats from "the family," Carlos's sudden appearance during the appointment with Billie Williams and the Moricks, the "follow-up" note he had wanted to send, mentioning the Moricks by name no less—it was all lies, it was all part of some insane, grotesque plan.

"Richard," Felice Fernandez was saying with a sad smile. "You are a good friend. Carlos will need you today."

Ashton looked away, silent. He glanced at the woman draped over the sick man's legs. He had seen her only once before, ten years ago when she had come, without Carlos's father to see her brilliant son graduate from the European Institute of Fertility in Paris.

"Felice, tell your mother that Don Rafael has died," he said. "We cannot save him."

Felice nodded and knelt down next to her mother, who had broken into still louder cries. Just to make sure, Ashton reached for his syringe and inserted the needle into the intravenous tubing.

The phone rang. The nurse answered it and spoke for a moment before she returned to the bed. "Dr. Sanchez is still away," she said. "The hospital operator doesn't think he's coming back until just before the surgery. We have a number where he can be reached. Do you want me to inform him of the death?"

"Please," said Ashton softly, remembering the years Carlos had trained as a surgeon before entering the field of fertility. And then the rest was clear: yes. Sanchez probably was planning to perform the surgery, but he most likely had no idea where the tissue was coming from. What neurosurgeon in his right mind would ever come near . . .

Felice was talking. ". . . thought he was with my brother," she finished, looking curiously at the nurse. The nurse shrugged helplessly, and Felice turned to Ashton with a little shake of her head. "It doesn't matter. He'll get the message when the priest sees Carlos, We're so fortunate he came when he did. Otherwise Papa would have died without his last rites."

Nodding, Ashton withdrew the syringe and started to move away. But Felice was still talking. He turned to her in time to catch the last of her words: ". . . he's just visiting from the States. I think he's leaving Santa Maria tomorrow."

Ashton looked at her blankly for a moment. Then he looked down at her father's head and eyes and neck. "When was the priest here, Felice?"

Tears finally escaped from her. "He left after he gave Papa his last rites," she said, wiping her eyes. "Papa died right afterward. They both must have known it was time."

"Did you say the priest is just visiting Santa Maria?"

She nodded. "He's blessing all the patients who are having surgery in the morning. But when he saw Papa, he was worried about him."

"How long was he here?"

"Ten, maybe fifteen minutes."

"Was he alone with your father?" Ashton said. "I'm just wondering if he could give a time of expiration for the death certificate."

"They were alone for a few minutes so Papa could make a last confession. That was only a few minutes ago. He left just before you got here."

Ashton nodded. "Maybe we can talk to him later." He moved to the bed, took hold of the bed sheet, and pulled it up to Don Rafael's neck as though he were just tidying him up. But even from a foot away, now that he was looking for it, he could see the wide stripe of pinkish skin where the band of pressure had been around the man's neck.

He straightened and began to back away. "Do you know where Carlos is?" he said to Felice. "I'd like to be with him now. It might be best if you stayed with your mother."

"Yes, but the priest said he would tell him to come to the hospital right away."

"I'm sure the priest being there when Carlos hears the news will help. But . . . I'm his friend. It's not the same."

She nodded. "He's at Dr. Valdez's laboratory. That's where the doctor from Mexico City is bringing the donation. I guess they had to prepare it there."

"Where's the laboratory?"

Hardly had she finished giving him the street name and directions when he was backpedaling for the door. He walked to the end of the hall, ran for the stairwell, and took the steps three at a time to the lobby. The same young woman was at the reception desk. Out of breath, he asked her to call him a cab. Then, thinking that maybe someone could take him in an ambulance, he asked her where the emergency room was. He took a step toward the emergency room and paused as one of the doors to the lobby flew open. Gallagher ran in, looking around as he went. When he was in the middle of the domed foyer, he stopped short.

"Godammit!" said Ashton. "Why'd you tell him about Sanchez?"

"Who?"

"*DeLozier*, who else? Now he's gone after him *and* Carlos."

"*You* told him! You said his name in your office. Every medical library in the world has books listing specialists and where they work. Anybody with half a . . . Why'd *you* send me off on a wild-goose chase? Sanchez's lab is locked and dark as hell. Now what? What the hell have you been doing?"

"Do you have a car?"

Gallagher was still nodding when Ashton bolted for the door, urging the younger man to "hurry the hell up." But out on the stone steps, Ashton suddenly stopped. Turning around, he stared up at the upper stories of the old hospital. "Wait a minute," he said. "I'll be right back."

TWENTY-SEVEN

Stepping from the rear entrance of the lab into the scrub room, then into the operating room, Carlos Fernandez felt his steps light and sure. Shortly he would be given seed—in a matter of hours Don Rafael would grow new life and lead the way. And he would watch his mother and Felice, as though it were a new field of corn or young coffee trees. It was the simplest of circles. Seed to tree, tree to flower, flower to seed, seed to life. For a moment he watched the flower cling to Josefina. Then he stepped out to begin a preparatory scrub. Now it was all so simple.

He took hold of the handle on the sink. His hand—moving back and forth, back and forth—slipped away. Cursing it, he went out the back door to his car and took a drink of whiskey. He felt it hot in his belly, felt it flow through him like fire. He brought the bottle in with him and began to scrub.

In the bright operating room, he took the flower into his arms. It squirmed, and he calmed it with a prick in its thigh. When it was limp, he laid it on the table and studied it. It was so beautiful, so full of life, so perfect. For Don Rafael it was . . . good enough. He took a bag of intravenous fluid, hung the bag and the tubing by the table, and took hold of a catheter. The catheter shook uncontrollably as he prepared to puncture the big vein in the flower's arm, and he steadied his hands on its belly. Finally he slid the catheter into the vein.

He took a razor and shaved off the flower's hair. Roberto brought him a basin of orange fluid, and he scrubbed its head in ever-widening circles, over and over, oblivious now to the rhythmic jerking of the sponge. While he worked, Roberto prepared the saw, the trays of instruments, the anesthesia machines, the canisters of liquid nitrogen to freeze whatever tissue would not be taken to the hospital. Just how much would go to Sanchez now, he had not yet decided. Certainly enough for Don Rafael to lead the way. But not one cell more.

When they were done, he turned the flower onto its belly and buckled straps across its shoulders and legs. Then he studied the back of its head, chanting to himself: "He loves me, he loves me not. One little cell for you, and one for me. One for you and *more* for me."

Roberto handed him a mask for the flower to breathe through. He placed the mask over its mouth and nose. He felt its muscles go even limper. The room was light, so wonderfully light and airy. Everything was clear and beautiful. He paused, wondering if he were ascending to . . . He heard noise—knocking—from the front of the lab. One of the operating-room doors was cracked open. "There's a priest here," said Manuel. "He says he needs to speak with you."

Dr. Valdez's laboratory was in a two-story rectangular brick building on Paseo de Montejo, a mile from Hospital San Pedro. There were two cars parked out front, as well as dim light showing through the first-story windows. Gallagher parked away from the other cars and looked at Ashton.

"There's no other choice," said the older man. "I can't wait out here. You can, or you can go call Lindsey or whoever and tell the police to come here instead of Sanchez's. I understand."

Gallagher shook his head. "We don't have time for that. He could be cracking her head right now." A cream-colored Audi 5000 sedan pulled in beside them. Its lights flicked off, the engine died.

"Then let the two of us go in. If one of us can't reason with him . . ."

"You can't reason with him if he's dead. That green car over there is a rental."

Ashton looked at him. "What do you want me to do, Brendan?"

Gallagher shook his head and opened the car door. Without responding he waited for Felice to join them.

They walked up the sidewalk silently. Just before the front step, the two men peeled off to either side and flattened themselves around the corners of the short walls that projected from either side of the door. Startled, Felice stepped back and looked at Ashton curiously; then suspiciously.

"Knock on the door, Felice. I want to surprise him."

She hesitated.

"Please knock on the door. We have to talk to Carlos *now.*"

She frowned, glanced around her, and knocked.

Gallagher saw a shadow coming toward the front window, and he moved closer to the building. Pressing up hard against the rough wall, he heard the blinds rattling, then footsteps. The door opened. A man began to respectfully address Felice, and Ashton pushed her through, with Gallagher right behind them.

They were in a small lobby, Gallagher registering the scene as though it were coming to him from isolated frames of slow-moving film: a short, scarred Mexican man, totally confused, was stepping back; a taller man behind him was conferring with a priest—DeLozier; DeLozier, taking them in at first, then reaching under his jacket; the Beretta, suddenly in the taller man's face.

Felice gasped; Roberto stepped back. "What is going—" Roberto started to say, but then turned to retreat as DeLozier pushed the gun at him shouting: "He's dead, I tell you! The man is dead!"

"Stop!" Roberto roared. "What is this madness! You come in here—"

"Listen to him!" said Ashton, stepping forward. "The priest is right—Don Rafael is dead. He passed away in his sleep only minutes ago. The hospital is trying to reach Dr. Sanchez so that the surgery can be canceled. I want to talk to Carlos. He's my friend. Tell him that Richard and his sister want to see him."

Roberto was studying Ashton when DeLozier moved toward the back corridor.

"Stop!" Roberto again, his face pale, his eyes flicking from DeLozier to the others. "What in God's name are you talking about?"

DeLozier moved forward, and Roberto blocked his way.

"Wait!" said Ashton to DeLozier. He looked at Roberto. "Listen to me! There has been a horrible mistake. We all know that. Don Rafael is dead. Carlos has no need for the baby. And if we're allowed to leave with her, the moment we step out this door, it'll all he forgotten. We'll be on a plane home this morning.

Roberto looked to be debating Ashton's words, but then they all heard the footsteps down the hall. Roberto turned toward the door, and Delozier lunged for him, bringing the gun up to his face. "Get out of my way!" he shouted, and pushed past him. He ran down the hall and into the back of the laboratory toward a set of double doors. Pushing through, he stopped short only feet inside the room, followed by Gallagher and Ashton. DeLozier pointed the Beretta once at Roberto and Manuel, and they pulled up, looking hesitantly from the operating room to Felice down the hall.

The room was ready for surgery, the trays of instruments neatly laid out around the head of the empty but sheeted table. A young woman was in one corner of the room trying to hide. Lauren was no where to be seen.

Gallagher glanced once at the woman, then quickly around the room. A line of plastic intravenous tubing was hanging off the side of the operating table, clear fluid still dripping out of its tapered end. The sheet beneath where it had been yanked out was spotted with fresh blood. Below the sheet on the floor were strands of short, fine brown hair. But the skull saw next to the table was clean, the suctioning tubes and basin empty. He ran for the side entrance to the operating room, saw that the scrub room was deserted, and yanked on the rear door. Exiting onto a cement landing he took two more steps and leapt for the burly man who was holding Lauren in one arm, and fumbling with the door of the silver Mercedes with the other. He caught him ten yards out into the street. Climbing onto his back, he slowed him, all the while yelling: "He's dead! Your father's dead! He died in the hospital! You don't need her!

Fernandez lumbered on, Lauren pinned to his side. Gallagher wrapped a forearm around his throat and squeezed. The big man gasped, staggered, and dropped the infant to the pavement as he reached for Gallagher's arm.

DeLozier scooped her up and ran past before he stopped to look at her. She was motionless, but breathing.

Gallagher and Fernandez fell wrestling to the street. As they rolled, Fernandez kicked the young man away and came up on his knees holding a wildly shaking arm.

"No, Carlos!" yelled Roberto, coming to a stop next to him. "Don Rafael is dead. He died in his sleep."

Felice ran up and went to hold her brother's head, but he lurched upward screaming: "You fools! Give me that baby! It's mine. We are one!" He stepped in the direction of DeLozier, and Ashton jumped in between them, yelling for him to stop.

"Richard!" Fernandez bellowed. "Don't do—"

ashton lunged for him, and Fernandez's hand came up, followed by a loud explosion that seemed to rock Ashton still. Then Fernandez's mouth fell open, and blood oozed from the hole in his neck. Ashton and Gallagher turned to see DeLozier, Lauren cradled in his left arm, his right hand trembling from the weight of the Beretta.

Fernandez began to jerk on the pavement, and Ashton knelt down to take one of his hands. Felice, her hands to her face moaning, slowly bent down, then reached for the other. Looking up at them, Fernandez tried to speak, but his efforts brought forth only bloody spittle, and he closed his eyes. "Forgive me," he finally managed. "I . . . did not want to hurt either of you. Try . . . to understand. That . . . that . . . that match was mine." A slight shudder ran through his body, and his breaths stopped.

For a moment all of them were still. Then Roberto stepped in, moved Ashton aside, and spoke softly to Felice. Bending down to lift Fernandez onto his shoulder, he staggered up and trudged over to the silver Mercedes. He dropped the body in the backseat, spoke briefly to the man who had opened the front door, got into the car, backed out, and turned up the side driveway. The other man waited for Felice to finish speaking with Ashton, then held the rear door of the lab open for her.

The Mercedes was screeching around the front of the building when Gallagher started for his car. He could hear Ashton and DeLozier yelling at him, but all he could think about was somehow diverting the police. Suddenly he stopped. Turning, he was transfixed for a second by the headlights that had just rounded the corner at the other end of the building. Then, even before he saw them accelerate, he was running once more.

DeLozier was running as well, but with the building on one side, and a high ledge and fence on the other, there was no place to go but down the alley. He made it to Gallagher, put Lauren into the younger man's outstretched arms, and wheeled to face the car as though it were some animal charging him. He planted his feet and crouched, the Beretta held away from his body between a hand and a white paw. One, two, three rounds crashed through the windshield. He squeezed off one more shot before the car hit him, sending him feet first into the air and onto the hood. The vehicle came to a quick stop, and DeLozier flew forward into the street. Roberto backed up, looked at Gallagher without expression, and maneuvered the car around DeLozier's head. Once more he turned the corner.

Ashton ran to the fallen man. After a moment he straightened and shook his head. Before he could speak, the faint sound of a siren came to them.

"Get out of here, Brendan," he said. "Get the baby home. I'll take care of this."

Gallagher began to move away, aware that Ashton was still talking to him.

"Remember," he was saying, "I could have had that fetus. One way or another, I could have caused her to abort."

The siren was near, and Gallagher picked up his pace. Lauren Morick was waking up.

EPILOGUE

The plane was on a steady ascent, the engine noise barely audible. Leaning back in his seat, he could feel the steady respiratory rhythm of the baby's chest against his own. He opened his eyes to look down at her. She was asleep, her face to him. He could see the fading forceps bruise on her forehead, the near-perfect lips and Cupid's bow. Suddenly her eyes opened, and she blinked. He smiled at her, watching his reflection in her eyes until her lids drooped, then shut.

He put his head back as the plane leveled out. He was exhausted, wanted to sleep, but the faces kept coming. With them were the words, the little pieces of this nightmare, spoken and unspoken. Ashton had been taking eggs for years, using the symbols in his records to track how many he had retrieved, how many had been fertilized, how many he had given away, and to whom. Mainly they were eggs left over after a successful fertilization, eggs that had been frozen as "backups." Mainly they had been given to researchers. Lindsey had more or less told him so in Garret's, but he hadn't put it together. Talking about Ashton's research, she had said; "I've heard him complain for years about not being able to study embryos and fetuses in more detail. 'That's where the answers are,'" she had said, imitating his voice and hand motions. "'If the goddamn politicians want cures, then they have to let us start at the beginning.'"

But from time to time, Ashton had intentionally gathered too many eggs, usually from patients who hadn't

277

given him permission to freeze them. And from time to time, he had known quite well that they weren't being used for research. For that he could not be forgiven.

Lauren stirred as they went through some turbulence. Stroking her head, Gallagher repositioned the both of them. He closed his eyes and forced his mind blank. But there was nothing to stop the flow. Everywhere there where faces, notes suppositions. Billie Williams's sweating gray visage loomed large, then faded as her husband appeared. Buck Williams: hateful and heartbroken, but rich with Fernandez's bribe to drop the lawsuit, which would have been tantamount to an investigation of *all* the Moricks' records. Wukich quickly followed. Wukich, with two fatherless sons.

He shut his eyes tighter and tried again. He imagined going home to see his family at Thanksgiving; he made a mental list of the work at St. Joseph's he had to catch up on. It was no use. Ashton's many poses came at him in dizzying succession, followed by the circles—open ones, dark ones, ones slashed dead. And he had seen only a fraction of them. Where were they? Where were all the circles now? Some were buried. But the others? Where were the open ones, the unfertilized eggs? Were they also long dead? Or were one, or two, or twenty alive and . . .

He opened his eyes, stared straight ahead. And now what in the name of God was he to do? Abandon Ashton? Support him? True, the man had not capitulated to Fernandez—he had never intended the nightmare he had helped initiate. Lauren moved, and he held her tight. He could take no more. Pushing all else away, he thought of Lindsey. Slowly his mind cleared. He fell asleep.

The jolts of the wheels smacking rock-hard concrete awakened her. She blinked, again and again, until the brightness faded. Suddenly she was turned over, the firm pressure shifting from her back to her arms. The shape above her matched a pattern that she had seen before, and she studied it, her mind sorting out the curves, the shades of lights and darks, the way it moved. A blanket fell over her, and she was turned again. For a brief moment all motion stopped. Then from all around her, shapes were rising, voices were crisscrossing above her. Sudden pressure, and she was moving upward, her face coming to rest on rough cloth, her body against another at a familiar angle.

She was moving, bouncing and turning with the force beneath her. The voices softened, almost quit altogether. For several seconds there was nothing but a rhythmic padding from the floor. Then a wave of noise washed over her. Voices came from every direction, in all tones and cadences. She lifted her head, searching for the sounds she had recognized. They came again, closer and louder. Her eyes opened wide. A short gurgle escaped. The familiar smell was all around her, the comforting grip clutching her hard against the sweet scent of familiar flesh. She heard the pounding, faster than she had ever heard it, but somehow the same. She cried once. Her head moved against the soft cloth. She closed her eyes and fell asleep.

AUTHOR'S NOTE

Fetal-tissue transplantation as a treatment for advanced Parkinson's disease, a progressive and debilitating neurological disease, is being studied in many medical centers around the world, including the United States. Because the main abnormality in Parkinson's disease is the dysfunction of a specific group of brain cells—the *substantia nigra*—it has been proposed that replacement of the diseased tissue with normally functioning cells could alleviate many of the symptoms. Fetal brain cells are advantageous because they are in a period of rapid growth, readily survive transplantation, and are less likely to be rejected by the recipient than adult cells. If the donor and recipient are closely HLA-matched—a method of determining tissue compatibility used in kidney and bone-marrow transplants—some of the remaining risk of rejection may also be avoided. Although research in this area has almost exclusively utilized young fetal brain cells, the exact age at which this part of the brain can no longer be successful transplanted is not known.

ABOUT THE AUTHOR

JOHN O'NEILL is a graduate of the Georgetown University School of Medicine and now practices medicine in the Washington, D.C. area. *Baby Girl Lauren* was his first novel and was widely acclaimed. *Blue Death,* his second medical novel, explores the intricacies of surgical pathology and deception. *Blue Death* has also been widely acclaimed, particularly within the medical profession. *Protocol Ichor,* his third medical suspense novel, will be published later this year.